By Moon Rise – Tielle St. Clare

After three years of working as a werewolf's personal assistant, Caitlin didn't think anything could surprise her. When she finds herself locked in a hotel room for two days with her wickedly handsome boss, she learns how wrong she is.

The moon is on the rise and only one thing will satisfy the wolf inside Luc—sex, and lots of it. It's a sacrifice Caitlin is oh-so-willing to make.

But when wilder, deeper emotions come to the surface, Caitlin fears she won't make it out of that room with her heart intact.

Dream Walker – Patrice Michelle

Erin Stein thought that discovering the ability to travel in time would benefit mankind. Never could she have imagined that moving through time would become so complicated.

Now that her invention has fallen into the wrong hands, she's on a mission to destroy her creation in order to save her world.

Little does she realize just how much the past, present, and future will come to mean to her.

One Night Stand – J.C. Wilder

Lucius deVille had the face of an angel and the body of an unrepentant sinner. He was the kind of vampire every woman dreamed of calling 'Lover' at least once in her life. The proverbial tall, dark and handsome male that was the fantasy of millions of women around the world and to top it all off, he was educated and possessed a wicked sense of humor that had charmed more than one woman out of her panties.

Tonight, Rachel was determined to claim Luc as her own.

Tail of the Tiger – R. Casteel

Hiding since her ill-fated birth, Kat—half woman/half animal—has lived in on a small tropical island all her life.

Upon the death of his father, Cedric Deverone learns of the evil his father has done and feels compelled to seek out this halfling creature and hopefully find the answers he is searching for and the purpose of his own existence.

In any quest, the answers found are not always to the questions asked, especially in matters of the heart.

Dragon's Law: Mace – Alicia Sparks

When Mace rescued Eleanora from the clutches of the dragon, he had no intention of mating with her, but fate intervened proving that sometimes the forces of nature and desire are stronger than willpower. In his fevered state, he has no idea that Eleanora has spilled her virgin blood on his cock until he wakes up, literally impaling her soft body.

Taming Jack – Angela Knight

Motorcycle cop Jack Ramsey hungers for revenge on the inhuman thing that murdered his beloved sister. So much so that his obsession drives him away from the woman he loves. So much, in fact, that he's willing to allow an alien energy being to possess him if it means gaining the power to kill his sister's killer.

Lark finds herself offered a similar devil's bargain – become a host to one of the energy symbiotes, in return for the power to save Jack from himself.

In his obsession, Jack has become a superhuman vigilante, absorbing the evil entities which possess killers like the man who raped and murdered his sister. But every time he kills one of the symbiotes, he runs the risk of spinning out of control.

Discover for yourself why readers can't get enough of the multiple award-winning publisher Ellora's Cave. Whether you prefer e-books or paperbacks, be sure to visit EC on the web at www.ellorascave.com for an erotic reading experience that will leave you breathless.

WWW.ELLORASCAVE.COM

ELLORA'S CAVEMEN: TALES FROM THE TEMPLE II
An Ellora's Cave Publication, May 2004

Ellora's Cave Publishing, Inc.
PO Box 787
Hudson, OH 44236-0787

ISBN # 1-84360-928-2

ISBN MS Reader (LIT) ISBN # 1-84360-927-4
Other available formats (no ISBNs are assigned):
Adobe (PDF), Rocketbook (RB), Mobipocket (PRC) & HTML

This book is a work of fiction and any resemblance to persons, living or
dead, or places, events or locales is purely coincidental. They are
productions of the authors' imagination and used fictitiously.

ELLORA'S CAVEMEN: TALES FROM THE TEMPLE II edited by
The Legendary "Queen of Steam" *Jaid Black*.
Cover design by *Darrell King*. Photography by *Dennis Roliff*.

ELLORA'S CAVEMEN: TALES FROM THE TEMPLE II

By Moon Rise
By Tielle St. Clare

Dream Walker
By Patrice Michelle

One Night Stand
By J.C. Wilder

Tail of the Tiger
By R. Casteel

Dragon's Law: Mace
By Alicia Sparks

Taming Jack
By Angela Knight

BY MOON RISE

Tielle St. Clare

Chapter 1

"We're *what*?"

Caitlin didn't flinch at her boss's outburst. After three years she knew Luc's temper flared hot but burned out quickly. She also knew his anger wasn't directed at her. She was just the messenger.

"Quarantined," she repeated with polite patience. Since the SARS outbreaks a few years before, world health organizations took immediate precautions when new viruses appeared. "The entire hotel is locked down for forty-eight hours. The virus takes twenty-four hours to incubate. We'll all be tested and if we're fine and showing no symptoms, we can leave."

"They can't just keep us here."

"Yes, they can. Ninety percent of the people who contract this disease die within three days. It's got everyone in a panic and since the last two cases have connections to this hotel, they've quarantined the whole building. Only health officials will be allowed in and they'll be in protective suits."

Luc dragged five fingers through his long black hair and spun away. His long legs carried him across the suite at a furious pace before he whipped around and came back.

"We have to go north." The bright glitter of his blue eyes warned of the ragged emotions humming through him.

Caitlin could understand his concern. His future wife was waiting for him. The bonding ceremony was only three days away.

"Don't worry. I put extra time in our schedule to deal with any delays. We'll make it on time."

"You don't understand. We can't stay."

"We don't have a choice," she countered. She knew he didn't like to be confined, but the suite they occupied gave them plenty of room—enough for some privacy and a little freedom. "And don't worry. It's a simple blood test to determine the existence of the virus. They won't notice anything different in your blood," she said in case that was his concern.

"We can't stay," he repeated. Something in his tone alerted Caitlin. He wasn't joking or complaining. He was dead serious. There had to be a reason. She waited. Finally Luc sighed. "Tomorrow night is the full moon."

Caitlin's stomach fell away. A full moon was the one time when werewolves couldn't control their change. That meant that sometime tomorrow night, Luc, third in charge of the Northern Pack, would sprout fur and grow very large teeth.

"I have to sneak out."

Caitlin shook her head. "They have guards posted around the building. They are really panicked about this latest outbreak." She bit her lip and began her own wandering around the room. "And they have your information. If you were able to get out, they'd come after you, and that could lead them to the Pack." Pack security was always the first priority.

"Either I make a run for it or we're going to be explaining how a wolf got loose inside an urban hotel." He rubbed his forehead. She could almost see the tension headache forming. "God knows what kind of damage he'll cause in a place like this."

Caitlin knew from talking with pack members that they had only vague memories of their times as a wolf. The passion and energy of the animal remained, but specifics were hazy.

"Isn't there a way to stop the change? Or delay it?"

Luc shook his head. "No. The moon controls it." He sighed. "And that means by moon rise tomorrow night, I'll be a full wolf."

Their paths intersected in the middle of the suite. She stared up at him, noting again the sheer masculine beauty—the long black hair flowing to his shoulders, the intriguing angles and shadows of his cheekbones and strong jaw, but it was his eyes that called to her. Eyes troubled and looking to her for answers.

"Call Fallon," Caitlin suggested. "Since becoming the Alpha he seems to have answers for everything."

Luc smiled grimly and agreed. "He does seem to have bits of arcane knowledge that he doesn't see fit to share with the rest of us until the precise moment we need it." Luc flipped open his phone and dialed the direct line to the head of the wolf pack.

Not wanting to eavesdrop on the conversation but knowing she might be needed, Caitlin lingered nearby as Luc went through the ritualized greeting of the wolves.

Then, Luc reported their situation. "So, is there anything that can stop a full-moon change?" He waited. Confusion crinkled the corners of his eyes. He looked over at her. "Uh, I don't think that's going to work," he said, his voice dropping. "I'm with Caitlin. I'm just not sure she's ready for that."

Caitlin straightened, pulling her shoulders back and extending to her full five-foot-six. Though not a werewolf herself, the Pack had become her family as well as her employer. She would do whatever it took to defend the Pack.

"Fallon wants to talk to you." Luc offered her his phone then quickly backed away.

What was this mystery activity? Did he need to feed on her blood? That sounded suspiciously like a vampire's cure and since werewolves and vampires had been mortal enemies for centuries, she doubted that would be it.

"Honor upon your house. Health and happiness for your pups, Alpha," Caitlin said.

Luc leaned against the wall and watched Caitlin. He'd always thought she was cute but he'd never allowed himself to look at her in a sexual way. Staring at her now, he could see her lush body—firm, full breasts, an ass with just enough curve to fill his hands. He ignored the tightening in his crotch and listened to Caitlin's conversation. As she talked, she continued to walk the width of the room. The Alpha's solution was unusual and risky. And it required Caitlin's full cooperation.

Luc could hear the faint rumble of Fallon's voice through the phone. And he knew the precise moment he explained what was needed. It was the moment Caitlin's cheeks turned red. She raised one finger and gnawed on the nail. It was a habit she had when she was thinking or nervous.

"Yes, I understand." She nodded and turned away. "Yes, thank you, Alpha." She snapped the phone shut but kept her back to him.

"Did he explain what you would need to do?"

Caitlin nodded and slowly turned to face him. "I'm to keep the room cool, feed you the rarest cuts of meat they can provide and…" The blush bloomed again in her cheeks. "And have sex with you whenever and however you desire it."

* * * * *

Caitlin paced the length of the bed, crushing the plush carpet into a squished path. She stopped by the window and glanced outside. The crisp clear winter day had faded to a brightly lit night with city lights and star bouncing off the fresh snow. It was a peaceful scene and did nothing to ease her frazzled nerves.

She'd agreed to do it. She'd agreed to offer herself to Luc and his wolf for sex.

According to Luc the pull of the moon began during the twenty-four hours prior to the rise of the full moon. That meant that sometime tonight, he should be calling for her. Could she do it? Could she actually have sex with her boss? Her friend?

The man she loved.

Her stomach fell away at the thought. She was able to conceal her emotions most of the time, but what was she going to do now? She'd been in love with Luc for almost three years but she'd never let that affect her work or her interactions with

Luc. It did no good to love Luc. Nothing would ever come of it. Early on, when she'd first joined the Pack, she'd learned that while some pack members chose human mates, rarely did those unions produce children. As a dominant male, Luc's duty to the Pack required him to mate with a dominant werewolf female and produce strong cubs. Luc's mate was already chosen for him by his Alpha.

So Caitlin had learned to hide her feelings and keep her distance. But tonight they were going to be as close as two people could get. The ache in her stomach moved lower, between her legs.

Before retreating to her room, Caitlin had asked, in an attempt to appear practical and nonchalant, about birth control. Not having planned to have sex on this trip, she hadn't brought condoms and hadn't been on the pill since she'd kicked her last boyfriend out of the house. Luc had assured her that only a True Mating between a human and werewolf could produce a child. True Mates were rare because the wolf had to fully accept the human. The animal's instinctive fear of humans made that unlikely.

Caitlin sighed and continued pacing. Birth control was actually low on her worry list. A broken heart was much more likely. The one thing that had helped her suppress her feelings for Luc was his platonic treatment of her. But to have him look at her with lust and desire...just the thought made her knees weak. What would happen after they'd had sex? Either she would be able to walk away having known the experience of loving him—

Or it would only serve to tighten the connection she felt for him.

Despite her fears, Caitlin couldn't stop the flutter of anticipation. For one full day—twenty-four hours—she would have him, belong to him.

And when the moon began to wane and the wolf was once again contained, she would have her memories.

Then she would leave. Caitlin planned to request a transfer as soon as Luc's Mate Bonding was complete. She knew she could never have him for herself, but she wasn't a masochist. Seeing him every day with the tall, elegant werewolf who'd been chosen as his mate was too painful for her to endure. She couldn't leave. Once a human was drawn into the Pack, they stayed — serving in whatever capacity the Alpha deemed. Fallon would understand and find a new place for her.

She just had to make it through the night — allowing her body to enjoy his but keeping her heart distant. *Yeah, right.*

Caitlin slapped her palms together and exhaled. It was past midnight and she hadn't heard anything from Luc. The rare steaks he'd consumed at dinner had made her queasy, but he'd enjoyed them. There was more almost-raw meat in the little hotel fridge. If what Fallon had said was true, the wolf would need more than meat.

She opened the door and walked into the main suite area. They'd agreed that she would have the private bedroom and Luc would sleep in the bed in the shared area. She knew he'd given her the bedroom so she had a place to escape to if the wolf got out of control.

When she walked into the room, he was sitting, staring intently at the television. He looked calm but there was an energy hovering around him that warned her he was fighting the inner demons that sought to control his body.

"Luc, how are you doing?"

He didn't flinch when she spoke, but then she hadn't expected it. With his extended senses, he would have known the moment she'd entered the room, no matter how silent she'd been.

"I'm fine," he said, without looking back.

"Are you sure? You said it would start sometime tonight and…"

"I'm fine, Caitlin. You should go to bed. I'll call you if I need you."

His voice was calm. There was no sign of tension in his long, strong body. Then she saw his hand move. It was slow and subtle as he dug his fingernails into the leather couch. His knuckles whitened and she watched four tiny tears follow the paths of his fingers.

"Luc—"

"Really, I'm fine." This time he turned and looked at her. He even smiled. "Go to bed."

Not knowing what else to do, she nodded and backed out of the room.

A faint growl reverberated from the couch as she shut the door behind her. She couldn't leave him like that. The Alpha had warned that the beast couldn't be allowed to take control. That once the animal gathered strength, it would be difficult to pull back. And it looked like it was getting a good grip on Luc already.

Caitlin stared at the door for a long time before finding the answer she needed. Luc was trying to fight it on his own. She would have to offer what he was hesitant to take.

Using the spark of nervous energy, she moved quickly, stripping off her clothes and stacking them neatly on the bed. An invisible band seemed to wrap around her chest making a long, deep, calming breath impossible. Her fingers shook as she fluffed her hair and put on a fresh coat of mascara. Luc probably wouldn't notice, but this was her one time with him. She was going to look her best. Thankfully she'd had a razor in her bag. It was one thing for Luc to turn hairy. She wasn't going to do the same.

She finished and stood in front of the hotel mirror. The muted lighting gave her skin a warm, golden tone and made her auburn hair look almost mahogany. The tips of her breasts were high and tight...and ready for Luc's mouth. She let the openly sexual urge slip through her body, allowing all her suppressed desires for Luc to bubble up. Moisture flowed into her pussy and her hips swayed gently to an unconscious sensual rhythm.

Before she lost the courage she'd found, she opened the door and stepped outside—ready to seduce a wolf.

Chapter 2

Luc tensed as the door opened for a second time. He'd listened to her move around the other room and hoped she was preparing for bed. And locking her door.

She had to stay away. He was controlling the beast, but just barely. Her presence wasn't helping. Her scent was driving him crazy. Though she'd been embarrassed and slightly fearful when the Alpha had explained what was required, Luc had also detected the faint scent of arousal. That delicious aroma had grown through the evening. And it caused him to respond in kind.

He'd always been scrupulous in keeping his distance from Caitlin. She was a sweet woman who also happened to be the best damn assistant he'd ever had. There was no way he was going to screw that up for a brief affair. Caitlin wasn't the type to sleep with a guy one day and then work for him the next as if nothing had changed. But she was devoted to the Pack and would do anything to protect its members. Even fuck one.

He had to send her away. Maybe there was another woman in the hotel he could use for his purposes. She would be well compensated. There had to be someone else. Caitlin was special. She was his friend as well as his employee. If he touched her, even under the influence of the wolf, he knew he would alter that relationship forever.

He spun around in his chair, prepared to order her back into the bedroom.

"Really, Caitlin, I'm—"

His throat seized up, like someone had punched him in the neck.

She was naked. Completely bare as she stood before him. The slight insecurity in her eyes tugged on his human heart and angered the wolf inside him. Didn't she realize how beautiful she was?

Unable to stop himself, he drew in a deep breath, pulling her distinctive scent into his body and holding it inside like a present meant for him alone. His stomach rumbled, but it wasn't physical hunger that created the sound. He licked his lips, anticipating her taste as his eyes fell to her curvy hips and the pale red hair between her thighs.

Again a mixture of fear and arousal blended into an intoxicating scent. The wolf inside him screamed, urging him on. The beast wanted Caitlin. And Luc found himself wondering why he was fighting the compulsion to take her.

"I can't do this. Not with you," he rasped, offering one last attempt at nobility—humanity.

Her lower lip trembled and the insecurity blazed in her eyes. She covered her breasts with her arm and placed the other hand down, shielding her pussy.

"I'm sorry. I just thought…"

"Don't ever cover yourself before me."

The harsh command came from a instinctual place inside him that he didn't quite understand. Caitlin jumped and took one tiny step away. His human-self winced, knowing he'd frightened her. The wolf inside him crouched, ready to chase if she ran. Somehow the wolf knew she was his prize for the night.

"Don't move," Luc ordered. "I have control over him right now, but if you try to run, he'll come after you."

His words seemed to renew the confidence she'd had when she walked into the room. Slowly, she lowered her arms and stepped forward. "I'm not going to run."

He shook his head. The dilemma was set. If she moved, the wolf would pounce. If she stayed, he wouldn't be able to resist having her.

"Do you understand what's happening to me?"

She nodded. "I know what I'm doing — what we're going to do."

Her declaration eased some of his concerns. She was here — if not from desire, at least with an understanding of what would occur. She waited naked before him and there was no choice but to allow the wolf his release. He wouldn't be denied.

Resigned, Luc vowed to go slow, to control the wolf that much as least. Caitlin had to be terrified. What human woman wouldn't be? But she was also aroused. He could smell her. The hot place between her legs flowed with moisture. He hungered for the feel of that cream on his tongue.

"Get on the bed." The low, almost animal-like sound of his voice warned him he was at the edge of his control. He curled his hands into fists and struggled to contain the beast.

Caitlin hesitated for a moment — long enough that he thought she'd changed her mind — before walking toward the huge bed stationed in the corner of the suite. Her soft, curved rump swayed as she moved away. Luc followed. His hands burned to hold that delightful ass — to squeeze it as he slammed his cock into her pussy or flicked his tongue inside her cunt.

The alluring scent of her sex beckoned him. His tongue practically hung from his mouth when she crawled up on the bed and rolled over onto her back. Without being told, she spread her legs.

The sight of her open pussy sent twin spikes of pain and need into his cock. He had to have her. He tried to slow his movements — not wanting to frighten her any further — but the wolf was grabbing at his throat and his genitals, screaming to be free. If he'd been at home or with the Pack, he would have released the wolf and reveled in the animal's form. But here, now, he had to keep the wolf contained. *Give the wolf what it wants* — that had been the Alpha's advice.

What the wolf wanted now was Caitlin.

Luc reached out and let his fingers wander across the sweet, soft flesh between her thighs. Keeping his eyes locked to hers, he stroked her from knee to pussy. Her breath caught as he brushed close to her sex. He wanted to speak—to sooth her with sexy, seductive words but the wolf clawed at his soul, desperate for the taste of her.

Reining in the wolf, he wrapped his hands around her hips and dragged her forward, placing her on the edge of the bed, sinking to his knees to match her height. He looked up. Caitlin watched him with wide, innocent eyes. A howl lodged in the back of his throat as he fought the impulse to fall on her like a ravening beast. The delicious arousal from her cunt filled his nostrils until he thought he would go insane with the need to immerse himself in her. He couldn't fight it. He leaned forward and placed his mouth against her hot, wet sex.

A jolt of recognition electrified his body. He pulled back. There was something different about her, but he couldn't stop to analyze it. He needed her too much. He opened his lips and gently kissed her, flicking his tongue out, gathering more of her flavor. The fiery taste exploded in his mouth.

Delicious. Addicting.

"Luc, please." Her breathless plea urged him on. The wolf howled its victory and the sound drove Luc on—needing to conquer and consume. Needing to feed the wolf.

He slowly traced the length of her warm, wet flesh with his tongue. She shivered. The wolf in him smiled. Luc drew back and tried to find again his control. His cock pressed hard against his fly, straining for release. The desire to possess her—to overwhelm her—ripped at him. He ground his back teeth together to keep from growling his possession.

The air was thick with the perfume of her sex. He didn't understand the driving urge but simply knew he needed her. He stroked her cunt with his tongue, gathering her flavor. The sensation was like his own private orgasm. He had to have more. And more of her.

Caitlin closed her eyes as his delicate caresses fluttered through her sex.

This wasn't what she'd expected. She'd imagined his pouncing on her, fucking her hard, but never this slow oral exploration.

"Luc, I...please..." She didn't know what she was begging for—only that he could supply it.

The light flicker of his tongue invaded her pussy with fire and need. She pressed her lips together, trying to hold back a cry—trying to keep a piece of herself separate, knowing that with each touch he would sink deeper into her heart. But the exotic caress of his mouth made him impossible to resist. Even knowing she would regret it later, she let her fingers drift into his hair, touching the soft strands—caressing him as she'd dreamed of doing many times.

"Please, Luc, more."

He continued his gentle approach to her sex. The touches so soft, so elusive, she thought she'd dreamt them. The long, slow glide of his tongue up her slit until he stopped a whisper away from her clit. She waited, tense, trying to prepare herself. But instead of moving forward, he sank lower and continued the teasing licks. He drew his tongue through her folds, tasting every inch of flesh, pushing into her sex. More liquid poured from her pussy, but she couldn't feel any embarrassment. There was only pleasure.

He moaned as he tasted her. His obvious enjoyment let her relax and indulge in the wild sensations. She spread her legs and shimmied farther down, opening herself even more. Luc raised his head and looked at her. The hunger in his eyes startled her. Gold glittered around the edges of his pupils.

Luc licked his lips—looking very much like a wolf anticipating his prey. His mouth kicked up into a half smile that sent shivers through her body. She wasn't frightened. But that smile warned her that he was in charge. He lowered his head back between her bent thighs and began again his slow banquet.

Thoughts bounced in and out of her head. Nothing settled. Heat flowed from his mouth through her body in delicious waves. She rolled her hips, silently begging for more. Finally, he swirled his tongue across her clit as if to soothe her. It only left her desperate for a harder touch.

"Luc!" Her plea became a command but Luc wouldn't be rushed.

The long slow caresses continued mixed with shallow dips of his tongue into her sex and more quick licks around her clit. Caitlin held her breath, waiting for the next touch. She twisted, knowing that if she could only move, find the one touch, then she could come. His hands held her down. He pressed her thighs wider, spreading her open, spearing his tongue into her wet pussy.

Caitlin fought against his hold, but he was too strong.

"Please, Luc. I need more." She whimpered as the pressure built. "I need to come." This cry seemed to reach him. He returned to her clit, sucking it lightly between his lips. Caitlin clawed at the sheets as he brushed his tongue across the sensitive bud.

Her body froze for one second before sensation exploded. Bright shimmers spiraled from her core, racing out into her limbs.

Gasping for breath, she stared up at the ceiling, trying to capture the remaining pieces of her sanity. How had he done that? She'd had orgasms before, but nothing like that. Her body felt used and electrified. As if he alone had the power to give her pleasure.

She lost track of how long she lay there—knowing only that Luc continued to lick her, comforting strokes of his tongue. As her heartbeat began to slow, he rose.

He stood beside the bed, staring at her spread legs. The wild light of the wolf haunted his eyes. Moisture from her pussy lingered around his mouth. He licked his lips and stared into her eyes.

"Your cunt is delicious." He placed his hand over her pussy, slipping one finger into her passage. "I'll have more." The promise sent a renewed fire into her sex. "Later. Now, I need to come inside you." He pushed a second finger into her. "May I have you?"

The question startled her for a second. She was lying on the bed, naked with her legs spread and he was asking permission to fuck her? He didn't move—just waited for her answer. Finally, Caitlin nodded.

He stepped back and stripped out of his clothes with an impatience that was thrilling. As he dropped his pants, his cock sprang free and she caught her first glimpse of his fully erect penis.

Oh my God — how is all that going to fit inside me?

"Slide up, baby," he said lifting his chin toward the headboard. "I mean to have you long and hard and don't want to risk falling off the bed."

Caitlin nodded and scrambled backward until she was in the middle of the mattress. Her eyes never left his cock. The long shaft stood out proudly from the nest of black hair. It looked delicious. Awe inspiring.

He crawled onto the bed and lay down beside her, close but not touching. She dragged her gaze away from his crotch and stared wide-eyed up at him as he cupped her breast and massaged the peak with his thumb. "I want to suck on your pretty little nipples—" His hand stroked down her stomach to the top of her mound. "—spend hours with my mouth on your skin, but now I need to be inside you. Spread your legs for me, baby." He continued his downward path, sliding his fingers through her damp flesh. "You're so wet for me. I have to have you."

He rolled over and pressed himself up until he was above her. Balancing on one hand and his knees, he guided his cock to her entrance and with a slow, deliberate thrust, began to ease inside her. Caitlin tensed as the first thick inches penetrated her.

"Sh, sh," he whispered.

She hadn't realized she'd made a sound.

He placed a soothing kiss on her mouth. "You'll take me. You'll hold me like no other." More of his cock eased into her. "You're wet and hot and delicious."

She stared down, watching the dark shaft slide deeper into her body. The heat was incredible, warming her from the inside out. He didn't pause—just kept steadily pushing until she thought she'd explode.

"All this fire is for me. Just for me."

"Yes," she moaned. "Just for you."

He whispered hot, wild words against her lips while he fed his cock into her. Caitlin tried to hold on to each sensation, wanting to keep the memories, but her senses were overloading. Every part of her body felt alive, felt touched by him.

He drove the final inches in, hard and fast. Caitlin groaned and gripped his shoulders, using him to steady her world. She took a deep breath and listened to her body. He was tight inside her, stretching her, but in the most delightful way.

He brushed her tangled curls away from her face, staring into her eyes as her body held him—just as he'd said. The warmth in his gaze inspired her tingling nerves to flutter. She was ready for more—ready to feel him pumping inside her.

She wrapped her hand around his neck and pulled him down, opening her mouth to his, accepting his tongue. Then, as they kissed, he pulled back, slipping almost out of her before sinking into her again.

The pace was slow but she would never call it controlled. The look in his eyes told her he was barely containing the beast. The thick head of his cock massaged her deep inside—until she thought she would go mad with it. The steady pressure built, teasing her with a release that was just out of her reach.

"That's it, baby," his whispered, his voice low and husky. He groaned against her neck as he pushed back into her. "God, you feel good. Your cunt was made for me."

His words filled her mind, making thought impossible. Instinct took over. She needed more of him. She ground her heels into the mattress and pushed up as he thrust down, moving satisfyingly deep. He wrapped his hand around her hips, holding her to him, holding himself inside.

"Not yet. I want to enjoy you a little longer." He pulled out and thrust in one more time. Pure pleasure rippled across his face. "I want to stay inside you."

"Luc, please." She fought his grip. "Please, I need to come." He bent down and licked her throat. The shiver that scorched through her body pushed her over the edge. "Damn it, Luc. *Fuck me.*"

Again that arrogant smile formed on his lips. Caitlin was too wound up to care. She needed movement and she needed it now. She placed her hands on the sides of his face and lifted his head until he stared directly into her eyes.

"Fuck me," she demanded. "Now."

The golden eyes of the wolf glittered. Luc hissed as if fighting an unseen force. He slowly pulled back. Just when she thought he'd leave her, he slid back in—deep and hard.

"Yes," Caitlin moaned. "Like that." He pounded his cock into her, filling her sex with long, hungry strokes. Caitlin closed her eyes and pumped her hips, meeting his downward thrusts. Yes, this was exactly what she needed. Hard, deep strokes inside her cunt, the heavy penetration massaging her clit with each stroke.

The pleasure that had lingered just out of reach became a desperate goal. She dug her fingers into his back, urging him faster and deeper. The sweet tightening in her pussy grew each time he came into her until she couldn't contain it.

"Luc!"

His name broke from her lips as the sharp bright tension snapped and sent her flying. For one brief moment, the world erupted in crystal clarity—everything seemed brighter and more distinct—and then it was gone and all that was left was the hazy drug of pleasure. She sagged back on the bed, her legs opening wider to hold him deeper.

Luc continued his furious pace, slamming their bodies together. The hot thrusts of his cock dragged each tendril of heat from her pussy. Another tiny orgasm hit her, shocking her already loose body. With a groan, Luc drove into her one final time.

The warm release of his cum started, flowing in hot spurts into her sex. Caitlin curled her knees up, pressing against his ribcage, holding him deep inside.

* * * * *

Caitlin rolled out of Luc's sleepy embrace as the sun crept through the curtains muted by the heavy ice fog that hugged the city. She shivered, imagining the cold just beyond their sanctuary.

Luc muttered an incoherent protest as she moved away, but let her go. Shallow twinges from her recently stretched muscles made her move slowly, sliding off the high mattress and placing her feet gingerly on the floor. Her legs trembled as she pushed up to standing. Her tired, well-loved body urged her to stay in bed but she needed a moment alone. Needed a moment away from Luc to deal with the overwhelming reality of what had happened.

The night had passed in a sensual blur. When he hadn't been actively fucking her, he'd stroked her skin and whispered hot love words into her ear. Even now, she could hear his voice telling her how beautiful she was, how sexy she was, how hard she made him.

Two separate yet equally powerful aches began in her body. One in her pussy, longing for the luscious sensations only Luc seemed able to create. The second in her heart, and the pain she knew would follow when he walked away. Logic told her it wasn't Luc making love to her—that the desire came from the wolf's needs—but that didn't stop her heart from latching on to the experience of holding him inside her body.

She forced herself walk away. The rustle of skin on sheets alerted her that he was awake. Though she'd spent the night naked, accepting him into her body, a sudden wave of shyness washed over her. She bent down and picked up Luc's discarded shirt. It would work until she could get a robe. She wrapped the shirt around her shoulders and began to work the buttons when a rumble from the bed stopped her. The low, animal growl was no sound ever made by a human.

Though she knew Luc would never hurt her, a wave of fear showered through her body. Slowly, knowing the wolf would react to sudden movements, she turned around. Luc watched her with glowing eyes and firmly set lips.

"Luc?"

"Don't ever cover yourself around me," he said in a low, almost threatening tone. "Take it off." He rolled over and began to crawl across the bed. Like he was stalking her, ready to pounce.

She swallowed deeply and reminded herself that this was Luc—her friend and now her lover. With trembling fingers, she pushed the material off her shoulders and let it fall to the ground. Luc stopped at the edge of the bed. A very wolfish grin formed on his lips as if there was satisfaction in being obeyed.

"I was just going to clean up," she said, feeling his seed slip from her body.

"Later. Come back to bed." He rested back on his heels baring his hard cock to her eyes. "I've need of you."

Seeing that massive shaft rising up to her, Caitlin felt a response in her own sated sex. And a separate hunger. She licked her lips and stared at him for a moment.

"I could...suck you off," she offered in a hesitant voice. As she made the offer she realized she wanted that. She wanted that thick cock in her mouth. To give him the same pleasure he'd given her. A long-suppressed feminine voice told her she could cloud his mind with so much sensation he would think only of her.

"And you will, baby, but first I want your delightful cunt again. It's been too long since I've come inside you." He held out his hand. Caitlin put her fingers into his palm and let herself be pulled forward. "You feel so good when I'm buried inside you."

The soft words seduced her back onto the bed. With the guidance of his hands, she rolled onto her back and spread her legs. There were no preliminaries, but her body didn't need them. He pressed his cock to her opening and she was wet and able to take him.

She groaned as the thick length slid back inside her body. She would be sore when this was over, but for now she wanted everything he would give her.

"That's it, baby. Let me have you again."

"Yes." Worried that her emotions would show too easily, she closed her eyes as he buried his cock deep in her pussy.

Luc stared down at the incredible woman beneath him. He wished she would open her eyes so he could see the deep hazel brighten as she discovered her passion.

Part of his soul wanted, *needed*, to thrust hard, to pound into her body and reclaim it as his. Luc listened to the quieter voice in his head that whispered being inside her was enough for now. He placed warm, gentle kisses on her neck and throat, stroked her hair. Seducing rather than fucking.

"So sexy," he whispered against her skin, the love words flowing off his tongue without ceasing. It was as if everything he'd ever said to a woman was practice for Caitlin. Something scratched at his consciousness—that this wild compulsion to fuck her, love her, wasn't normal.

It had to be the wolf and its need. *Surely any woman would create the same reaction.* But as he stared down at Caitlin beneath him, a quiet voice in his head warned him that she was different. Special.

She arched her neck, silently asking for more kisses and Luc felt his cock harden even farther. She didn't understand how vulnerable she was in that position. The wolf in him growled at the blatantly submissive posture. He couldn't resist. He leaned down and nipped at her skin, knowing he would leave a faint mark. The delicious taste reminded him of the flavor of her sex. He laved his tongue across the spot, soothing the tiny wound.

Her cunt tightened around his cock as if it too felt the slow stroke of his tongue. Slowly he began to move inside her. The long, heavy slide of his cock filling her again and again urged him to drive harder and deeper. But he held back, wanting her sighs as well as her screams. He continued the slow deep fuck, loving every inch of her cunt with his shaft. He lost track of time, knowing only that the sun was rising and Caitlin was beneath him.

Her delicate whimpers and the soft contractions around his shaft warned him she was coming. He watched it move through her body, ending with the heat filling her startled green eyes. Her quiet climax triggered his and he tossed his head back and groaned. Long moments later he collapsed down on the bed, crushing her to the mattress.

The room was silent around them. He lay on top of her, his cock half-hard and still embedded inside her pussy. The wolf pushed at him to have her again, but Luc rejected the animal's urgings. He tensed, preparing to struggle for control of the body they shared. Surprisingly, the wolf backed down. As if it was content now that they'd had Caitlin.

Luc knew he had to take advantage of the situation now. Though the sun had risen, the wolf would still feel the draw of the moon until moonrise tonight. That meant twelve more hours.

Caitlin would need her rest.

A soft snore drew his attention. He smiled.

Masculine triumph filled his chest as he watched her sleep. He'd exhausted her.

He slipped out of her and rolled off the bed, his cock hardening as he looked at her sprawled legs and his seed dripping down to the mattress. A strange possessiveness he'd never felt with any other lover curled like a fist into his gut.

He wanted her, again. He dragged himself away from the bed, pacing the room silently, not wanting to disturb Caitlin. She needed her sleep. Each trip across the floor brought him closer to the bed. Like a physical ache, he needed to be near her—touch her.

The muscles in his neck tightened and he rolled his head and shoulders to try to ease the tension. He'd battled with the cravings of the wolf before but it had never been like this.

Finally, unable to fight the need any long, Luc crawled back into bed and pulled Caitlin into his arms. She groaned softly but rolled with him, settling her head on his chest.

Her unruly curls tickled his nose but he loved the sensation. He closed his eyes and enjoyed the delicious scent of her hair. The wolf sighed in pleasure. There was no way he could sleep—too much energy flowed through his body—but he would give her as much time as he could before the wolf would demand more of this woman.

Chapter 3

The tap on the door pulled Caitlin from the dazed stupor she was living in. On legs barely strong enough to carry her to the door, she staggered out of bed and across the room. Her entire body ached but she had the satisfaction of knowing they'd succeeded. The moonrise had begun and with it the wolf would begin his slow retreat. Caitlin had few clear memories of the past twenty hours—her mind, body and spirit had been consumed by Luc and his need to drive the wolf back.

As the moonrise had grown nearer, his lovemaking had become more ferocious—demanding more, giving more. Pale marks from his hands, his lips—his teeth—decorated her skin. She shivered as she remembered a nip on her shoulder as he'd ridden her from behind, driving hard into her pussy.

She heard Luc shift in the bed and knew he was watching her. She made no move to put on a robe—not after the last time she'd tried that.

The soft tap on the door repeated and had to be answered. Every four hours they checked on the hotel's guests to see how everyone was feeling. So far, no one in the hotel was showing signs of the virus. She hid herself behind the door and opened it a crack.

"Good evening Ms. Bennett. How are you tonight?" The attendant in the white plastic suit and mask greeted her with cheerful eyes. "I'm making my rounds and delivering dinner." He winked. "I hope I'm not interrupting."

"It's fine." Exhaustion claimed her and she leaned against the door. She offered a weak smile and brushed her matted hair away from her face.

"Are either of you exhibiting any of the symptoms listed? Any rash?" Caitlin shook her head. "Coughs? Numb extremities?" Again she replied negatively. "And I need to see your husband, just to confirm that he is also in good health."

Caitlin glanced back at the bed. Nothing obvious revealed that Luc was a werewolf, but she wasn't sure he looked completely human either. He looked wild—his beard darker, his eyes the mysterious gold of the wolf's. She raised her eyebrows in silent question. With a sigh, Luc reached over and dragged a sheet across his waist. When he was minimally covered, she opened the door, keeping herself hidden behind it. The attendant stepped just inside the room and saw Luc. What a picture he made—long black hair loose around his shoulders, his bare chest gleaming with the sweat of their recent lovemaking, and the slash of white covering his hips barely masking his erection.

"Uh, yes, sir, it's good to see you're in good health."

"We're both in *excellent* health. And we're busy."

The man glanced down to the sheet that was doing less and less to cover Luc's growing cock. "Yes, I can see that. I'll just leave your meal outside." He backed away. "I'll let you get back to your…your…well, to whatever."

He practically leapt out the door and slammed it shut.

Caitlin spun around and glared at Luc.

"Did you have to do that?"

"What? Let him know that he was interrupting me while I was fucking my woman? Yes."

The openly possessive statement knocked the air out of her chest. She stared at the frustrating, sexy man for a long time while she tried to figure out how to escape from the hotel without running into that attendant. How mortifying.

Getting out of this room with her heart intact was impossible. She could have at least hoped for keeping her dignity.

Luc raised his eyebrows and watched her, the heat from his gaze reaching across the room and sinking into her chest. He still wanted her. The sun was set; the moon had risen—but the wolf must still be in control. Caitlin let her head tip back against the door and closed her eyes. He was so beautiful. The power of his spirit infused the physical perfection to make him irresistible. Damn, she couldn't look at him. It was too painful. She could never have him—and his image was burned into her memory.

A strange ache sparked inside Luc as Caitlin closed her eyes and leaned against the door. It wasn't jealousy. Caitlin belonged to him. He knew it and soon she would accept it. But something about the way she closed her eyes—when he entered her, when he made love to her—ripped at his heart. As if she was trying to avoid looking at him.

Or was imagining another filling her body.

The animal's basic level of logic assured him she was his—he'd marked her with his teeth, his scent, and his seed—but the human recognized the signals. Through all the fucking—every touch and caress—there had been something missing. She'd let him have her in any way he'd desired—but still he felt like she was holding back.

She was his. She belonged to him.

As the words entered his head, he realized they were true. She was his mate. Every strange emotion that had assailed him because clear. That was why she seemed familiar when he'd first licked her delicious cunt. She was the one destined to belong to him. His True Mate.

She didn't understand that yet, but she would soon. Luc threw back the sheet he'd reluctantly used as a cover and stepped off the bed. She was doing it again. Hiding her eyes. Hiding from him. She was running. If not physically, then emotionally.

A growl welled up in the back of his throat. And it didn't come from the wolf.

He tracked her scent across the room, stopping inches in front of her. Her eyes popped open when he placed his hands on her hips. In one quick move, he flipped her around and slipped his cock between her barely spread thighs. Hot liquid trickled from her cunt and coated his shaft. All her heat, her fire, belonged to him. And she would acknowledge that.

She gasped as he skated his fingers across her pussy, dipping lightly into her open flesh. He pumped his shaft between her thighs, loving the feel of her flesh around him.

"Who do you think about when I fuck you?" he growled in her ear. She shook her head, as if to brush him away, but he wouldn't be denied. Someone was in her head—in her heart—and he would find out who. "Who do you think about when I drive my cock into your body?" he asked.

She groaned as he thrust against her, not entering her—just moving between her thighs, brushing lightly against her clit.

It wasn't enough. He needed to be joined with her—some instinct beyond his control, even beyond the wolf, commanded that he enter her. Luc spread her legs and pushed his cock into her pussy. The slick walls of her passage told him she wanted him.

He reached around her waist and collected her hands in his. With a slow, deliberate movement, he placed her palms against the door, then pulled her hips back.

She belonged to him—he'd claimed her, she'd accepted his cock and his seed. Now, he would push any other lover from her mind.

"You like it when I fuck you from behind, don't you?" he asked, beginning a slow, forceful thrust into her cunt. "Don't you, baby?"

"Yes," she groaned.

She would scream it before he was done. He continued to slide into her, listening to Caitlin's shallow breath as she accepted him. She held him so perfectly. But he didn't stop to linger. He pushed hard, letting the wet grip of her pussy lure him deeper and harder inside.

Still it wasn't enough. He needed her to scream his name — he needed to hear the truth from her lips.

"Who do you want? Whose cock do you want in your tight little cunt?" Her fingernails clawed at the door as she pushed back against his solid thrusts. "Tell me, my pretty Caitlin, who do you want fucking you?" he asked, the answer suddenly vital to his existence.

"You," she groaned, pumping her ass against his stomach. "Only you."

"Tell me," he commanded. He peeled his lips back and contained the howl that threatened. She belonged to him and damn it, she would say it .

"Only you. I want only you."

"More, baby. Give it to me. *Tell me.*"

He didn't understand it but her desire, her need, wasn't enough. He couldn't back down. He drove into her sex over and over again, needing to release his seed inside her but needing her words even more. He continued to demand her answer.

"Tell me, Caitlin. Come on, baby. You know what I need to hear."

"I love you," she sobbed, leaning against the door. "I love you. Please, Luc."

Her admission loosened the fear inside him — an emotion he hadn't recognized until it faded. The wolf growled its satisfaction.

"*Again.*"

"I love you."

He reached around and placed his fingers on her mound — sliding them down to tease her hard clit. Light, gentle touches and he felt her tremble in his arms.

She sagged against the door. He picked her up before she fell and carried her to the bed. She clung to him, easing the tension inside him a little more. As he placed her on the mattress, he drove his cock back into her. She took him. As she had all weekend. Her legs curled around his hips, squeezing him and pulling him deeper.

"Tell me," he whispered. He bit down on her throat, leaving a mark for the world to see. "Tell me," he repeated.

"I love you. Luc, I love you."

The words soothed the animal within him. And gave the human peace.

He rode her deep, sinking into the body made to hold his until he heard her shattered cry. It wasn't an incoherent moan. It was his name that left her lips as she climaxed. Throwing his head back, he howled as his seed flooded his mate's womb.

Chapter 4

Caitlin woke again as the sun brushed across her pillow. She shifted in the bed and groaned as her muscles rebelled — screaming at her for their overuse. While her body whimpered, her mind raced. Nothing made sense. The wolf had retreated shortly after moonrise, but Luc had become no less intense — fucking her through the night.

Until they'd finally fallen asleep as dawn arrived.

She turned her head and looked up. Luc lay next to her — awake and watching her. The golden wolf eyes had disappeared and the familiar vibrant blue had returned. She felt a blush move across her cheeks. All the things they'd done together came back to her in a flash. Though some of the memories were passion-fogged, others were crystal clear — the explosive orgasms, her cries for more, and Luc's voice, whispering softly his pleasure at being inside her. Unbelievably her pussy fluttered in anticipation of more. Her blush deepened.

"Good morning," she said, her scratchy early morning voice reminding her that reality was just minutes away. Holding herself as still as possible, she took a shallow breath, hoping to calm the rabid butterflies that had invaded her stomach.

"Good morning." The deep rumble of his greeting sent a new tingle into her sex. "How do you feel?" He smoothed his hand over her cheek, an unusually gentle action considering the hard fucking they'd indulged in throughout the night.

"I'm fine," she assured him. And she was. Physically, she was sore and tired, but she would recover. Her heart — she didn't know.

As she'd feared, having sex with Luc had bound her heart even more tightly to his.

He combed his fingers through her hair, staring at her face as if he'd never seen her before. The intense scrutiny made her uncomfortable. And the emotion in his eyes was too tempting. It was too easy to imagine it to be something more than it was. She couldn't let herself believe that.

She knew Luc. His loyalty was to the Pack. He would never allow anything to interfere with the Mate Bonding.

She couldn't stay here any longer—she had to get away, save what was left of her heart.

"I'd better get cleaned up, " she announced briskly, reverting to her efficient assistant's voice. "They'll be calling shortly with the test results and we should be free to go." She threw back the sheets and climbed out of bed.

"Caitlin, wait."

She stopped a few steps away. It took more courage than she thought she possessed to turn around. Luc sat in the bed, looking gorgeous and confused. And a little hurt.

"We have to be ready when they end the quarantine." She swallowed deeply. "Your mate is waiting for you in the north."

"But about last night—"

She had to stop him from saying anything sweet. The memories were going to be hard enough to deal with. She didn't need platitudes. Not from him. She straightened her spine and offered him a strained smile.

"I'm glad I was able to assist the Pack in this manner."

Luc stared as she all but ran into the bedroom.

Assist the Pack? Pain stabbed him square in the chest. Her groans of pleasure hadn't been to assist the Pack. Her orgasms hadn't been to assist the Pack. And her vows of love had nothing to do with assisting the Pack.

He glared at the closed door.

Caitlin was trying to run. She obviously didn't understand that when one ran from a predator, the predator gave chase.

* * * * *

Caitlin tapped her fingers impatiently on her folded arms as she paced the hallway outside the Alpha's Chambers. Though a modern man, Fallon maintained the trappings of the past. Pack headquarters was a labyrinth of halls and corridors, rituals and elaborate ceremonies.

A door opened at the end of the hall and Luc entered. A dainty beta female followed behind him. She smiled flirtatiously as she turned and walked the other direction. Caitlin watched the blatant flip of her hips as she strolled away.

"Has he called for us yet?" Luc asked as he approached. He flipped his damp hair out from beneath his collar. He'd just climbed out of the shower—Caitlin could smell the soap on him—and perhaps some sexy female werewolf's bed?

Luc had contained the wolf's primary rise, but Caitlin knew that things got wild and sexual around the Pack during the days surrounding a full moon. There was more bed hopping amongst unmated werewolves than a group of bunny rabbits. And the thought that Luc might have driven ten hours with her, and then crawled into another woman's bed, made the hair on the back of her neck stand up.

A possessiveness she'd never experienced before flooded her chest. Caitlin felt her lips pull back in a growl. She stopped herself before she released any sound. It was a reaction she'd seen many times between Pack Members. But she wasn't a member of the Pack. She was human. She had to remind herself that being human meant she couldn't have the one thing she craved—Luc.

After today, he would belong to another. As a human, she was allowed to witness all but the most private ceremonies. As Luc's friend, she would be expected to attend his Bonding Ceremony.

The Mate Bonding was a ritual similar to a human wedding but with fewer restrictions. It allowed for the wolves involved to take lovers, so long as the children produced from the union came from the mated pair.

She found the ceremony simple and elegant. But that was before she knew she would be witnessing Luc's.

A deep snarl broke free, creeping out between her tightly clenched teeth. *His mate* wouldn't mind if he hopped into a pretty werewolf's bed, but for some reason that thought made Caitlin want to rip someone's throat out. Preferably Luc's.

"What's wrong?" Luc asked, watching her with concerned eyes.

"Nothing. Glad to see you're still easing the wolf's needs." The words came out prissy and uptight but Caitlin couldn't stop them — or the tone.

Confusion streaked across his face. Then he looked down the hall, following the female with his eyes. He smiled. "Don't worry, baby. I showered because I was hot from the drive. Not to wash off another's scent."

Caitlin told herself she didn't care, but that didn't stop her from taking a deep inhale to see if she could detect any foreign smells — any lingering traces of perfume.

"The Alpha will see you now." The Secretary's announcement stopped any further conversation. Or analysis on Caitlin's part. It shouldn't matter to her if Luc slept with every female in the Pack. It wasn't any of her business.

When Caitlin didn't move, Luc put his hand on her back and nudged her forward. This audience was supposed to be his final preparation for the Mate Bonding, but instead, Luc was going to have to tell his Alpha that he couldn't Bond with the lovely werewolf from the other pack. And that he'd taken a human for a mate. Fallon wouldn't be happy with the change of plans.

They entered the room and Luc immediately went to the Alpha Wolf. With a movement that had little to do with humbleness and much to do with respect, Luc dropped to one knee and lowered his eyes.

"Greetings, my Alpha. I renew my vow to protect your Pack, your mate, and your person, and I bow before your wisdom."

"Arise."

Luc followed the command and came to his feet.

"Those words just stick in your throat, don't they?" Fallon asked with a smile.

Luc accepted the offered hand with a chuckle. "Only when I get to the 'wisdom' part. I grew up with you, Cousin. I know exactly what sort of wisdom you gained."

The twinkle in Fallon's eye calmed Luc. Fallon was the Alpha Wolf. He was also a friend. He would understand.

"You and I need to talk."

Confusion and a touch of concern marked Fallon's expression. Then he nodded. He turned to Caitlin and held out his hand. "You have once again delivered your charge safely home. Thank you, Caitlin."

He greeted her with a polite kiss on the cheek.

"I'm glad I was able to assist the Pack." Caitlin politely bowed her head.

There was that phrase again. Luc felt his upper lip curl back, but cautiously pulled it down. He did the only thing he could—clung to the words she'd screamed when he'd been pounding inside her body. *I love you, Luc.*

"If I might have a few minutes of your time, Alpha, when the ceremony is done?"

"Of course, my dear."

Luc couldn't help rolling his eyes. Fallon was barely three years older than he was and that made him only six years older than Caitlin. The fatherly tone and attitude didn't suit his age.

"Fallon, I need to speak with you now," Luc announced, using a commanding tone that few would dare direct toward an Alpha. Fallon raised his eyebrows in question. "It's important,"

Luc added, knowing Fallon would recognize the seriousness. Fallon nodded.

"Oh good, you've arrived." Everyone in the room turned as a unit to greet the Luna. Her pale hair was draped casually down her back. Luc bowed respectfully, but quickly, anxious to drag Fallon away. "How are you, Caitlin? You look lovely. You always look lovely of course, but still...have you done something different to you hair?"

Caitlin shook her head.

"Well, there is something different about you. I just can't put my finger on it."

She spent the weekend fucking a werewolf...

Luc kept his snide response to himself.

"Fallon," Luc said with clenched teeth.

"Merina," Fallon addressed his mate. "Would you visit with Caitlin while Luc explains to me what is so blasted important?"

Merina nodded and Luc was finally able to lead Fallon to the far corner of the room.

"We have a problem," Luc began.

"So I gathered. What?"

"I can't go through with the ceremony."

"What?!"

The harsh question was like a shot through the room. Luc glanced over to Caitlin and Merina. Both women were looking their direction.

"Going to tell me why you're backing out of a mate bonding that both packs have agreed to and that has great potential to increase the strength of both bloodlines?" Though Fallon kept his voice down, there was no mistaking the intensity.

Luc stared directly into Fallon's eyes, almost daring the other wolf to challenge him. "Caitlin's my mate."

He watched Fallon's mouth fall open. And Luc couldn't stop his smile. It wasn't often that one caught the Alpha Wolf unaware.

"How did you not notice this before?" Fallon demanded after a moment's hesitation. "A true biological mate is supposed to be *obvious* to the werewolf in the pair. How did you miss this?"

"I kept myself away from her. You were the one who told me not to mess with my staff. And I haven't. It wasn't until this weekend and we were fucking that it became crystal clear."

"Is there any chance you've made a mistake?"

Luc understood Fallon's reluctance, but he knew the truth. "No."

"Maybe it's just residual lust from the moon—combined with your appreciation. It could make you..."

Luc shook his head. "When we got here, I went to my room, Angelina was waiting for me. Naked." Every male werewolf in the Pack understood the significance of that invitation. Angelina was known for her oral skills. She could suck the chrome off a bumper. "I sent her away."

Fallon's eyes widened. "Wow."

"Exactly."

"I hate to interrupt—" Merina said. Both men jerked. They hadn't noticed her approach. "But I was eavesdropping and I thought you should know—you've got one other issue to deal with." She leaned closer and dropped her voice to a whisper. "Your little mate is newly pregnant. Her body's just kicking into overdrive."

It was Luc's moment to be stunned beyond speech. *Pregnant?* They'd made a baby? Though *he* had no doubts about it—a True Mating could be proven only by the birth of offspring. That she'd already conceived would go far in having the Pack accept her. This was direct proof she was his destined mate.

All three werewolves turned and looked at Caitlin. As if sensing their appraisal, she looked up.

"Is something wrong?"

"Uh, no," Fallon answered after a moment. He left the little group and walked back to her side. "You had something important you wanted to discuss with me as well."

Caitlin thought about putting it off, but she had Fallon's attention. "Yes." Knowing Luc's superior hearing would make it easy for him to eavesdrop but relying on the wolf's natural courtesy, she lowered her voice and spoke. "When the Ceremony is over, I'd like to discuss a transfer."

"What the hell are you talking about?"

Caitlin spun around at Luc's furious question. He all but pushed Fallon to the side and took Caitlin's shoulders in his hands. "You're my mate and that's my child you're carrying so don't get any ideas about going anywhere but home with me."

"That was subtle," Merina muttered.

Luc ignored her. So did Caitlin. "What did you say?"

"You're heard me. And don't try to change the subject. A woman's place is with her mate."

There was a wildness in his eyes she'd never seen before—and it had nothing to do with the wolf. She stepped back and glared at him. "What are you talking about? What's this about mates and…" Her mind caught up with the conversation. She slapped her hand across her stomach. "Did you say child?"

Fallon stepped in and placed his arm around her waist. Caitlin didn't know if it was to comfort her or to stop her from lunging at Luc.

"Yes, my dear, it seems that you and Luc are fated to be mates. True Mates. You've conceived."

"Bu-bu-but—" Surprise locked the words into her throat. "I thought humans couldn't mate with werewolves. I *thought*," she said, regaining her composure and glaring over the Alpha's shoulder toward Luc, because he had given her this information, "that children couldn't result in those unions."

"I told you it was rare but that if the human and wolf were destined to be mates, then it could happen." Luc leaned forward, staring down at her. For a moment she almost pulled away but stopped. Luc wouldn't hurt her, no matter how intimidating he wanted to appear. "I don't see what the problem is," he continued. "You love me. You told me so."

Caitlin straightened, trying to remember when she would have spoken those words. She'd been so careful to keep her feelings hidden. Or so she'd thought. But it seemed, at some point, she'd told Luc. Probably when they were fucking.

Not that it mattered.

"I'm not going to be your mate just because that animal inside you likes to fuck me," she snapped, forgetting for a moment that Fallon and Merina were listening. Then she decided—*what the hell?* Fallon knew what had happened this weekend. It had been his suggestion. And obviously Merina knew as well. "I deserve more than a man who marries me because of a biological urge!"

Luc shook his head and stared at her like she was speaking Russian. "What?"

All the anger slipped from her body and she shook her head sadly. "Luc, you and I both know that it wasn't you fucking me all weekend. It was that damned wolf. But that's not a reason to be together. For the other twenty-nine days of the month, you'd be stuck with me."

"But that's what I want."

"No, you don't."

He placed his hands on her shoulders, holding her steady beneath his stare. "Caitlin, the wolf was urging me on but I was in complete control of him all weekend. From the first moment my mouth touched your cunt—"

Caitlin choked, then was relieved to see that Fallon and Merina had stepped away.

"—I knew precisely what I was doing. Baby, the wolf just gave me the strength to fuck you all weekend. The desire was all mine. You're the woman I want."

Caitlin tried to slow the thoughts swirling through her head. "You've never thought so before," she pointed out.

He lifted her hands to his lips. "I always knew you were someone special. I couldn't let myself have you knowing I would have to bond with another woman. But then the wolf chose you as his mate and I knew there was no one else for me."

Her heart ached to believe him.

"Perhaps you two would like to continue discussion…in private," Fallon suggested. "I'll go make our explanations to the other pack. A True Mating takes precedence over a typical bonding."

Caitlin let herself be led away, down the hall to Luc's bedroom. The huge four-poster bed that dominated the room caught her attention. An elaborate carving of wolves running across a meadow decorated the headboard. She pulled out of his arms and stepped away.

"Are you sure about this? You're giving up a lot. You'll never be Alpha, not with a human mate. And it's probable that our children won't be able to change."

Luc smiled and reached out, brushing her hair away from her face. "I have no desire or anticipation of being the Alpha. Fallon's too healthy and too damn strong to give up that position before he's old and gray. And as for our children…" He shook his head. "It doesn't matter to me if they can change or not. They'll be perfect just as they are. Just like their mother."

Her heart melted. "Oh Luc."

He bent down and kissed her. It was soft and gentle. Nothing like the deep commanding kisses he'd given her throughout the weekend. There was something sweet and decidedly sensual in the light press of his lips to hers. He opened his mouth but didn't attempt to push his tongue inside. The delicate kisses made her heart ache. He sampled her mouth as if he'd never tasted anything so delicious and wanted to linger over the flavor.

Their bodies moved together, her legs automatically opening to cuddle his erection. His hands smoothed down her back and hips, retracing the territory he'd claimed. He spread hot kisses across her neck and chest, still soft and gentle–the light touches equally as arousing as the hard, driving caresses from before.

"I need you," he whispered against her skin. "It's been too long since I was inside you."

He lifted his head and looked at her. The silent question hung in his eyes. He was letting her know this wasn't the wolf needing comfort. This was the man asking for her to be with him.

"Make love to me, Luc."

In the heavy silence of the room, he stripped off her clothes, caressing each inch of skin as it was revealed. When she was bare, he ripped off his own clothes and carried her to the bed.

He placed her in the center and arranged her limbs, spreading her legs, massaging the tired muscles inside her thighs, easing the knots from her calves with his magic fingers. Caitlin watched him as he touched her. His movements were slow and dreamy. And focused solely on her.

And when she was relaxed and limber, he lay down beside her and licked the peaks of her breasts, soothing the sensitive tips with his tongue before gently biting down on the pert nipples. He kissed his way down her body, trailing his tongue across her rib cage and belly.

He caressed her skin with lips and tongue, with words and praises — telling her of her beauty, and the delicious taste that filled his mouth. Knowing that her heart was safe, Caitlin let herself sink into his power one more time.

He licked the soft curve of her stomach then placed a gentle kiss at the top of her sex, as if thanking her and asking permission to worship her. Moments later she felt the soft lick of his tongue across her clit. The touch was so tender and loving, it brought tears to her eyes.

Every touch was new, every caress sweet. It was as if he was paying homage to her sex. The pleasure built slowly with languid caresses and gentle touches, until he placed his lips over her clit and gave a soft suck. The sweet pull of his mouth sent an unimaginable ache into her center. She pushed her hips up, trying to get more, trying to find a release.

"Luc, please," she moaned.

"May I come inside you?" he asked, kissing her stomach and her ribs. "Or are you too sore?"

"No."

He leaned back and stopped his upward progression. Though he moved with his usual grace, she felt tension explode in his body and realized he thought she was rejecting him.

"No, I'm not too sore," she said, smoothing her hands up his chest. "I need you." The tension fell from his body and his relief was only partially masked by the trademark arrogance.

He moved over her, covering her breasts and neck with kisses, finally pressing his lips to hers. She opened her mouth and eagerly accepted his tongue. Long drugging kisses made her head spin. She wanted him, needed him, but he held back.

Instinctively knowing what he needed, she spread her legs, opening her pussy to him.

"Come inside me," she whispered—and he was there, thick and hard, the head of his cock gliding into her cunt.

Hours of desperate fucking had taught her body to accept his. To crave the sensations only he could create. But this was no frantic mating. He loved her with gentle touches and soft words. Caitlin felt the slow rise of her orgasm—a long powerful wave that started in her pussy and rolled through her body, flooding her soul with love and need.

"*Luc!*" She gripped his shoulders, trying to hold herself in this world.

He thrust into her again and again, his muscles clenching beneath her hands. She felt him come inside her, then the heavy weight of his body on hers.

As she waited for her heart to slow to a reasonable pace, she stared up at the ceiling. Luc thought everything was settled, but they still had things to discuss.

He desired her but what about...

"I love you." He followed the whispered declaration with a soft kiss on her shoulder.

"What?"

He raised his head and looked at her with twinkling eyes. "I was just thinking I hadn't actually said that and you might still be wondering. So I wanted to tell you. I love you."

"Oh."

He grimaced and pushed himself up on his elbows. "You could say it back."

"You said I already had." She squinted suspiciously up at him. "And just when did I make this statement?"

Luc smiled and a hint of red stained his cheeks. "Well, darling, it seems you'll confess anything under the power of really hot sex."

She kissed him and shook her head. "Not anything. Just the truth."

"Tell me," he said.

She heard the need shimmering behind his arrogant command.

"I love you, Luc. Only you."

About the author:

Tielle (pronounced "teal") St. Clare has had life-long love of romance novels. She began reading romances in the 7th grade when she discovered Victoria Holt novels and began writing romances at the age of 16 (during Trigonometry, if the truth be told). During her senior year in high school, the class dressed up as what they would be in twenty years—Tielle dressed as a romance writer. When not writing romances, Tielle has worked in public relations and video production for the past 20 years. She moved to Alaska when she was seven years old in 1972 when her father was transferred with the military. Tielle believes romances should be hot and sexy with a great story and fun characters.

Tielle welcomes mail from readers. You can write to her c/o Ellora's Cave Publishing at 1337 Commerce Drive, Suite 13, Stow OH 44224.

DREAM WALKER

Patrice Michelle

Chapter One

"Great, just great. Even Mother Nature's not on my side tonight."

Erin Stein gripped the steering wheel tighter as thunder rolled and lightning splintered the night sky above her. The smell of rain combined with the cool breeze blowing through her car vents caused goosebumps to form on her arms. Electricity hung in the air, the impending storm almost upon her.

As if on cue, the sudden downpour hammered against her windows. Erin glanced in the rearview mirror as the rain streaming down her back window magnified the bright lights of the truck gaining on her. She clenched her jaw and returned her gaze to the road, her shoulders tense and her heart pounding out of control.

I have to shake them, she thought, her mind whirling for alternate routes she might take. *I have to get to Kian. He'll know what to do.*

Her neck snapped back as her car jolted forward, jerking her out of her musings. Fear radiated through her at the sound of metal crumpling and plastic cracking as the truck rode her bumper, revving its engine. Holding back the scream that threatened at the violent turn of her situation, she shifted gears and slammed the pedal to the floor. Her car shot forward, fishtailing on the muddy road. She counter-steered to straighten her vehicle, thankful she'd been able to put at least a car's distance between her pursuers and herself.

"You idiots! If you kill me, you get nothing," she called out with a hysterical laugh.

Thunder rumbled, shaking the ground and even her car in its intensity.

"A miracle would be nice," she murmered at the same time a bolt of lightning struck the road twenty feet ahead of her.

As gusts of wind buffeted her car, rocking the sedan back and forth, Erin looked up and saw a tall oak tree on the side of the road sway, then begin to fall. Gunning her engine once more, she swerved against the wind and let out a sigh of relief when the tree slammed hard on the road behind her. She glanced over her shoulder in anticipation to see the truck slide across the muddy dirt road right into the tree.

"Take that!" she exclaimed in triumph, a wide grin on her face as she quickly turned back to face the road.

When her gaze landed on the huge rock lying directly in her path, Erin's smile faded and her adrenaline spiked once more. Her chest tightened with fear as she jerked the wheel to avoid the obstacle. Too late. Her car's front tire caught the edge of the rock and sent the vehicle careening straight toward the woods along the side of the road.

When she entered the woods and her car plummeted down a steep ravine, she screamed. As tension gripped her entire body, she clung to the steering wheel, her arms locked in position. It may have been fruitless, but the action gave her the false sense of security that she had a modicum of control over the situation. While tree limbs sped past, leaves and branches clawing at her windows and reality hurled toward her at an accelerated speed, Erin accepted her fate. Regret washed over her that she had failed. Squeezing her eyes shut, she prayed for a swift, painless death.

The sudden, jarring impact caused her head to slam into the steering wheel. As excruciating pain pierced her skull, a fleeting thought occurred: *why the hell didn't the airbag…*

She didn't get to complete the thought as she succumbed to blissful oblivion.

* * * * *

Erin awoke to the sound of men yelling. A man's voice called out, then faded in the distance as if he quickly moved away. Sharp pain entered her head as she tried to turn toward the noises she heard. Torrential rain beat down on the roof above her, while every single drop echoed in her aching head like a jackhammer.

She slowly opened her eyes to see a man, his long, dark, wet hair plastered to his head and shoulders, grab the man trying to open her car door. Erin gasped and pulled away when she recognized the bald man right outside her window as one of the men who'd been chasing her.

The stranger yanked her pursuer back and threw him twenty feet into the woods as if he weighed no more than a pillow.

She squeezed her eyes shut, then opened them again. Did she just see what she thought she saw?

While she started in shock, the stranger tried to open her crushed car door. When the door didn't budge, determination filled his expression. Apprehension gripped her as he grasped the handle and yelled out as he yanked hard, pulling the whole panel off its hinges.

Her eyes widened and her heart jerked at the superhuman strength. Oh yeah, no way did she miss that one!

She shrunk away when he leaned in the car and started to unbuckle her seat belt.

"You just pulled my door off my car as easy as a soda can tab." Her words came out in a croak but she needed to hear it said out loud in order to believe it.

The stranger flashed her a sheepish smile, then shrugged. "Adrenaline, I suppose." Gently touching her forehead, he asked in a concerned tone, "Are you all right?"

"I—I think so." Her hand shook as she tried to raise it to her sore head.

He clasped her hand in a warm, firm grip. Glancing at her, he used his other hand to touch her forehead once more. "You have quite a knot here."

His fingers lingered on her hairline, and then moved to her temple. Through the fog of the surreal situation, Erin realized he touched her in a familiar manner, as if he knew her. She stared at his handsome face while she marveled at the warmth his fingers emanated despite the cold rain that soaked his body. How could he be so warm?

"Let's get you out of here before these men come to," he said as he released her hand and unbuckled her seatbelt.

When he lifted her out of the car, cold rain drenched her white button-down blouse and floral rayon skirt. She clung to his broad shoulders and leaned closer to his warmth. Even through his wet chambray shirt, heat radiated off him as if he were her own personal furnace.

Setting her feet on the ground, he held her arms to steady her. As the man regarded her, Erin had to look up to meet his striking emerald gaze. Even in the dark his eyes appeared to reflect a depth in them she'd never seen in another person before. Man, he had to be at least six feet five, she thought. At five feet nine inches, she didn't run across many men where she had to make an effort to meet their gaze.

"Can you walk?"

"I think so." She started to take a step and stumbled, gasping at the dizziness in her head.

He quickly picked her back up in his arms, replying in an amused tone, "I think maybe not quite yet."

She wrapped her arms around his neck. "Thank you for helping me, um, I don't even know your name —"

The distinct clanking sound of metal slamming against metal drew their attention. They both stared at the tranquilizer dart imbedded in her car's side door less than a foot away — a little too close for comfort.

"We need to go," the dark-haired man said in a serious tone as he shifted her in his arms and threw her across his shoulder before he took off into the ravine at breakneck speed.

The deeper into the woods he ran, the denser and darker it became until a different kind of fear began to well up inside her. He may have just saved her life, but the man was still a total stranger. And she was alone with him. Erin stiffened against him, her heart racing despite the pain in her head.

"Where are you taking me? And...and...I still don't know your name," she managed to wheeze out between the jolts to her body caused by his running.

The stranger slowed his pace. When he finally stopped, he let her body slide down his chest until he cradled her in his arms once more. He met her gaze, his dark eyebrows drawing together. While his head briefly sheltered her face from the driving rain, Erin took advantage of his intense perusal and stared back, mesmerized by his striking emerald gaze.

Cold rain ran off his straight nose and high cheekbones in rivulets, the trails of water landing on her throat and chest as he spoke, "I heard your vehicle crash and came to investigate. When I approached, I saw two men surrounding your car, holding guns." He paused. A muscle jumped in his jaw as if he tried hard to remain calm before he finally continued, "I sensed they meant to harm you." He looked up and started walking again. "My home isn't much further."

Somewhat relieved at his explanation, Erin peeked over his shoulder to see if the men had pursued them. But the rain came down so hard around them she couldn't see more than three feet in front of her.

The seriousness of her situation—the fact that her boss had betrayed her, was even willing to use violence to get what he wanted, sank home as this stranger carried her to his secluded house. Having lost her adoptive parents to cancer and old age within five years of each other, she had no one to turn to except Kian. The fact that her car looked like an oversized accordion, didn't inspire confidence she'd be seeing him any time soon. Trust. She had to trust someone. Did she really have a choice?

"I'm Erin Stein." She braced herself for the inevitable ribbing her name always wrought. As a brainy physicist, her first initial and last name, E. Stein, had been the bane of her existence and the butt of way too many Einstein jokes that stuck over the years. Half her colleagues called her Ein instead of Erin.

He stopped walking and his dark gaze searched her face once more before sliding down her neck to the wet shirt clinging to her breasts. "Eriana. I like your name."

Oh right, this man had no idea what she did for a living! As evidenced by his heated look. Otherwise, he'd have probably been turned off. Warmth infused her cheeks and her breasts tingled at the electricity in his gaze. Her name might be Erin, but who was she to correct him. He had a nice, soothing voice, laced with an unusual accent that made her new name sound poetic when he spoke. She wished she could place the accent. Maybe he was Native American. With his defined cheekbones, darker skin, and pitch-black hair, he could certainly pass for one.

He gave her a sexy smile as if he knew her very thoughts. Dipping his head, he said in a formal tone, "My name is Kian."

Chapter Two

Shock slammed through her. Kian! The man who had somehow stumbled across her research theories for time travel? The man who had been emailing her for the past month trying to convince her that the world wasn't ready for time travel and never would be?

She hit his shoulder. "Why didn't you tell me who you were right away?"

He frowned. "Because we needed to concentrate on getting out of that dangerous situation, not stand around making introductions."

Erin laughed at Kian's statement. That was so like his email persona. Blunt and to the point. The introduction line in his first email to her: *I admire your brilliance, but you have to stop trying to discover the ability to time-travel.*

"Do you know I almost deleted your first email, thinking it was a joke one of my colleagues dreamed up. But when I reread your message, I realized you had knowledge about my project that none of my coworkers could possibly know."

"I have a bit of foresight," he commented with a smile.

She regarded him, still unsure how he fit into the whole picture, but something inside her made her want to trust him.

"Well, you did say something worth listening to when you told me to head in this direction if I ever got into trouble — that you'd find me." She shook her head in bemusement. "Man, you do have foresight, don't you?"

He chuckled at her comment. "Only when it comes to you, Eriana."

She smiled and relaxed against him as he began walking once more. Just like his emails, Kian radiated a confidence that had at first provoked her anger via cyberspace. Strangely, that same confidence comforted her in her current situation. She hadn't felt so safe since this whole nightmare began, she mused as she pressed closer to his warmth.

True to his word, Kian approached a small log cabin in less than ten minutes.

Once he carried her inside the one-room cabin and kicked the door shut, Erin expected him to set her down. When he held on to her and started toward his bed, she tensed once more. "Um, I can walk and the couch will do—"

"No, your mind isn't ready yet," he ground out, his tone forceful and clipped as he tightened his hold on her.

She instantly stiffened at his tone and Kian relaxed his grip, saying in a calmer voice, "You need to get warm, Eriana."

Erin wanted to argue but now that the danger seemed less eminent, her teeth chattered and her entire body shook. God, she was chilled to the bone. No fire burned in the fireplace and the cabin felt cool as well. The fall wind howled, blowing hard against the wooden walls outside.

"I'll start a fire." Kian laid her down on the bed and started to move away.

A fire would be nice, she thought. Nice and warm and cozy. *The smoky smell of a fire always makes me smile—smoke!* Smoke would draw the attention of the men pursuing her. His cabin was so secluded more than likely the men wouldn't know it even existed as long as Kian and she didn't do anything to draw anyone's attention.

"Wait!" she called out, propping up on her elbows. The fast movement cost her and she quickly laid back down, her head reeling.

Kian stood over her once more, his gaze clouded with concern. "What's wrong?"

"No fire, please," she begged him.

His frown reflected his disagreement. "The fire will warm you."

She glanced at the lamp he'd turned on near the bed, paranoia setting in. "No lights either. They'll find me."

Kian nodded his understanding and walked into the kitchen area to retrieve a couple of candles from the rustic-looking cabinet. The kitchen and living room took up half the cabin while the bathroom and bedroom took up the other half. The only room in the cabin with a door was the bathroom. Every other room in the house flowed into one another.

She noticed he didn't have a kitchen table or a TV. But he did have a big soft brown leather sofa that faced the stone fireplace. The only other furniture in the room, other than the bed, was a wooden rocking chair, an oak chest of drawers against a far wall and a matching nightstand next to the bed.

As Kian lit the thin, taper candles he'd set in metal holders on the nightstand, he said, "Get out of those wet clothes."

When he turned off the lamp, Erin started to unbutton her shirt, but she hesitated when he didn't move away.

"Er, I know the cabin isn't set up for privacy but..."

"Don't be shy about your body, Eriana. The clothing we wear only covers who we really are," Kian murmured in a dark, seductive voice.

For some reason, she didn't fear him. Well, it's not like he'd be interested in her body anyway, she thought with an inward smirk. She might be tall, but even as a teenager she'd never been super-model thin. Reaching thirty hadn't changed that fact. Of course, having mouse-brown hair and "nothing to write home about" features to boot didn't make her very inspiring on the sexual attraction scale. Nah, he wouldn't be interested in her.

"I give you my word I won't touch you unless you wish it, Eriana." His words rocked her world as he raked his heated gaze down her body.

When his emerald gaze locked with hers in the sputtering candlelight, he reached up and started to unbutton his shirt.

Despite the chills racking her body, as she watched him peel away his shirt, an inner heat began to swirl inside her belly. The heat radiated to her breasts and pulsed to her sex in throbbing waves of awareness. Never had she had such a swift, gut-wrenching reaction to another person.

Her lips parted and she held back a gasp of admiration when he peeled away his shirt to reveal broad, muscular shoulders. His well-formed biceps flexed as he drew his shirt completely off, then dropped it on the floor. Unbidden, her gaze lowered from his smooth chest to his washboard stomach as he started to unbutton his jeans.

"I'm way ahead of you," he said in a light tone, amusement lacing his words.

Erin's breathing turned choppy as he unbuttoned his pants and kicked off his shoes before he pulled his wet jeans all the way off.

When he straightened, she greedily admired his sculpted form—his thick chest, narrow waist, muscular thighs. And to think she'd spent a month dodging his emails. Oy! Her gaze traveled over his smooth olive-toned skin, not a single tan line to be seen. Oh yeah, Indian! She'd put money on it.

He was a masterpiece to look upon and his perfection made her even more conscious of her own not-so-perfect body. She'd purposefully avoided looking at his groin. She didn't want to see the evidence of his lack of desire for her. Her fingers stilled on the buttons of her top.

"I'll get undressed in the dark." She leaned over to blow out the candles.

"No, Eriana," he commanded as he approached.

His intemperate tone stopped her short, but she kept her eyes on the candles, refusing to meet his gaze.

Warm fingers grasped her chin and tilted her head. "Look at me."

The softening of his voice slid over her like a sensual purr, surprising her. Erin met his intense gaze.

Kian ran his thumb along her jaw line, then traced his fingers down her throat, causing a shiver to race down her spine.

"I know you have a beautiful mind and now I want to see the gorgeous body that goes along with it."

She bit her lip and started to shake her head when Kian reached down and clasped her hand. His gaze never left hers as he took her fingers and wrapped them around his very hard, very impressive erection, while his other hand moved to the buttons on her blouse.

"We want the same, Eriana," he said in a low, husky voice.

Raw desire reflected in his gaze as he unbuttoned the top button of her blouse, then another and another. Erin's stomach clenched and her heart raced as he finished unbuttoning her shirt.

Maybe if she distracted him, he wouldn't notice her barely indented waist or her less-than-a-handful breasts. She clasped her hand around his cock and smoothed her thumb over the plumb tip, giving him a tentative smile.

Kian's breath hissed out and he rocked his hips against her hand several times, his motions primal, but control evident as he ground out, "No." Grasping her hand, he removed it from his erection.

Uncertainty swirled through her. Fearing she'd disappointed him, Erin bit her lip and looked away.

Kian pulled her to her feet. "If we can't use the fire to warm you, I have a better idea."

Before she could respond, he handed her a candle and scooped her up in his arms. When he carried her toward the bathroom, she began to struggle. Oh no, a bath? She'd have to reveal her entire body to him. She wouldn't be able to jump underneath the covers as soon as she was naked.

"Calm your fears, Eriana. You need to get warm quickly and this is the best way."

When he entered the bathroom and she saw he only had a shower stall, Erin panicked. She obviously couldn't take a shower without his help since she had a hard time just walking. As her breathing increased, her head began to throb.

"Just give me lots of blankets, Kian. I'll be fine."

He lowered her feet to the floor in the bathroom and took the candle from her hand. Setting it on the sink, he shut the door and turned the shower on full blast. As the warm steam began to fill the room around them, Erin closed her eyes while Kian slowly removed her clothes. She didn't want to see the disappointment reflected in his gaze when she stood naked before him.

When he'd removed her clothes, she stood there feeling completely exposed and vulnerable. Embarrassed heat suffused her cheeks despite the chills that racked her frame from head to toe.

I want him to touch me, she thought wistfully.

Erin drew in a sharp breath of surprise when a warm mouth closed over one of her nipples. Her back naturally arched and her hands instantly moved to cradle his head as he sucked hard, pulling her nipple deep within his mouth, then lightly nipped at the pink tip. As heat infused her body from his attentive ministrations and her pulse began to rise, Kian moaned against her breast, lifted her in his arms, and stepped under the spray of warm water.

She wasn't a small woman, but as the hot water pounded down on them, Kian held her as if she weighed nothing. Erin clung to his broad shoulders, reveling in the erotic sensation of his wet, naked flesh against hers. He felt hard and smooth and, God, she wanted to run her hands all over his body — feel every single dip and swell of the well-formed muscles that covered his frame.

Before she could work up the nerve to act on her fantasy, Kian sat down on a bench built into the wall of the shower and leaned against the wall. Pressing her back against his chest, he kissed her neck and then her jaw. When she turned her head toward him, he captured her lips with his.

The glide of his tongue against hers, dominant and aggressive, told her exactly how this man would make love. Lurid thoughts of his body pounding into hers, giving everything and expecting just as much in return, entered her mind. Her heart hammered at the combination of his physical and her mental stimuli.

When he pulled a bar of soap from the dish above their heads and slowly rubbed the edge of the bar across each of her taut nipples, the tips hardened, causing warmth to spread to her sex. Suds began to form on her breasts and the heat of the shower and the exotic smell of the soap engulfed her senses, changing the source of her shivers from cold to sensual awareness.

As she watched Kian use the bar to draw a seductive line down the center of her body to the nest of dark curls between her thighs, her heart skipped a couple of beats before increasing to a wild staccato rhythm.

He slid his hand up her waist and across her belly until he cupped her breast, his touch possessive and firm. Erin bit back a gasp at his thoroughly intimate gesture, but when he rubbed his thumb across her nipple, she couldn't resist reacting. She arched into his touch.

The rough pad of his finger dragged across the soft, pink bud. Her breath caught at the erotic sensation. She laid her head back on his neck in complete submission, enjoying every single sensation: skin against skin, wet and warmth, the heat of his body surrounding her, the building, spiraling, out-of-control desire raging through her body.

"Beautiful," he murmured against her temple. "How can you not see how desirable your body is, Eriana?"

Chapter Three

She shook her head and moaned when he slid the fragrant bar into her curls, brushing the edge against her clit—once, twice, three times—before he dropped the soap to the floor of the shower.

Clasping her thighs in his large hands, he pulled, silently directing her to put her feet on his knees. Erin did as he bid, her breathing changing to a rapid pace as her body throbbed in intense need to be touched, to be caressed, to be...

Possessed.

Kian's hand slid into her soapy curls, his finger brushing down the front of her clit. He played with her sensitive bud, back and forth, toying with her, creating a wave of desire swirling within her body that mimicked the steam curling around them. Erin rocked her hips, giving in to his masterful strokes.

Kian tweaked one of her nipples while he rolled the sensitive bud of her clitoris between his thumb and forefinger, and rasped in a very aroused voice, "*Kruma, a nara.*"

Heat radiated in her lower belly at his foreign words and she instinctively knew he'd just told her to let go. Erin curled her toes on his legs, gaining purchase as she pressed against him and sought her climax.

Her movement caused her backside to brush against his erection. Over the sound of the splattering water, Kian groaned low and deep near her ear. His hand moved from her breast to her mound and he immediately plunged two fingers deep inside her core.

Erin called out his name as he gave her body exactly what it needed. Her sheath instantly contracted around his fingers and her heart raced as she moaned in pure pleasure. Through half-closed eyes, she noticed the shadows on the shower walls change as the candlelight sputtered and dimmed. Even the warmth and wetness of the shower seemed to fade until only the heat of Kian's body, the brand of his touch, and the promise of fulfillment, dominated her brain. She rode her climax, arching against him in total, blissful abandon, moaning her pleasure against his neck.

With her heart still racing and the final spasms of her orgasm throbbing throughout her body, Kian swiftly stood with her and turned her around to face the wall. Taking her hands, he pressed her palms to the white tile as his cock nudged against her moist entrance from behind.

Erin had never had sex in this position. For that matter, she'd never had sex in a shower before. The entire experience made her feel wanton, dominated and oh-so-ready to be fucked…she'd worry about protection in another life. It's not as if someone like her often got a chance to meet someone like Kian, let alone have passionate sex with him.

Excitement shot through her as he kept one hand over hers on the wall. His chest pressed against her back while he whispered in her ear, "Trust and know that I can't give you a child this way, Eriana."

She gave a doubtful laugh and panted out in a sarcastic tone, "I'd like to know your idea of how you *could* impregnate me then."

"Where I come from it takes more than a joining of bodies," he said in a rough voice as he kissed her neck then entered her body in one forceful thrust. His aggressive action sent any thoughts of trying to make sense of his words right out of her mind.

She cried out at the full stretching of her inner walls, the depth of his penetration, but Kian didn't give her a chance to pull away. He slid a hand down her lower belly and pressed against it as he withdrew and thrust back inside her again and again. With each plunge he took, he hit her hot spot inside while the counterpressure from his hand on the outside of her body only heightened the sensations rocking through her. Erin keened her delight and rocked her hips, pushing back against him, accepting his forceful pistoning with reckless abandon.

"Kian!" She screamed his name as her body began to pulsate around him.

"*Shimnara,*" he groaned as he bit down on her shoulder and rammed into her once more.

Never in her life had a sexual experience compared to being with Kian. The erotic sensation of being bitten while in the throes of a full-blown orgasm only fueled her libido further.

Erin's heart threatened to burst from her chest. She moaned long and loud as a deeply satisfying climax rippled throughout her body. When she opened her eyes it was to see the entire room slowly fade to black. Surrounded by pure darkness, the only sensation she felt was Kian surrounding her with his heat, filling her with his body while her walls contracted around his cock.

The last thing she remembered before she succumbed to the lightheadedness racking her brain was the screaming sound of a large wildcat off in the distance.

Grrrrrooooowl.

* * * * *

When Kian sat down on a stool in the bathroom with her in his arms Erin opened her eyes. After he'd rubbed a towel all over her body and her hair, he stood her up and opened the bathroom door. Running his hand across the mirror above the sink, he wiped away the steamy mist.

"What do you see? he asked, his tone low and quiet.

She looked up at his handsome face, his dark eyebrows, his long, thick, wet hair slicked back from his head, making his angular features that much more dominant and downright sexy. "I see a tall, handsome man named Kian," she responded, not sure what he wanted from her. *Well, other than to be with a woman who could stay conscious more than a half hour,* she thought with a wry smile. Did she really faint from that orgasm?

Kian reached around from behind her and touched her jaw, turning her gaze until she saw herself in the mirror.

"No, Eriana. What do *you* see?" He repeated his question, patience evident in his tone.

Regretfully she pulled her gaze from his in the mirror to look at herself. "I see an average looking woman with shoulder length blah light brown hair and hazel green eyes."

She met his gaze in the mirror once more, sighing. "I'd rather look at you."

Kian's eyes narrowed and his jaw hardened. He brushed his finger down her cheekbone. "High and defined."

He then slid his finger across her chin. "Strong and determined."

Moving his thumb to her mouth, he said as he brushed her lower lip, "Full and sweet." He leaned close and whispered in her ear, "I can't wait to feel your lips around my cock, sucking me long and hard."

Erin's heart jerked in her chest at his lurid words. She'd never been more turned on in her life.

His warm breath fanned against her check as he continued. "Did you know your eyes turn the shade of Aradan jade when you're aroused? Look and see."

Erin quickly glanced in the mirror. Even in the dim candlelight, she could see her eyes were a shade she'd never seen before—a beautiful shade of dark green.

Her lips parted in surprise at the discovery of herself the way Kian saw her. She closed her eyes when his hands came around and cupped her small breasts, then plucked at her nipples.

"Responsive in every way," he said in a hoarse voice before he swiftly turned her around. Grasping her upper back, he pulled her close and captured a nipple in his mouth, sucking the tip, nipping at her until she clung to his shoulders in sheer ecstasy, her body primed to be taken again.

Flicking her wet nipple with his tongue, he gave her a devilish look. "More than a mouthful is wasteful, *a nara*. My mouth is only *so* wide."

Lifting his head, he slid his hands to her waist and pulled her against him, saying in a serious tone, "I like a woman who can handle my weight, not one who's going to break underneath me."

Tears filled her eyes at his words. The knowledge that he found her desirable in every way sent a tingling sensation zinging through her body all the way to her toes.

She slid her fingers through his wet hair and pulled his head close. "Then I'm your woman," she whispered right before she touched her lips to his.

Breaking their kiss, he slid his hands down her spine, clasped her rear, and pressed his erection against her belly. "You *are* mine, Eriana. In so many ways you have yet to comprehend," he finished as his mouth covered hers once more.

Erin's head reeled at the possessive nature of Kian's kiss, how well he wove his seductive web around her. She melted against him and almost forgot the candle when he picked her up in his arms to carry her out of the room.

Kian let her set the candle on the nightstand before he tugged back the burgundy down comforter and laid her in the bed. Crawling in beside her, he leaned against the headboard and pulled her between his legs, leaning her back against his chest.

Kissing her on the neck, he slid his hands down her chest to fondle her breasts. "Tell me what happened. Your cryptic email of "'You were right. In five minutes I'm en route to the destination you recommended,' doesn't necessarily tell me everything."

As he kissed a path from her collarbone to the sensitive spot behind her ear Erin answered him in a breathless voice, "You just *have* to hear how right you were, don't you?"

"No." He stopped his seduction of her body and turned her face until she looked at him. Brilliant green eyes locked with hers. "I think it'll ease your fear if you talk about it."

A shudder passed through her that he seemed to know her so well yet had only just met her. She turned away, confused but oddly comforted that someone else understood just how scared she was. Over the past several days, she'd had to hide her fear behind a mask of professional academic acceptance as her 'scientific discovery' came crashing down around her.

Kian wrapped his arms around her, surrounding her with his warmth. He whispered in her ear, "Tell me."

She sighed and tried to suppress the shiver of apprehension that started in her body as soon as she thought about the recent past. "A few days ago I sent off an email to my superior at the University to tell him I had finally succeeded in my research."

"Creating the ability to time-travel," he interjected.

She nodded. "I thought time-travel would be a wonderful tool for mankind. The future holds many discoveries, hopefully including medical advances. A cure would be found for every illness eventually. So why not benefit our race today and make those discoveries sooner...er, with a little help."

Her voice turned bitter and her entire body tensed as she thought of the domino effect her breakthrough had wrought. "But little did I know just how politically active the head of the Physics department was. I later learned Daniel Haughten had been involved with a secret military defense organization for years. When he read my email about the successful outcome of my research, he immediately realized the potential time-travel could have for giving our military an advantage and pounced on it."

Kian splayed his hand over her ribcage and rubbed his thumb under the curve of her breast in a rhythmic motion as if his touch alone could soothe her frazzled nerves. "Wouldn't the military personnel's memories be lost, too, when they came back to the past—all they'd learned for naught?"

"That's the theory, yes. Why do you think I'm running? Not only did I not give them the entire process it takes to create a rift in time in my initial documents—I retained the code key to turn on the energy source—but my boss insisted I also create a 'vacuum' that wouldn't be affected by the change in the time continuum. He was right. That was something I had initially overlooked in my haste to successfully establish the ability to time travel."

"A vacuum? You mean like a room?"

"No, they just wanted a vial, something small that would fit in a person's hand—a place where a digital chip could be hidden. That way when they came back from the future, the information they'd collected couldn't be erased in the trip back in time."

She turned to face him, her gaze searching his. "Think about it, Kian. If Daniel's group were able to retrieve advanced weapons from the future, entire nations could fall. The balance of world power could so easily be shifted in their favor until there would be only one dominant country."

Kian nodded as he ran his hands down her arms and across her belly. She turned away once more, tremors of anxiety making her voice quiver. "All because one nation would have the ability to bend time."

Leaning her head back against his neck, she continued in a sad tone, "Daniel was so blinded by the potential military aspects that could benefit from time-travel, he didn't even consider the whole point of my discovery…a world without disease."

Kian had begun to massage her neck while she spoke, but his hands stilled at her last words. "That's where you're wrong, Eriana."

Chapter Four

"Huh?" she said, turning her body around to face him and tucking her knees underneath her. Her heart raced at his revelation.

He reached up and brushed a tendril of hair away from her cheek before rubbing his thumb along her jaw. The reverent look on his face made her heart constrict with emotion. With every word, every touch…he made her feel more and more cherished.

"I'm not from your world, *a nara* – " he began.

She leaned back with a grin, letting amusement reflect in her gaze. "You can say that again, hot stuff. No way would I see someone like you roaming the labs at the University."

A look of sheer determination filled his gaze. "That's not what I meant." Clasping her shoulders, he stared at her as if willing her to believe.

She let her gaze roam his body.

Gimme a break. He looks human. Okay, there was the strength he'd displayed earlier by ripping my door off my car as if he were popping open a can of chips, but he did *mention adrenaline. God knows he* feels *human,* she thought with an inward chuckle as she remembered how well his cock filled her body.

Kian clasped her chin in his hand and elevated her head until she looked at him. "And I won't let you forget how well I fill you, Eriana, as I plan to again and again."

Warmth rushed to her sex at his adamant statement while her eyes grew wide with shock as realization dawned on her. *Had he just read her mind?*

"Yes," he replied, his expression impassive.

Erin shook her head and scooted away, refusing to believe. "You *look* no different from any other human man."

He raised an eyebrow. "What? You expect me to look like a little green man?"

She folded her arms over her breasts in a defensive manner and glanced around the room accusingly as she said in a loud voice, "No. What I think is..." She paused and raised her voice in case she was being recorded, "someone is playing a cruel joke on me."

Kian moved toward her on his hands and knees, stalking her, his expression intense, almost feral. "What will it take to convince you?"

Read my mind, Mr. Man-From-Planet-Gorgeous. I want to know what your *mouth feels like on* me, she thought with a smirk.

Erin had barely completed the thought when Kian clasped her ankles and jerked her legs toward him, pulling her flat on her back.

"I've never had a more appealing request, *a nara*." An arrogant look crossed his face as his mouth descended to her mound.

Erin's heart hammered out of control as his tongue made contact with her body. She arched her back and raised her hips closer to his warm, moist mouth. Kian nuzzled her vaginal folds, then lapped at her slit from bottom to top while a humming sound surrounded her so completely that her body vibrated.

Where was that noise coming from? she wondered as she grasped the covers and gave over to the tide of emotions welling inside her. God, he was good. He'd begun to lick her sex in long, tantalizing strokes, each lap of his tongue slightly rougher than the last.

Man, his tongue felt wonderful. She didn't remember his tongue feeling rough when he'd kissed her, but now that it was stroking her entrance, she felt every abrasion against her sensitive skin and reveled in the unique sensation that only heightened her pleasure.

After he ran his rough tongue over her clit and she keened out her pleasure, Kian spoke. *You've only seen some of my powers. Now look at me*, he demanded.

She realized he'd just spoken in her mind and the knowledge made her meet his gaze in amazed disbelief. The humming sound grew louder as if it was her own blood rushing through her veins—the beat seemed *that* rhythmic, *that* close, *that* seductive.

All thoughts of the strange noise invading her senses fled when he clamped his lips on her clit, sucking hard, at the same time he slid two fingers inside her channel. Erin locked her gaze with his and the raw sexual hunger in his eyes sent her over the edge. His gaze reflected the candlelight like an animal's—glowing, hypnotic, exotic…erotic.

Erin screamed as she came, rocking her hips against Kian's mouth and hand. He was relentless as he withdrew his hand and clasped her ass, yanking her even closer. Pressing his face against her body, he groaned as he swallowed the warm juices that flowed with her orgasm.

Again! he commanded in her mind. *I want more.*

Is this for me or you? she thought in exhaustion as her heartbeat started to slow.

This time is definitely for me, he mentally ground out while he continued to lave at her nub and slid a finger inside her. His enticing touch igniting her once more, Erin dug her heels in the bed for leverage as her breathing turned choppy and her heart rate kicked up.

Kian withdrew his finger and slid it down her wet slit, pressing on the skin between her vagina and her anus. *When I enter you again…where do you want my cock? Here…* He thrust his finger deep inside her channel once more, causing Erin to moan in ecstasy. *Or here*, he finished as he withdrew his finger from her core and trailed it down to her anus and circled the entrance.

Erin gasped at the foreign, erotic sensation. She'd never been touched there before. *Would it feel good? Or strange?*

Never be afraid to explore every part of your body, a nara, he whispered in her mind, the deep timbre of his voice dark, enticing, seductive, as he applied light pressure.

Though her mind considered the potential pleasure she might derive, her body instinctively tensed. Kian chuckled in her mind. *We'll save that lesson for later. That time will come, Eriana, and so will you. Put your feet on my shoulders.*

Erin threaded her fingers into his wet hair and clasped his head as she lifted her feet and placed them on his shoulders, her pulse racing out of control.

As Kian laved at her sex, he plunged two fingers in her core, withdrew and thrust them inside again. When her body began to tense as her impending orgasm coiled within her, Kian withdrew his hand from her body, grasped her buttocks, and pressed his chin against her folds, sucking her clit relentlessly.

While Erin thrilled at the additional pressure against her body, her heartbeat roared in her ears. Her entire body tuned to the sounds around her and that was when she heard the humming again, but this time she felt the vibration against her sex as if...as if Kian were a living vibrator!

The sensual thought caused her world to splinter around her and Erin gave over to the jolts of pleasure streaming through her body. As the candlelight sputtered and finally extinguished, dousing the room in total darkness, the distinct smells of candle wax and faint smoke were the only sensations she could distinguish other than Kian's masculine scent and heated touch — the only ones that mattered.

Long after her tremors had ceased, he continued to lave at her sex. But his ministrations seemed different, more attentive than sexual, she thought as she combed her fingers through his slightly damp hair, enjoying the brush of his thick, long locks against her inner thighs.

Kian finally moved and relit the candles. Climbing back into bed, he crawled over her body, blocking her in. A devilish smile tilted his lips. "Do you believe me now?"

Erin grinned and nodded as she tucked his hair behind his ears so she could see his handsome face. "Oh yes. That was definitely out-of-this-world, Kian," she answered with a chuckle.

He frowned. "I think you need to be spanked for your impudence, *a nara*."

Before she could reply, he had her face down over his lap, his hand on her back holding her in place. Amidst bouts of laughter, Erin struggled to get up until a resounding slap landed on her backside.

"Ouch!" She tried to jerk around to frown at him.

"I come from Aradan."

Smack!

"...A world without disease."

"Damn it, Kian, let me up!" Erin started to struggle in earnest.

"Not until you accept what I tell you," he replied in a gruff voice.

Smack!

Her backside had started to sting with that third slap. "Kian!"

"I'm here because your people *did* eventually travel to my planet. They didn't care about our medical advances. Instead, they all but destroyed my race."

"But...but my invention only made time-travel possible, not space travel." Guilt washed over her, despite the impossibility.

"Your invention was the catalyst, Eriana. Daniel used time travel to go forward in time to bring back advanced weapons of mass destruction to his time. But to retrieve information on creating those futuristic weapons, he used your invention as a bartering tool. Everyone was happy—the people in the future got your 'time-travel' data and Daniel got his weapons."

She looked over her shoulder and met his gaze, her tone adamant. "Like I said, my invention only impacts time-travel not space."

His brows drew together. "You're only aware of the limits of physics by today's standards. There are discoveries in the future that, when combined with your invention, allowed your future descendents to travel much greater distances than they would ever have been able to do without it. That's when Aradan was discovered. Once your descendants learned of our capabilities, they held our loved ones hostage while they treated the ones with the strongest powers as lab rats."

The depth of emotion and pain in Kian's voice, the rigid way he held his body, made Erin cease her struggles. Her heart ached for all that his people had gone through...all because of her. She went limp against him, waiting, accepting her punishment.

Anticipating another hard smack, she jumped when Kian's hand brushed gently against her backside. He kneaded the soft flesh, then clasped her cheek in a possessive manner.

"I don't blame you, Eriana. Your intentions were altruistic. I have learned from your people, barbaric though they were. Without your invention I would never have known how far our galaxy extends. But, for the survival of my race, we must undo what should have never been."

He rolled her over and cradled her in his arms, kissing her forehead. "I'm here to help you complete your mission to destroy your invention—to ensure the ability to time-travel is never discovered."

Lying down on the bed, he turned her back to his chest and tucked her body against his before pulling the comforter over them. Her heart raced as the realization of his alien status sunk in. But as quickly as it raced in excitement, her stomach tensed when she realized his time with her might be limited. She rolled on her back and touched his jaw, tears sparkling in her eyes.

"You have to go back, don't you?"

He gave her palm a tender kiss before he met her gaze once more. "Yes. I'm a leader for my people. Though I know they'd do fine without me, they seem to have grown attached to me."

He clasped her hand and laced his fingers with hers. "Are you ready to let me help you disable your invention?"

She stared at the man above her. He made her forget her apprehension at the very thought of going back to the University and her lab where Daniel had posted his men, effectively imprisoning her until he got what he wanted. At least now she wouldn't have to do it alone. She slowly nodded her assent.

Kian grinned, his white teeth flashing in the dim light. "Rest for now. You'll need your strength soon enough."

She frowned. "But I'm not tired."

"Rest, *a nara*," he commanded.

That was the last thing she remembered before her eyelids grew too heavy to hold them open any longer.

* * * * *

Erin awoke to Kian's voice as he nuzzled her neck. "It's time to wake, Eriana."

She sighed and snuggled against him. She'd never get tired of hearing him say her name like that.

He swiftly stood and held out a hand to her. "Now that you're rested, we need to go."

Noting that he must've put on his pants while she slept, she asked, "Go?"

"Destroy your invention," he reminded her.

Disbelief rocked though her that he'd want to leave now, in the middle of a storm...er, wait a minute. It wasn't storming anymore. As a matter of fact, it was eerily quiet outside.

Kian looked toward the window with a grin. "Yes, the storm does appear to have stopped," he said as his gaze returned to hers, beguiling her. Clasping her hand, he pulled her to her feet to stand in front of him.

"Your clothes are dry now. Get dressed and let's go save these power-hungry humans from themselves."

She smiled and started to speak when bright lights flashed in the windows accompanied by the sound of a helicopter flying right over the cabin. Panic seized Erin once more and she pulled away from his grasp.

Kian gave her a determined look and held out his hand once more, his tone quiet yet commanding. "Ignore the lights and sounds, Eriana. Concentrate on me."

She bit her lip. The lights circling the cabin combined with the *whoosh, whoosh, whoosh* of the helicopter's blades seemed to beat in time with her hammering heart. Fear engulfed her. She put her hands over her ears and cried out, "How can I ignore them? They've found me!"

Kian walked to the door and opened it, changing the muffled sounds outside to a deafening roar. Facing her, he held out his hand once more and spoke in her mind. *Trust me.*

The bright lights outlined his powerfully built body in an almost ethereal glow. The wind whipped his long hair around his face, making him look like a warrior standing on the edge of battle, ready to face the enemy.

I need your strength, she thought as trepidation rooted her where she stood.

Kian's expression turned tender as he lowered his hand and called out over the noise. "Know that you'll always have my strength and my love, *a nara*." As soon as he finished speaking, he walked outside and closed the door behind him.

"No!" She screamed out. *He can't leave me*, she thought, her mind frantic. Shoving aside her anxiety of being captured and heedless of her naked state, she ran toward the door and pulled it open.

Chapter Five

Erin awoke to bright lights shining in her eyes through the window's half-closed mini-blinds while the sound of a helicopter's blades almost drowned out men's voices yelling outside. Surveying the stark, antiseptic-smelling room around her, and the single hospital-type bed underneath her, total confusion caused her body to tremble.

Where am I? she thought as panic began to set in. *And where is Kian? God, don't tell me everything I just experienced was a dream.* She drew in a quick breath at the deep sense of loss that realization caused.

When she tried to raise her hand to her mouth to muffle her sobs, a sharp pain drew her attention. She looked down to see an IV taped to the back of her hand.

I'm here, Eriana.

Erin jerked her head up at the voice and peered around the darkened room, looking for the source. The helicopter swept by once more, its lights gliding across the walls and floor. Empty. No one was in the room.

Oh God, not only have I had a vivid, oh-so-real dream, I've just invented an imaginary friend to boot, she thought miserably, totally questioning her sanity.

The man chuckled in her mind. *I wouldn't classify myself as a friend, but you can consider me your playmate if you want.* His tone turned clipped and urgent when he spoke again, *Get up and run!*

His exigency spurred her to action. *So what if a new personality has somehow emerged from my brain. Apparently, my old personality got me into this mess in the first place.* The self-deprecating thought crossed her mind as she threw back the covers and set her feet on the cold tile floor.

Lightheadedness and weakness washed over her in waves. Erin fought the need to sink back onto the bed and tried to take a step, but her knees gave out under her. Before she slid to the floor, she quickly grasped the edge of the bed for support.

Cold air brushed her backside when she leaned over the bed and took deep, steadying breaths. The hospital gown did little to cover her body as a cold sweat broke out all over her skin, making her shiver.

"I—I can't. I'm too weak," she moaned out in frustration.

Remember my promise, Eriana. I will give you my strength, he replied at the same time she felt a surge of energy rush through her body, washing away the weakness. She stood and tested her legs, amazed the weakness had disappeared.

Marvel later. Now move that lovely ass of yours! We haven't much time.

As she turned toward the door, his voice entered her head once more. *Find the stairs. Take them to the roof.*

She peeked out the door and saw one security guard reading the paper and the other one flirting with a nurse sitting behind the desk right outside her room. Opening the door another inch, she strained to see down the hall. A silent sigh of relief escaped her when she saw a red exit sign hanging over a door at the end of the hall.

Biting her lip, her heart thudding in her chest, Erin slowly opened the door. Just when the door reached a point she could finally slip through, the hinges creaked, drawing the guards' attention.

Throwing open the door, she bolted down the hall as fast as her feet would carry her. One man yelled out for her to stop while the other one talked into his walkie-talkie. "She's out of her coma, sir, and trying to escape. We're in pursuit."

A coma? she thought in shock as she reached the exit door and pushed it open. *Oh boy, no wonder I made up an entire fantasy. But why am I going to the roof? There's nowhere to go once I'm up there!*

No voice with a witty answer entered her head as she rushed up several flights of stairs. The sounds of men's booted feet trampled the metal stairs behind her.

When she reached the roof and closed the door, Erin looked around. The helicopter was heading straight toward her. Oh God! She began to run across the building to hide behind a utility unit and mentally groused, *Why the hell would my own new split-personality suddenly abandon me in a crisis. Oh, yeah, because it's chicken-shit!*

Such skepticism, Eriana. Where's the trust? Kian's amused voice entered her head. *Run to the edge of the building as far from the door as possible. Wait there.*

Now I truly am losing it, she thought as she veered away from her original destination and ran toward the edge of the building. Not that she could explain it, but somehow she trusted the confident voice echoing in her head.

When she reached the edge, the helicopter now hovered above the building. Its bright spotlight made her wince as the two soldiers opened the door to the roof and stepped outside.

Out of the corner of her eye, she saw a black blur rush past her, and then the helicopter pitched sideways as if it'd been knocked by a heavy force. The sudden tilt made the blades come dangerously close. To avoid the danger, Erin threw herself to the ground, her adrenaline pumping through her body as her breathing turned choppy and erratic.

The helicopter pitched once more and this time its blades took a large chunk out of the building, causing the aircraft to nosedive straight to the ground. When the helicopter landed with an earth-shaking thud, exploding on impact, she screamed and covered her head as fire and debris shot to the sky and against the side of the building. Glancing up at her pursuers, she noticed the explosion had knocked the two soldiers down to the ground.

As the men quickly scrambled to get up, a huge black panther emerged from behind the utility building, his powerful shoulders rising and falling with each step he took toward them.

He walked with a steely confidence, his entire bearing demanding respect for his size and lethal nature.

The animal's gaze never left the men as he moved to stand between the soldiers and Erin. His long black tail hung nearly to the ground, the tip of it twitching back and forth as if he waited to attack.

One of the soldiers radioed his commander. "Um, we have a panther up here on the roof, sir."

The radio clicked off.

"A what? Repeat soldier," the gravelly voice came across the line.

"A huge, black jungle cat, sir," the man clarified as he trained his gun on the cat.

Before his commander could reply, the cat let out a loud roar and dove toward the men. She watched in shock at the speed with which the cat moved. In a matter of two seconds the men were down. Not a single shot had been taken. Though very little blood was spilled, neither man moved.

She shuddered at their swift deaths and stood up on shaky legs, her heart ramming in her chest. Then the panther turned and started to walk toward her his movements swift and purposeful. Oh God, she was next. She could try to run but the panther was too fast. She knew if she ran it would only encourage the large predator to hunt her down.

As he approached, the raging fire behind her reflected in the panther's striking green eyes, reminding her so much of Kian. An ache settled in her chest. Why couldn't he have been real? As the animal stalked toward her, he reared up on his hind legs, letting out his wildcat's roar. Before her eyes, he changed to a man's form. Kian's beautiful, handsome form.

As she succumbed to total shock and her knees crumbled underneath her, Erin's whole world went black once more. She felt Kian's arms catch her and heard his voice from far, far away.

"We'll have to work a little harder on this 'staying conscious' thing, *a nara*."

* * * * *

Erin jolted awake at the sound of car horns honking. The crisp fall breeze blew through the window and the scent of smoky fires teased her senses. Smoky fires…the thought made her memories come rushing back.

"Kian!" she called out and sat up quickly, her rapid heart rate causing her entire body to jerk in time to its thudding rhythm.

"I'm here," he responded in a quiet tone from a chair near the window.

She turned at the sound of his voice. Kian wore faded jeans, a black t-shirt, and boots and had his long hair tied back away from his face. But his eyes, God, his jewel-toned eyes mesmerized her.

He stood, opened a thermos, and poured the liquid into a cup. Walking over to the bed, he handed her the cup saying, "Drink this. You were in a coma for three days. This should help you get your strength back."

The orange liquid smelled so good, like tomato soup with elusive spices she couldn't quite place. Her hands shook as she tried to raise the cup to her lips. With concern reflected in his gaze, Kian sat down on the bed and held the cup for her so she could sip the broth.

As the delicious soup slid down her throat, Erin stared at him over the rim of the cup, wondering about his feelings. If everything she'd experienced was a dream, they'd never physically touched, let alone made love. She realized he'd somehow created a safe, secure place, a fantasy for her so she could overcome her fears and emerge from her coma. Then why did it hurt so much to look at him?

His green eyes darkened and his gaze slid hungrily over her body. She followed his gaze and realized the comforter pooled around her waist, revealing her naked flesh. Embarrassment swiftly set in as she pulled the covers back up to cover her chest.

"Remember what I said about covering your body," he warned.

"*Your* skin seems to have an even deeper layer, doesn't it, Mr. Panther?" she responded defensively with a half-laugh.

"It's who I am," he sighed. "I have feline blood in my genetic make-up. All Aradanians do. I'm also a dream walker, Eriana."

His reminder of their time together, even if only in her dreams, embarrassed her further. She needed a layer of protection. "Where are my clothes?"

He nodded to a set of clothes on the table. "I collected some things from your house to prepare for when you finally awoke from your coma." Returning his gaze to hers, he continued, "While you were unconscious, I brought you to this hotel and bathed every inch of your body."

His lips quirked at the heat that rose to her cheeks. Then his expression turned serious and intense. "It was the only way I could touch you and not get physically involved. I assure you, I enjoyed every brush of my hands on your skin."

Tormented emotions swirled in his gaze: frustration, sexual hunger, regret. "Your dreams were as real to me as they were to you. I've never become physically involved in another's dreams, but you were pure temptation, *a nara*. I've watched you for a month while this whole thing stirred to its inevitable conclusion, but once I entered your dreams, I couldn't resist. I had to touch you, make love to you, even if only in our minds."

She finished the broth and set the cup down on the nightstand. Meeting his gaze, she touched his arm, hurt stabbing at her heart. "You talk as if it's a bad thing...you touching me."

He moved swiftly, putting his hands on the bed on either side of her, blocking her in. His expression angry, intense, almost...explosive. "I want nothing more than to spread your soft thighs and slide my cock into your warmth. To fuck you again and again until your body contracts around me, milking me dry. I'd want us both totally satiated and exhausted until neither can move," he replied in an intemperate tone.

The emotion in his gaze and the ferocity of his words told her just how much he wanted, but she didn't understand.

"Then why— "

"If I get physically involved with you, I might impregnate you. Then when I return to my time, I would leave behind a part of my race in your time and your world," he bit out angrily. Kian pushed himself away. Standing up, he clenched and unclenched his fists as if it took supreme effort not to act on his wishes.

"Get dressed, Eriana. We've got to get back to the University and destroy your creation."

Kian had never felt so powerless in his life. He was a commanding leader among his people, yet here, in the presence of this one woman, he felt both impotent and enraged.

As Eriana got dressed and ran a brush through her shoulder-length light brown hair, he watched through a hooded gaze, coveting every movement. He desperately wanted to see her hazel eyes turn that beautiful shade of green when she came in his arms. He knew they would.

While she dressed, she argued, "Are you certain, Kian? I use the monthly pill. Surly that's enough protection."

In his heart he wanted to believe. He might come from a very advanced race in many ways, but his people still held on to certain superstitious beliefs. Her birth control might not work and he'd never leave behind a cub.

Dressed in a short black skirt, a lightweight white sweater and tennis shoes, she stood in front of him, a confused expression on her face. "Why did you pick out a skirt?"

Kian flashed an unrepentant grin. "I might not be able to touch but I may as well enjoy the view while I can."

She frowned and backed away. "That's just cruel, Kian."

Hiking her skirt, she pulled down her underwear saying, "Well, two can play at this game."

Kian set his jaw. The idea of her running around with nothing covering her sex would drive him nuts. Already he smelled her arousal.

"Not a good idea, Eriana. Put your underclothes back on," he ground out.

She twirled her underwear around her finger with a challenging look in her eye. "Make me."

Kian knew that if he touched her, he'd have her bent over and his cock thrust deep into her warmth, his hips meeting hers as he stroked in and out of her body, faster than she'd ever been taken. It would be too late for him. He'd be bound to her and her world.

His chest constricted at the thought, for his heart already belonged to her. But he had a duty to fulfill and fulfill it he would, even at the expense of his own personal sacrifice—losing his one true mate. Their mental connection was too strong to be otherwise. In his race it took both a strong mental and physical connection to conceive a child. For that reason, each birth was a rare and precious gift on his planet.

He'd been physically attracted to Eriana from the first moment he saw her. But he couldn't have anticipated the special mental connection they'd have. Even now, outside of her dreams, he could still hear her thoughts. She wanted him.

Fuck!

He liked that human word he'd discovered in his studies of Earth. He liked the versatility of its uses. But right now all he could think about was fucking his mate again and again. Lust seared through his body, tightening his balls, knotting his stomach.

Kian took a couple of deep breaths, opened the hotel room door, and mumbled, "Suit yourself. Let's go."

Erin put her hand on his arm and pulled him back in the room. "Not so fast, Kian." Shutting the door behind him, she gave him a seductive smile as she reached for the waistline on his jeans and pulled him against her. "I believe there's one fantasy we didn't fulfill."

Chapter Six

"Eri—" he started to warn, but instead he ended up sucking in his breath when she grabbed his balls through his jeans and held him in a firm grip.

Standing on tiptoe, she whispered in his ear, "I want you to know what my mouth feels like on your cock. I want you to have your own fantasy before you leave."

Kian fisted his fingers in her hair and pulled her head back, intending to push her away. His anger, borne of unfulfilled sexual frustration, rose until he stared down into her eyes—eyes the color of Aradan jade—beautiful, desire-filled eyes. They stripped him bare. Goddess, he wanted her.

She released him and slid her palm up the front of his jeans. The pressure against his throbbing cock was almost more than he could bear. Her floral scent filled his senses as she kissed his jaw and then his neck before she pulled open the buttons on his jeans. His heart stuttered in his chest when she slid her fingers from the sensitive tip of his erection all the way to the base of his shaft.

"You're much bigger then you led me to believe in my dream," she chuckled, her voice filled with delighted surprise.

Her words warmed his heart. Thank the Goddess she wasn't fearful of his size.

"I didn't want to scare you away, *a nara*," he said in a dry tone.

"No worries there, tiger," she teased.

"Panther," he growled back as she briefly let go to slide his pants to his ankles. When she stood up once more, she encircled as much of his wide cock as she could, pumping her hand up and down his shaft.

Kian moved his hips, thrusting into her hand, anticipating what her warm mouth would feel like on his erection. He closed his eyes and leaned heavily against the door, rocking into her.

His entire body jerked when her heated mouth closed around the tip of his cock even as she kept her hand on the base of his shaft.

Nothing compared to the reality of the warmth of her mouth around him.   The real, physical sensation slammed through him confirming how right he'd been. Their connection was real...stretching beyond their mental link.

During her dreams their emotions were so strong, so involved and in tune with one another that each time either one of them came, his concentration stuttered. He'd had a hard time maintaining objects in her dream world other than himself when all he wanted to do was make sure she felt him as deeply as he did her.

Hmmm, she hummed against him and the pleasurable vibration brought his focus back to the physical as Eriana almost drove him over the edge. As much as he wanted to know what she was thinking, Kian stayed out of her mind while she slid her tongue around his shaft and ran her mouth up and down, sucking and tasting him.

He wanted to anticipate, to *not* know what her next move was going to be. When she slid her hand past the base of his cock and grabbed the ridge of hard flesh just beyond his balls, then massaged and pressed against it, Kian's knees bent. He had to work to keep from sliding to the floor while wave after wave of sensual pleasure jolted thought his groin.

"Goddess," he hissed out. He fisted his hand in her hair, palming her head to guide and increase her pace to match his desire spiraling out of control. In the haze of lust surrounding him, his own need so great, he forgot to block Eriana's thoughts.

If this is all I'll have from him, I want to know what he tastes like.

That was all it took.

His heart racing, his thigh muscles flexing, Kian groaned his pleasure and came hard and fast. As the last shudders of his orgasm dissipated, he welcomed the release of coiled sexual tension from his body.

Eriana didn't let go until she'd swallowed every last drop. His heart swelled with love for her. After she reached down and pulled his pants back up, he pulled her to him, intending to kiss her.

She pushed away with a sad smile. "We need to get going," she began, then glanced at the clock on the nightstand before returning her gaze to his. "It'll be daylight soon."

Kian wanted to argue. He wanted to pull her in his arms and kiss her until she begged him to take her, but he knew she was right—even if it didn't sit well with him that she'd been able to push him away so easily.

* * * * *

"The next shift should change in a hour and a half," Erin whispered to Kian as she pulled him along a darkened hall.

"What is this area?" he asked.

"It's being renovated. Due to my time-travel discovery, Daniel expects more funding, more personnel," she said, her tone sarcastic. "I explored this area late one night while one of the guards had fallen asleep. I was looking for an alternate escape route when the timing was right."

"So that's how you got away?" he asked, his hand tightening around hers. Erin could feel the tension, the anger radiating in his body.

Moving further down the hall, she finally reached the secluded place she'd been looking for. She opened the door and pulled him inside the empty closet, shutting the door behind them. "For obvious reasons, we'll have to sit in the dark."

Pushing the button on her watch, she noted the time on the illuminated background. "I'll keep checking the time so we can slip in during shift changes."

"Don't you think they'll anticipate you trying to come back here?"

She shrugged, then realized he couldn't see her in the dark. "It's possible, but I only need a few seconds to destroy the files and the disk with the key code on it."

"You mean it's been in the lab the whole time?" he asked, his tone incredulous.

She chuckled, then tucked her skirt underneath her legs and sat down in the cramped space. "What better place to hide it than right under their noses? It's the last place they'd expect to look."

She heard a shuffle as Kian sat down as well and leaned against the opposite wall.

"What will you do when you go back to your planet? Find a mate, have a few cubs, and live happily ever after?"

His answer came swift and fast. "I've already found my mate."

Erin's heart sank at his words. "Oh." But even though he was mated to another, she still wanted to know what he felt like inside her, shafting her body with his large cock, his mouth on her breasts, biting and teasing her nipples. Her sex throbbed at the thought. She pressed her hand against her mound to dampen her desire, thankful for the pitch dark so Kian couldn't see what she was doing. *Think about something else, God, anything but making love to Kian.*

As the quiet stretched out between them, she heard that humming sound from her dream. Erin looked around the room, sightless in the dark. It seemed to be coming from everywhere, surrounding her completely, making her associate the sound with making love to Kian.

"Do you hear that?" she asked as she started to raise her hands to cover her ears, to shut out the things the noise made her think about. But she didn't get that far as Kian grabbed her hand and pulled her forward slightly.

She tried to pull her hand away when his tongue took a long, seductive stroke against her fingers, then took another lap. Oh God, the same fingers she'd had against her sex. The humming sound seemed to grow louder as his tongue traced in and around her fingers, making her nipples harden and warmth rush between her legs.

Kian groaned and before she realized his intent, he'd grabbed her ankles and pulled her flat on her back. His swift action caused her skirt to ride up to her hips and as she started to push her skirt back down, his warm lips touched her mound. Erin gasped, then put her hand over her mouth to muffle her cries of pleasure.

As Kian's mouth vibrated against her sex, tears formed in her eyes. She realized that all that time, the humming sound she'd heard...Kian was purring, as any cat would do when highly excited or happy. What they had shared up until now may have been a dream, but the way he made her feel was very, very real.

When he licked a path along her sex and that rough tongue hit her clitoris, Erin bucked and keened her pleasure behind her hand. Again and again he laved at her body, bringing her to heights of passion over and over, yet never enough for her to come.

Just when she thought she'd go insane from the need clawing in her groin, Kian spoke in her mind, his voice seductive, and dangerous, *Tell me how much you want to be my mate, Eriana.*

"You can't do this, Kian," she whispered as happy tears trailed down her temples. "You have a mate already and you said you won't go back home if we make love."

"*You* are my one and only mate," he replied in a low, gruff voice before swiping his tongue across her sex once more. "Now tell me what I need to hear, *a nara.*"

She felt him move over her and clasp her thighs with his hands. Spreading her legs, he prepared her as he bit out, "I see your tears, Eriana. I know you're holding back. Tell me," he demanded.

She jerked her gaze in the direction of his voice, surprised he could see her as she put her hands on his shoulders.

"Yes, I can see you, I can hear you, I can smell you, and I want you very much," he replied as he pressed his cock against her entrance.

"Yes," she moaned at the feel of him against her body. "Yes, I want to be your mate, Kian. I—I love you."

Kian leaned over and kissed her as he thrust inside her in one swift plunge. Erin saw stars at the pain his shafting her caused, but as soon as he entered he began to move in and out of her body in slow, deliberate strokes, and the pain quickly turned to waves of pleasure.

Erin lifted her hips and met each plunge measure for measure while he paced the thrust of his tongue against hers with a dominate, aggressive sensuality he'd not been able to duplicate in her dreams. Nothing compared to the feel of him inside her, taking her breath away. Her heart hammered in her chest and her lower belly tensed in anticipation as her body's tension built.

Thugam vu, m'nara, he whispered in her mind, then said in her language, *I love you, my mate*.

Kian's words, combined with his forceful thrusts, sent her spiraling right into a fulfilling orgasm. His mouth muffled her cries of pleasure as his own movements changed to a quicker, more urgent pace.

With each thrust, Erin felt a change take place. As he slid inside, his erection felt smooth but when he pulled out, his shaft rubbed against her walls feeling slightly rough. The erotic combination sent her libido into overdrive.

"Oh God, Kian!" she called out at the waves of pleasure rolling through her body.

Kian clamped his hand over her mouth and whispered against her neck, "I know it feels strange to you, *m'nara*. Just let my body bring you to pleasure as yours does mine."

As soon as he spoke, Kian groaned and clamped his teeth on the skin between her shoulder and her neck, holding fast as he pistoned into her. Erin's heart seemed to take on a mind of its own, beating at a pace she'd never felt before, making her lightheaded and woozy as her body clenched around Kian's once more.

In the throes of her second orgasm, she heard the panther's *grrrroooooowl* in her head right as Kian came inside her, his warm semen shooting against her inner walls, filling her body.

He was here to stay.

Chapter Seven

An hour later, Erin and Kian snuck into the lab while one of the guards took a pee break and the other was on the cell phone being dressed down by his wife for an affair she's apparently just discovered.

"We have maybe five minutes before the sound of the reactor in full swing will draw their attention."

Kian nodded as she booted up her computer and flipped on the reactor's master switch. While the large machine hummed to life, she began to type in the passwords to get into the system.

"I'm in," she said as she swiftly began deleting files.

"You'd better hurry," he called out over the noise. "The guards are on their way down the hall. I hear them radioing for back-up."

Erin's heart raced and her entire body began to tremble as she punched in the rest of the files to be deleted as fast as her fingers would allow.

While she worked, Kian moved two desks in front of the door, creating a temporary barricade. But through the glass walls, Erin saw at least twenty military men bearing down on them, carrying their machine guns. Daniel led the pack, his face a picture of pure rage.

She looked at Daniel with a smile on her face and hit the delete key on the last file.

Nothing happened and Daniel still kept coming.

Shocked slammed through her. *Why? Why? Why?*

Then she remembered, she'd made a back up file, burned it on an unlabeled CD, and tossed it in her desk along with a few others.

As the men started to batter the door, Daniel yelled and pointed to the glass. Erin jerked open her desk drawer and looked at the CDs. Which one? She frantically grabbed one and broke it in half as machine gun fire shattered the glass walls between them.

Kian had moved to stand between her and Daniel's men when Erin picked up three CDs at once and broke them over her knee.

Time seemed to stand still as she watched the men vanish before her eyes—she assumed to wherever they would have been if she'd never discovered the ability to time-travel. Kian turned to her with a smile and she started to walk toward him, a grin on her face. Suddenly his body started to flicker and Erin began to panic.

"No!" she screamed and ran toward him. He gave her a puzzled look as if he didn't understand why she was upset.

Then he was gone.

Erin fell to the floor where he'd been standing and curled up on her side sobbing. She grabbed her belly as the sharp pangs of deep loss began to wrack though her body. She couldn't have lost him—a man who loved her just as she was, imperfections and all. She cried until her head hurt and her entire body was a ball of tightly wound nerves.

She wasn't sure how long she lay there. An hour, two? Eventually, she told herself, *I need to move on. I may carry Kian's child, our child.* With that thought to bolster her spirits, she wiped her tears and forced herself to sit up and finally to stand.

"I will be strong," she said out loud as she took a step toward the doors and then collapsed.

* * * * *

Erin awoke with a sense she was falling. She quickly grabbed her desk and righted herself on the stool. Looking at her computer screen, bleary-eyed and totally exhausted, she realized she'd fallen asleep at work. Several coffee cups littered her desk as she glanced down at her paperwork, then at her computer screen once more.

Blinking once, she rubbed her eyes several times and checked the date on her computer. The email she had started to compose on her computer was the one she'd outlined to her boss where she'd finally succeeded in creating the ability to time-travel.

She'd been putting in a lot of overtime, busting her rear to get this research and her project to succeed and she must've succumbed to her exhaustion before she hit the send button.

Erin shook her head in disbelief. Had it all been a dream? Was Kian just another character in a long, involved dream? But her memories seemed so real. She shivered as she vividly remembered her lover's scent, the way he felt inside her, and a deep ache filled her heart.

He had to be real, she insisted in her mind as she grabbed the mouse and clicked through her email inbox, her heart racing. Erin scrolled through several hundred emails, but she didn't find a single one from Kian.

Maybe what I just experienced in my dreams was a premonition of the future, she thought as she glanced again at the unsent email to Daniel.

She pulled up all her research files she'd yet to make a secret CD backup for and moved the mouse to highlight them all.

Her curser blinked back at her, winking, waiting for her to make a final decision.

Erin's heart thudded in her chest as her finger suspended over the delete key. All the hard work, all these years of research, and it all comes to this one pivotal moment. *If I do this and Kian was real, then I'll never get to experience his touch, feel him moving inside me, know his love.* The fleeting, selfish thought crossed her mind for all of two seconds before she dismissed it.

She sighed. *If Kian does exist, he would agree this is the only right thing to do,* she told herself as she let her finger land on the delete key.

Are you sure you want to delete these files? her computer read as if playing devil's advocate.

Setting her jaw, she hit the "enter" key.

A wave of relief washed over her when she deleted the files and the unsent email to Daniel. As she started to clean up the Styrofoam coffee cups and toss them in the trash can, a thought struck her: *Trashcan!*

She needed to empty the trashcan on her computer, too. Moving her mouse over the "trashcan" icon, she clicked to empty the recycle bin.

Are you sure you want to permanently delete these files? the computer asked her once more.

Argh! Her computer was mocking her, she thought as she hit the "enter" key with a determined tap.

As soon as she lifted her finger off the key, a bolt of lightning slashed across the empty lab and a vortex opened up right in front of her. Strong wind flew through the room, disturbing papers, whipping her hair around her.

Erin held her hair away from her face and stared in shock at the swirling dark blue void before her. When Kian walked through the portal and held out his hand to her, she literally fell off her stool.

He stood there wearing a black leather vest and black fitted pants with a gold embroidered ceremonial-looking sash around his trim waist. His long black hair flowed down his shoulders, drawing her attention to his thick chest and muscular biceps.

Kian chuckled as he scooped her up in his arms. "At least you're conscious this time, *m'nara.* You didn't think I'd leave you behind, did you?"

Happy tears spilled down her cheeks as she wrapped her arms around his neck, holding him tight. Pulling way, she met his striking green gaze and said, "But your memory would have been erased when you went back in time and none of this has really happened yet."

Kian raised an arrogant eyebrow. "Ah, but I didn't go back the way I came. And as for you thinking something as simple as a space and time continuum could erase my memory of you..." He paused and gave her a stern look. "I think you'll need to be reminded why you are my mate in all ways."

He turned and stepped into the vortex saying, "Here on Earth, you were way ahead of your time, Eriana. Come home with me where you belong."

About the author:

Patrice Michelle welcomes mail from readers. You can write to her c/o Ellora's Cave Publishing at 1337 Commerce Drive, Suite 13, Stow OH 44224.

Also by Patrice Michelle:

Harm's Hunger: Bad in Boots
A Taste For Passion
Cajun Nights
Dragon's Heart
A Taste For Revenge

ONE NIGHT STAND

J.C. Wilder

Lucius deVille had the face of an angel and the body of an unrepentant sinner. He was the kind of vampire every woman dreamed of calling 'Lover' at least once in her life. He was the proverbial tall, dark and handsome male who was the fantasy of millions of women around the world and to top it all off, he was educated and possessed a wicked sense of humor that had charmed more than one woman out of her panties.

Tonight, Rachel was determined to claim Luc as her own. For the evening, at least.

She slipped through the open doors of the *Chat Noir*, a popular restaurant and jazz club. To the left was the restaurant. Every table was crammed with Halloween revelers dressed in every kind of costume imaginable. A group of over-aged, underdressed cheerleaders hoisted their cocktails in a boisterous salute while the table next to them was filled to overflowing with costumed nuns and empty shot glasses.

To the right was a cramped seating area for patrons who consumed cocktails while they waited for their tables to be vacated. It, too, was crammed to the hilt and Rachel grinned as a naked man sauntered past dressed only in a body condom and an inebriated smile.

God, she loved living in New Orleans.

She threaded her way through the crowd and headed straight for the bar where she knew Luc was most likely to be stationed. She spotted her prey at the end of the bar talking to a redheaded waitress. With his elbow propped on the polished wood, he leaned against the bar and looked to be completely at ease in the midst of the madness going on around him.

Topping out at several inches past six feet, he was a masterpiece of hard-muscled male and barely leashed sensuality. His shoulder-length silky black hair was pulled back from an autocratic face with a narrow strip of black leather. Thick, dark lashes framed his mesmerizing blue eyes and his nose was thin with a slight bump at the bridge betraying the fact that it had been broken at least once during his human life.

His mouth was wide and sensual, bordering on feminine for such a masculine face. The lean planes of his cheeks and the sharp line of his jaw saved him from being mistaken for anything other than one hundred percent male.

A pointy elbow landed in her ribs and the unprovoked strike jerked her out of her contemplation. She scowled and allowed her lips to draw back from the needle-sharp incisors, knowing any mortal would believe them to be false. Halloween was the one night of the year vampires could flash their fangs and no one would pay them any attention.

Her molester was a drunken human dressed as a gladiator. He gave her a lopsided smile, tripped over his own feet, staggered and fell against his friends who were dressed as he was. He grabbed his crotch and leered at her.

"Hey babe, wanna bite this?"

His friends roared with laughter and then shoved him toward Rachel. She was forced to grab him or risk being knocked to the ground by his substantial weight.

Laugh at her, would they?

She snagged his collar and hauled him up until he was on his tiptoes, high enough to gain his attention without anyone else around them noticing. His eyes bulged and his knees knocked against hers as he flailed in an attempt to gain his freedom.

She smiled and flashed her fangs. His human strength was pathetic when compared to her vampiric abilities.

"Not without a rabies shot, little man." She released him and pushed him toward his laughing friends. It was only a gentle nudge yet it sent him barreling backwards into the others and forced them all back a few steps.

A wide-eyed blond man grabbed her victim by the arm. Giving Rachel an apologetic smile and a bobbing nod, he pulled his spluttering friend into the crowd leaving the others to follow.

Smart man.

Turning away, she moved through the crowd to the bar. When she passed Luc, he was still deep in conversation with the waitress. Rachel's gaze moved over him and she couldn't help but notice how handsome he looked in his pirate costume.

His feet and calves were encased in knee-high cuffed leather boots while tight black velvet pants covered his muscular thighs and slim hips. A red silk sash was tied around his waist and the jeweled dagger at his hip added a touch of danger. His oversized white shirt was open to mid chest allowing tantalizing glimpses of hard, muscled flesh beneath. The sleeves were long and full and the cuffs were trimmed in white lace. A gold hoop earring glinted in his left ear.

Luc looked good enough to eat.

Rachel snagged the only open bar seat and slid onto it. When she'd moved to New Orleans several months ago, the Chat had been one of her first stops. Known for good food and stellar accommodations for the preternaturals, the *Chat Noir* was a must-see for both residents and tourists.

Like the restaurant, the bar was packed with both mortals and others like her. Several werecat males were seated at the bar surrounded by a flock of mortal women. She grinned. The sexual appetites of the werecats were legendary in the preternatural world and she knew several of those beauties would be very happy women in the morning.

A group of young vampires headed for the noisy darkness of the jazz club in the back of the building. No doubt they were looking for some cool jazz and hot blood, though not necessarily in that order.

"Evening, Rachel." From behind the bar, Tom, the assistant manager of the bar, offered her a wide smile. He was a big, rangy werecat with thick golden hair, dark brown eyes and a quick, easy smile.

"Good to see you, my friend." She waved her hand to indicate the crowds. "I could barely get in the door tonight."

"We're always packed on Halloween." He reached for a black china mug that was used to serve their vampire guests. "Would you like your usual?"

"No, I think I will..." she smiled, allowing the tips of her fangs to appear. "Kick it up a bit."

His golden brow rose. "Are you sure, Rach? You aren't much of a drinker."

"I'm on a mission this evening, Tom. Besides, I'm feeling a little adventurous." She tilted her head, enjoying the unfamiliar feel of her long hair against her back. She almost always kept her hair up in either a ponytail or a twist to keep it out of the way. But not tonight.

He winked. "Your outfit tells me that."

Rachel's smile increased. She knew the tight black dress looked like it was painted onto her body. Her breasts threatened to spill from the deep V neckline. The high hemline barely covered the lace tops of her thigh-high stockings and. Her feet would be sore later, but the four-inch spiked heels made her feel sexier, more feminine.

She knew the outfit was hot, but Tom wasn't talking specifically about her clothing. Her index finger brushed the slim velvet choker that encircled her neck. The strip of red velvet advertised that she was a vampire on the hunt for a man.

She propped her arms on the bar. "I've achieved my goal then."

"In spades, babe." Tom leaned toward her and spoke in a low tone that only she would hear. "Do you want cat or wolf?"

She'd thought about this long and hard before leaving her cozy home earlier. The blood selection for the evening was an important one, as ingesting werecat or werewolf blood would achieve two very different purposes.

The wolf blood would hype her nervous system and possibly drive her into a frenzy if she ingested too much, while the werecat blood would do the exact opposite. Werecat blood would remove any inhibitions she had about enticing Luc into a one-night stand.

Her lips brushed Tom's cheek and she whispered, "Bring on the kitty."

A rumble of laughter sounded in her ear. "Your wish is my command."

Tom turned away to take care of her order. She shifted until she had a good view down the length of the bar. Luc had concluded his conversation and now leaned against the wall just several feet away. His alert gaze moved over the crowd and, while his body was still, she sensed he was ready to spring into action should the need arise.

It was just over a month ago when she'd first seen Luc in the flesh. She'd heard of him, of course, as the vampire community was a close-knit bunch for the most part and they loved nothing more than a good gossip. Several years ago, Luc had been involved in a very high-profile affair with a Russian actress that had ended with her suicide and his sudden disappearance from public life.

Rumored to be a French Viscount of old, he'd abandoned his self-imposed seclusion to come to New Orleans and lend a hand to Sinjin, the owner of the *Chat Noir*. Recently engaged, Sinjin and his fiancée, Vivian, had left on a long overdue vacation and Luc was keeping an eye on the place while they were away.

From the moment Rachel had seen him, she could barely take her eyes off the vampire. Drawn by his latent sexuality and air of mystery that surrounded him, she'd become a frequent visitor to the Chat, hanging out just to catch a glimpse of him. Not that he'd ever noticed her. What man would look at a mousy CPA when other, more beautiful, women surrounded him night after night?

None.

She smiled and propped her chin on her palm. Tonight would be different. Tonight, Luc couldn't overlook her, she'd make sure of it.

According to Tom, Sinjin was scheduled to return within the next day or so and, all too soon, Luc would be leaving New Orleans for parts unknown.

Rachel nibbled on her lower lip. Knowing he was leaving and that she'd never spoken to him—not once—nagged at her. She had only one chance left to find out what it felt like to be in this man's arms and she was going to grab that opportunity with both hands or make a fool of herself trying.

She wasn't interested in finding the elusive, happily-ever-after relationship that most women dreamed of. She'd thought she'd found it once long ago and, in the end, she'd lost Wyatt anyway. No, she was interested in Mr. Right Now. One night of unrestrained passion, enough to sustain her through the long, lonely, cold nights that lay ahead. Luc was the obvious choice as he was the first man in forty-three years who had interested her enough to bring her out of her self-imposed celibacy.

"Hey Luc," Tom called. "Do you have the key?"

Her heart leapt into her throat when the vampire turned his dark head toward Tom.

"Sure thing." Pushing off the wall, Luc walked toward them. With each step, her breathing grew shallower. Luc had a confident, easy walk; one that proclaimed he was comfortable in his own skin and in his place in the world.

He stopped near Rachel and she inhaled deeply. Heat swirled through her belly when she discerned his masculine scent through the myriad aromas in the room. It was dark and musky, sexual, a mixture of heated spice and warm male flesh.

"I need to run down the cellar; we're almost out of chardonnay." Tom gestured toward Rachel. "The lady would like a drink."

Luc turned toward her and she braced herself for the magnetism of his stare. The moment his midnight gaze landed on her face, she felt as if a hot poker had slid under her skin. Fighting for a cool demeanor, she lowered her arm and wondered if he'd recognize her as a Chat regular. His dark eyes showed definite interest in her as a woman, but she couldn't detect any flash of recognition. It was amazing what a little makeup could do.

A slow smile curved the handsome sinner's mouth. "It would be my pleasure to assist the lady."

A warm, liquid heat ignited in the pit of her stomach and her palms grew moist. Luc retrieved a slim silver key from his pants pocket and unlocked a narrow door built into the wall. Inside the cubbyhole were two black carafes, each marked with either a cat or wolf paw print in bright red. He reached for the one with the wolf imprint.

"Excuse me. I'd prefer the other, please." Rachel said.

His dark brow arched and the corner of his mouth hitched as his hand veered toward the one marked with the cat print. Picking up one of the black mugs, he set it on the bar.

"Not too many women search out this particular brand." He filled the cup halfway.

"Indeed." Rachel reached for the mug and pulled it toward her; her senses already on high alert at the first scent of the rich, warm blood. "I guess I'm not like many women."

His smile grew and Rachel's legs went watery. "I would have to agree that you're not like many women I've known."

A rush of pleasure moved through her and she smiled. "Oh, I can guarantee that."

He laughed and the warm, rich sound poured over her senses like sun-warmed honey. Dizzy with her success, she picked up the mug and tossed the miniscule contents back like a pro, or how she'd imagine a pro would do so.

The moment the liquid hit her mouth, she reeled. Unlike the familiar taste of mortal blood, the werecat blood was oddly spicy — almost to the point of being overwhelming. She felt as if someone had hooked her tongue to a car battery and then administered a series of short jolts. She swallowed hard and her eyes were watering when she set the cup down with a clatter.

Oh my…

She heard Luc chuckle.

"First time?"

She blinked and his handsome face slowly took shape. She scrubbed at her eyes and realized she'd just made a complete fool of herself. She'd only look more ridiculous if she denied her inexperience so she settled for a jerky nod as she struggled to not cough herself silly. She could feel her cheeks grow red from the strain and she forced herself to stop rubbing her eyes. She could only hope her mascara was as waterproof as the package had claimed.

His big hand covered hers. "It's not a good idea to toss back werecat blood like that." His fingers moved to encircle her wrist. "Think of it as brandy to a human; it is a delicacy that should be savored."

She cleared her throat. "So I see." Her voice came out low and husky. "I won't make that mistake again."

She was disturbingly aware of his flesh against hers, the heat of his skin and the strength of his fingers. His thumb gave the inside of her wrist a soft stroke and her heart stuttered. Liquid warmth in the pit of her stomach ignited and spread through her system, causing her to become hypersensitive to everything going on around her: the noise of the crowd, the dim lighting overhead and the heady sensation of this man focusing his complete attention on her.

"To properly enjoy the experience, you should take your time when indulging yourself." His voice was low, sensual. Luc released her wrist and she immediately mourned the loss of his touch. "Take pleasure in it." He reached for the carafe and refilled her mug before retrieving a mug for himself. "Were-blood, like lovemaking, should be savored."

Rachel reached for her drink. "So you're a man who believes lovemaking should be savored?" Amazed that she'd managed to speak of sex without stuttering, she raised the glass to her lips while she mentally praised the effects of the were-blood on her self-confidence.

He nodded. "Much like a fine wine or a rich meal." He propped his elbows on the bar and leaned forward until his mouth was barely an inch from hers. His breath was warm upon her lips when he spoke. "New Orleans is a city that possesses the twin vices of sin and pleasure." His gaze flicked over her mouth. "The city, like a good woman, should be indulged."

She lowered the glass and offered him a suggestive smile. "Or a good man." She tilted her head, enjoying the soft buzz from her drink and the long-dormant arousal that surged forth. She pressed her thighs together in a vague attempt to ease the burgeoning ache. "What about you? Are you a good man, Luc?"

His lips quirked. "Some women have said that I'm a good man." His gaze dropped to her mouth again. "While others might disagree."

She ran the edge of her cup against her lower lip before setting it on the bar. "Well, I don't trust the judgment of other women." She shrugged and allowed her arm to come down, then watched as her hand landed on his wrist. "I guess if I really want to know, I'll have to find out myself."

* * * * *

Luc couldn't tear his gaze from the beautiful woman who'd just propositioned him. Her long dark hair was a riot of curls and they framed a delicate heart-shaped face. Her eyes were sea-green and thickly lashed while her nose was small and pert. But it was her mouth that drew him. Wide and painted scarlet—nearly as scarlet as her velvet choker—her lips were slick with gloss. He wondered how those plush scarlet lips would look wrapped around his cock.

The temptress raised her glass to her mouth and took a small sip, her sexy-sleepy gaze never wavering. When she lowered the glass, a thin stain of blood marred her lower lip.

Never one to let an opportunity go to waste, he leaned forward and licked the liquid from her lip before taking possession of her mouth.

He felt her start of surprise a second before he lost himself in the lush sensuality of her kiss. Her lips were soft and warm against his tongue. He suckled the plump, lower lip, tasting both woman and the exotic flavor of the were-blood. She opened for him and he nipped at her tongue. She made a soft sound of either alarm or acquiescence, he wasn't sure, but he assumed the best as she made no attempt to move away.

The kiss continued and the noises from the bar faded to the hiss of white noise. All that existed for him was this enchanting creature and her luscious mouth. Their tongues tangled and their breath melded as they tasted and teased each other. The faint mewling sounds she made caused his blood to heat and his heartbeat to accelerate. His cock gnawed at the fragile zipper of his pants when she gave his tongue a strong, earthy suck. A low growl sounded from his throat as he reached for her. Her soft curls brushed the back of his hand when a loud voice intruded upon the sensual haze she'd woven around him.

"Jeez, get a room, Luc." Laughter laced Tom's words.

Luc pulled away from her tempting mouth, cursing the fact he'd forgotten where he was. Inattention to his surroundings could cost him his life, though in that moment he wasn't too sure he wouldn't sacrifice himself for another kiss.

Across from him, the wide-eyed beauty looked both dazed and aroused. Her lips were rosy and damp from his kiss while her sleepy gaze gleamed with a mix of amusement and arousal. He couldn't wait to kiss her again…and again. And again.

He cleared his throat. He wanted to get out of the Chat and take her with him, to spend some time with this intoxicating creature. But he couldn't—not yet. He glanced at his watch. Only one hour to go until his business meeting and then they could leave. Together.

"Shall we go listen to some jazz?" He was surprised his voice sounded so normal considering he was hot and hard as a pike. He did not relish having to walk out from behind the bar.

"That sounds lovely." Her voice was husky and just the sound of it aroused his senses even further.

Willing his body to cool down so as not to embarrass him, Luc topped off their glasses before locking the carafe up and tossing the key to Tom. Once he felt more in control of his anatomy, he walked around the bar to approach her from behind. His breath caught in his throat when he saw her dress.

Mother of God…

The slim curve of her back was exposed almost to her waist and her creamy pale skin was dusted with something that caused it to shimmer ever so slightly. His palms grew hot.

She swiveled the seat around then slid off the edge causing the hem of her dress to slide up enough to allow him a flash of pale thigh above her black thigh-high stockings. Her high heels looked lethal and, even with them, she barely came to his chin. He put out his arm to steady her when she swayed.

"Careful." He knew she'd be feeling the effects of the were-blood. She'd downed enough in her first shot to make any grown vampire stagger.

"I'm fine." She picked up her drink. "Do you think we'll get a table in the club?"

"I have a private table upstairs."

A slow smile curved her lush mouth. "Just how…private?"

"Very."

Her smile grew wider and he took her hand before picking up his glass. He led her through the crowd to a door near the club entrance before releasing her to unlock the door. After ushering her through it, he allowed the door to slide shut behind them.

The darkness was complete and the sounds of the club were muffled and indistinct. Her scent, warm woman mixed with vanilla, teased his senses and took his breath away. He reached for her and then forced himself to stop, knowing he had to move or risk taking her at the bottom of the stairs like a dog in heat. He took her hand and with their fingers twined, led the way up the narrow steps to a small, private balcony overlooking the club floor.

Barely eight feet by eight feet and surrounded by a wrought iron rail, the intimate space sported a small table and a comfortable padded bench seat built for two. A single white candle burned on the table and the tablecloth was blood red in the golden light. He stepped to the side and ushered her toward the seat.

"This is wonderful." She set her drink on the table before sitting down. "Who knew this was up here?"

Luc slid in next to her, relishing the feel of her warm thigh pressed against his. "Who knew?" he murmured, raising his glass to his mouth and taking a small sip.

On the stage below, the band was playing a wild Zydeco dance tune and, under the colored lights, the dance floor resembled a cast of extras from a B horror movie. Two zombies in tattered costumes and several werewolves—the real kind— cavorted with some outrageously dressed witches. In another corner, a group of women were dressed as football players while their male cheerleader dates sported short skirts and very bad wigs.

He grinned. New Orleans. There was no place like it.

Luc's gaze returned to his new-found friend. Her eyes were wide as she watched the show below. Her lush lips were parted and her expression was completely enraptured.

"Do you like the music?" He had to lean in to ensure she could hear him over the band. Her scent caused his cock to throb and his lips brushed the tender curve of her ear. He felt her shiver as he inhaled her vanilla-scented hair.

Her grin was wide when she turned toward him. "I love music and there's no city like New Orleans when it comes to music and food. It's the only place in the world where you plan your dinner while sitting at lunch and there's music on every street corner."

The strip of scarlet velvet looked erotic against the pale flesh of her throat. He reached for her, his fingers touching both the velvet and her skin and he couldn't decide which was softer.

"What's your name, beautiful?" he whispered, leaning toward her.

"Rachel." She licked her lips and the blood rushed to his groin.

* * * * *

Rachel didn't know how it happened. One minute she was watching the band and the next Luc was kissing her. His hands seemed to be everywhere at once and yet it still wasn't enough. She climbed into his lap, her hands stroking his broad chest while she leaned into him. Her thighs straddled his and his cock nudged at her aroused flesh with an insistence that was not to be ignored.

His mouth was hot on her throat while he slid his hands inside the deep vee of her dress. Lightly holding her breasts, Luc began to rub his thumbs over her nipples before he captured her mouth and kissed her deeply.

She moaned. He swallowed the sound as they kissed and she flung her arms around his neck. The unfamiliar feel of heated male flesh and warm silk against her breasts was both erotic and empowering at the same time. Her fingers fumbled with the thong that held his hair. When she managed to release the leather, she slid her fingers through the silk, tangling in the soft strands as she angled his head for a deeper kiss.

His big hands eased the bodice of her dress down to puddle around her waist before he broke the kiss and cupped her breasts. "I want to see you," he rumbled.

Rachel released her grip on his hair, hesitating for a moment before moving back a few inches. His dark gaze moved over her breasts and while she saw nothing but acceptance and pleasure, suddenly shy, she moved to cover herself.

"Don't." He caught her wrists and moved her hands to rest between them. "You're exquisite." His lips grazed the tip of her nose. "And you're mine, Rachel. And I claim you."

Her breath caught in her throat at his possessive tone. Her gaze dropped to his hands. They looked big and dark against her pale flesh as he cupped her breasts, lifting them gently as if to weigh and measure them. Rachel knew her breasts were too big for her slim frame but Luc didn't seem to mind at all. In fact, he seemed to enjoy them just fine.

He ran his thumbs over her hardened nipples. She shivered at the riot of sensations he ignited from that simple touch. He repeated the movement again and again until her breathing grew shallow and her thighs clenched against his hips. She felt the release of damp heat deep in her vagina.

Luc's dark head dipped. He took her nipple into his mouth, sending a bolt of sensation down her spine. She gripped his head, fearing for a moment that she'd faint when his wet tongue laved at the hardened tip. Soft mewls locked in her throat as she tipped her head back and leaned into the edge of the table, reveling in the mastery of his touch. Her head swam. Here — here — was the man she'd desired above all others and soon, very soon, she'd call him "lover".

He rolled the hardened nub against the roof of his mouth then suckled hard enough to wrench a cry from her. Her fingers knotted in his hair and she made a sound of protest when he lifted his head until she realized he was only moving to her other breast. She moaned and pressed her hips into his lap when he took the other nipple into his mouth and subjected it to the same masterful seduction.

After a few moments, he released her nipple and raised his head. His pupils were wide and his hands moved to her splayed thighs. His thumbs dug into her inner knees.

"Open for me," he commanded.

Unable to resist, she forced her thighs to relax then parted them. He shifted his hand to her hip then slid his fingers under the slim elastic band of her panties.

"I'm sure these are lovely." His voice was low, harsh. "But right now they're in the way."

He removed the dagger from the waist sheath and held it up so the candlelight gleamed over the steel blade. Their gazes remained locked as he lowered the dagger and slid it under the slim band. With a flick of his wrist, he cut through the elastic and then moved to do the same at her other hip. Rachel held her breath as the final band was cut.

Her tongue felt thick as he urged her upward to slide the destroyed garment from between her legs. The scrap of scarlet lace looked tiny in his big hands. With a wicked gleam in his eyes, he raised the crotch of the panties to his nose and inhaled. Her heart almost stopped as a smile of pure satisfaction curled his sinner's mouth.

"You're wet for me," he said. "That's good." He replaced the dagger in its sheath and dropped the shredded panties beside him on the bench. "Let's see if I can make you even wetter."

He ran his hands up her thighs and even before he touched her, she was arching toward him, her lust overruling whatever scant inhibitions might have remained. When his fingers brushed the soft curls between her thighs, she moaned and reached for him.

"Is this what you want, Rachel?" His breath was hot against her throat. With his free hand he caught her before she could touch him. He parted her dampened flesh to zero in on her clit. "Release?" His fingers began stroking her hardened flesh in a slow, sensual dance.

"Yes," she moaned. Her hips followed his touch and her eyes slid shut. The feelings he aroused were so powerful she felt as if she would fly apart.

"Tell me, Rachel." He increased the pace. "Tell me what you want from me."

"Make me come," she moaned. "Please."

His laughter was deep, throaty. "My pleasure."

Her hips moved in the sensual dance as old as time as he stroked her aroused flesh, his movements increasing in intensity. Soft moans built in her throat as the effects of the were-blood and his wicked, knowledgeable touches made her delirious. This was the man she desired over any other and her capitulation was inevitable. The pressure started in her lower belly then worked its way down into her thighs before shooting upward.

Her back arched and she came with a startled cry as her body was overwhelmed with the force of her release. The spasms seemed to go on for several long minutes until, finally, they slowed and then stopped. Released from the sensual hypnosis, she leaned into Luc's chest gasping for air.

After a few moments she sat up. He removed his hand from between her thighs.

"We need to get out of here, Rachel. Contrary to what you might be thinking, I didn't bring you up here to seduce you." His heated gaze moved over her face. "When I take you for real, I want you flat on your back as I enter you."

She shivered at the powerful images his words evoked and gave him a light kiss on the mouth. "That sounds like a plan. Shall we go to your place?" She knew he was living just down the street from the *Chat Noir*, much closer than her place across town.

He glanced at his watch. "First I need to take care of some business, but that should only take a few minutes." He dropped his hands onto her thighs and began rubbing them. "After that, we'll go home to my bed where I'll spread you out on silk sheets and worship you from head to toe."

Rachel slid her arms into the straps of her dress as she tried to stifle a groan. While she was a little disappointed that his business would cut into their limited time together, she'd waited forty-three years before taking another man to bed. She supposed she could wait a few more minutes.

*   *   *   *   *

He had to be mad.

Rachel sat in the shadows of the window seat, her long, spectacular legs stretched out before her. Her attention was completely captured by a coffee table book dealing with the architecture of old New Orleans. She nibbled her lower lip as her rapt gaze moved over the words. She was easy on the eyes, intelligent and he was completely smitten — smitten to the point he was reluctant to let her out of his sight even for a moment.

He glanced at the grandfather clock.

It was almost midnight.

Damn you, Reg, you'd better be on time.

He fixed his gaze on the check, which lay in the center of Sinjin's desk. His gut clenched. It had taken him many years to save up a million dollars but now his dream was about to come true. In a few minutes he'd purchase back the property that had been stolen from him in the early eighteenth century by an unscrupulous lawyer. He smoothed his fingers over the neat type. Soon *Belle Maison* would be in the hands of its rightful owner.

The clock struck midnight and as if on cue the intercom buzzed. He pushed the talk button.

"Yes, Sheila?"

"Mr. Darramond and his associates are here to see you."

"Send them up." His lips twitched. Mister indeed. In the old days Reg had been known as Crybaby for his unfortunate tendency to burst into tears when he became enraged, which then had been quite frequently. Luc slid the check into its envelope and then laid it on the desk.

Heavy footsteps on the stairs marked the progress of his visitors as they approached. Rachel looked at him and he gave her a smile.

"Just a few more minutes," he said.

She nodded and returned her attention to the book.

Reg swept into the room with all the pomp and circumstance due to a Head of State. His short, squat body was clad in an immaculate Versace tuxedo complete with diamond button covers on his shirt and black gloves. His black floor-length cape was lined with red silk and it provided a theatrical flare that Reg had no doubt anticipated.

"Lucius," he boomed.

Luc rose from behind the desk. "Reg, I'm glad you could meet me here." The men shook hands and Luc waved the other man toward one of the two chairs before the desk.

Several other men filed in behind Reg, all dressed in black from head to toe and sporting ear pieces that enabled them to communicate between themselves. Reg was very much into personal security these days.

"Do you have the check?" Reg arranged his cape to expose the blood-red silk.

"Do you have the paperwork?" Luc countered.

The other man didn't crack a smile and with barely more than a flick of a finger one of his flunkies came forward with a leather portfolio that he laid on the desk.

"I'm sure you won't mind if I look this over," Luc said.

Reg flashed his fangs and it wasn't a pleasant sight. "As soon as my assistant verifies the check."

Luc nodded. "Fair enough." He handed the envelope over then opened the portfolio and scanned the documents. His heart raced as his gaze absorbed the contents of the documentation. It was as they'd agreed; the house, grounds and contents of *Belle Maison* were detailed in neat black type along with the negotiated price of one million dollars.

He sat back. It was all here for the taking.

"I think you will find it to your satisfaction," Reg said. "There are two copies of the documents. All you have to do is sign both sets and that monstrosity you've coveted for so long will once again be yours."

Fighting for an impassive expression, Luc picked up his pen and signed his name to both copies. The scratching of the pen sounded loud and when he was done he laid the pen down.

It was over.

Reg's assistant came forward and picked up the portfolio. "These will be filed first thing in the morning, Monsieur deVille. By twilight the deed and the keys will be awaiting you."

"Thank you for your assistance, Douglas." Luc nodded at Reg. "And thanks to you Reg, *Belle Maison* has been restored to my family."

Reg waved his words away. "*Belle* never meant as much to me as it did to you. " He shrugged. "To me, it was yet another house; to you, it was a home."

Luc smiled. "Well, thanks anyway."

"Never forget, my friend, lest you lose her again, what one treasures, one must fight to protect. Remain vigilant for there are those who seek to take that which belongs to us." Reg's eyes glinted with unspoken emotion. "We must be on our way…" He rose from his chair and when he caught sight of Rachel, he stopped. Surprise flitted across his face. "You didn't introduce me to your friend, Luc." His tone was gently admonishing.

"You'll have to forgive me but I was anxious to get our business taken care of first." Luc rose but the other man beat him to Rachel's side. Reg took her hand and helped her to her feet. "Any friend of Luc's is most certainly a friend of mine." He kissed the back of her hand. "What is your name, beautiful?"

"Rach—"

"Mine." Luc slid his arm around Rachel's waist. His gaze clashed with Reg's and, for a moment, Luc wasn't sure the other man would release her hand. After a few tense moments, Reg released her.

"Indeed." Reg's gaze moved over her face. "So the lion has been bearded in his den has he? You must be quite a special lady."

Rachel tilted her head back and her long hair licked at Luc's arm. Promise glittered in the depths of her expressive eyes. "I don't know, Luc, am I special?" Her tone both teased and aroused him.

He opted not to answer and instead brushed his mouth against her temple. In response, she leaned into him and slid her arm around his waist.

"I can see that I'm in the way." Reg gave him a mocking bow before heading for the door and his security people scrambled to follow. "Remember what I said, deVille. Protect what you treasure." He paused in the doorway and looked back at Rachel. "No matter what that treasure may be."

* * * * *

Luc swept her into his arms and kicked the car door shut. Rachel flung her arms around his broad shoulders and kissed his neck as he bounded up the front steps. He smelled of cinnamon and warm, healthy male flesh. Encouraged by the growl he emitted when her lips touched his neck, she nipped at his skin, excited by the taste and proximity of him.

"Have mercy, woman." He spanked her smartly on the backside. "Wait till we get inside at least."

A bark of laughter escaped her as he released his hold on her legs as if to put her down—but there was no way she was letting him go that easily. She wound her legs around his and clung like a limpet to his broad frame.

"You are playing with fire, little girl," he growled.

Rachel pulled back and gave him what she hoped was a sexy smile. "Promise?"

His breath hitched, "Oh yeah."

The door swung open and he stumbled in, hampered by her twining legs. She laughed when she almost ended up on the floor, her heart near to bursting with excitement. Luc slammed the door and plunged them into darkness relieved only by the glow of a small lamp somewhere in the back of the house.

They kissed and Rachel sank into a pit of desire. He braced her back against the wide oak door, pressing the ridge of his arousal against the apex of her thighs. Dear God but she wanted him. With every fiber of her being she wanted this man to possess her with a need so ferocious it could no longer be contained.

Luc's breathing was urgent as he leaned heavily into her, pressing his erection into the softness of her body. He slid the straps of her dress off her shoulders, shifting her away from the door long enough to slide the garment out of the way. His fingers tangled in her long hair, pulling her head back to accept the deep thrust of his tongue into her mouth.

She whimpered into his mouth, restlessly moving against him in a vain effort to appease the growing ache between her thighs. She ached for him to fill the emptiness inside her, the same emptiness that was rapidly growing damp with need.

She slid her hands into the open neck of his shirt. Warm male skin, damp with sweat, awaited her touch. She kneaded and stroked the thick pads of muscle that rippled under her hands. Her fingers found his flat male nipples and a groan burst from his throat as she flicked each nipple. Greedily she swallowed his cry and sucked hard on his tongue.

Not wanting to end their torrid kiss but needing to feel more of him, she pushed his face away. He gasped for air and she leaned back to wrench his shirt from his pants. Grasping each half of his shirt, she yanked and the buttons flew in every direction. She pushed the tattered garment from his shoulders to expose his broad torso.

She licked her lips, tasting the essence of Luc and their passion before pulling his head back down to hers for another kiss. His mouth was hard as it nipped at hers. Her head reeled at the sensations he aroused and she clung to him to keep from floating away.

She sighed when he cupped her breasts and ran his thumbs over their taut tips, setting off another explosion that caused a moan to break from her lips. As if he understood what she needed, he broke the kiss to slide an arm underneath her buttocks and lift her higher. His mouth unerringly found one pointed nipple and he took it into his mouth and sucked greedily.

Rachel cried out as the symphony of sensations raced through her body to pool at the apex of her thighs. She arched against him as if to drag him closer or push him away, she didn't know which. He responded by pulling her tighter against him, grinding his erection into her. The erotic rocking motion set off a chain reaction. A high keening cry broke from her lips as the tension spiraled tighter, coiling low in her belly. As his left hand plucked at the erect peak of her breast her release exploded throughout her system.

She clutched at his broad shoulders as she convulsed against him, cries escaping her lips as the powerful orgasm washed over her in sharp waves. Her breath raged in her lungs and her head fell to his shoulder as the residual tremors moved through her. She clung to the man who held her gently cradled against his chest.

"That was the most beautiful thing I've ever experienced," Luc murmured against her shoulder.

Rachel roused herself to chuckle. "How can you say that? You can't see anything in here."

"I can see more than enough."

That's what I'm afraid of…

Her throat constricted. "Make love with me," she whispered.

"With pleasure." Luc pushed away from the door. Instead of heading up the steps, Rachel was surprised when he walked past them and into the living room. He gently deposited her onto the back of the couch.

"What about the bedroom?" she asked.

"Too far away, we'll never make it." Luc branded the damp skin of her throat with a hot, open-mouthed kiss.

Rachel purred as she felt the muscles shift beneath his skin. That she could make this strong man lose control was a very heady thought indeed. She wanted to sing with the sheer power of it. She stroked his back; muscles contracted beneath her touch as her hands caressed every inch of exposed flesh she could reach.

He shoved her skirt up and the cool air tingled across her exposed skin. Luc seized her by the back of the knees and she reveled in his strong grasp. He pulled her thighs apart and insinuated himself between them.

Luc reached for his zipper. She stopped him by sliding her hands over his velvet-covered erection, cupping him. His hands fell away and his eyes narrowed as he gave an involuntary thrust against her palm.

"If you keep doing that, this will be over too soon," he groaned.

Rachel laughed, a soft throaty chuckle. "And the problem with that is…"

His gaze claimed hers. "I want to be inside you when I come."

Her mouth went dry and her breath caught. She wanted that more than anything else in the world. She wanted this man buried deep inside her.

With hands that shook, she finally managed to unzip his pants to allow his engorged flesh to spring free. She slid her hand around his cock and the air hissed from his lungs. Gently she stroked him from the broad head to the root, marveling over his size and the feel of him in her hands. The silk-over-steel feel of him transfixed her as she stroked and she watched, entranced, as a bead of fluid escaped from the blunt tip.

"I think you'd better stop now," he hissed.

"If you insist..." With one last stroke she slid her hands up his hard belly to tease his nipples with her fingertips. She lightly pinched one and he jerked beneath her touch.

He pushed her dress up to press the broad tip of his erection against her damp flesh. "I want to come inside you, now." Sliding his hand between her thighs, he caressed her clit with long slow strokes until she writhed in his arms. He slipped a finger into her pussy and sank into her damp flesh.

Rachel shuddered at his touch; instinctively drawing her knees up to take him deeper. Desire threatened to engulf her.

"Just like that." Bending over her, he tenderly explored her cunt, coaxing and teasing, preparing her for his entry.

A moan escaped her as his thumb brushed her clit. She wound her arms around his neck, drawing him closer to her as the world tilted wildly beneath his knowledgeable hands. His slow strokes grew more rhythmic and her hips rocked in response, her inner muscles subtly clasping his finger as she answered his mating call.

Suddenly impatient, Luc removed his fingers and replaced them with the broad head of his cock. As he entered her, she moaned, arching against him, taking him so deeply she feared she would burst.

He slid his hands down the outside of her thighs. Catching her beneath each knee, he drew her legs up higher. The tiny shift in position allowed him to bury himself to the root. Her breath caught in her throat as his cock hit her clit dead on, sending chills over her body.

Fire rippled through her body and pooled between her legs as he thrust. She closed her eyes, concentrating on the sensations that rocketed through her veins. Strong hands held her steady as he hammered into her, each thrust taking her higher than the last. Her nails dug into his shoulders as he forced her body into taking its release.

She screamed with the force of her orgasm, her body arching against his. He continued to move, slow rippling movements of his hips that prolonged her ecstasy. Sensation flowed through her again and again, rolling over her in waves of pleasure until…finally…they slowed.

"Good?" he whispered.

"Yes…"

She'd barely caught her breath when he began thrusting in earnest. Within seconds, another cry was wrenched from her as a harsh groan exploded from Luc. With his head thrown back and his face contorted, she held him tightly as he came deep within her.

* * * * *

Luc awoke to the sensation of a hot tongue on his cock and his eyes flew open. Rachel was between his thighs and her scarlet mouth nibbled at the broad head of his cock. Her eyes sparkled with devilment when he moaned and she released him. Kissing his lower belly, her mouth was hot and her silky hair tickled when she lapped at his belly button. His stomach clenched and she continued her way up his body. Her breasts, crowned with fat, rosy nipples, scraped along his rib cage.

"Luc," she purred.

"Yeah, babe." His throat was dry and he could barely form the words. He reached for her, wanting to taste her, kiss her and fuck her all over again.

"I want to fuck you with my mouth." She guided his hands to the headboard and curled his fingers around the brass rails. "I want you at my mercy."

His tongue went thick and he gasped, "Trust me, I'm already at your mercy."

She chuckled and kissed her way down his body, pausing to lick at his belly button again. He squirmed because it tickled and she tossed her head back and laughed.

"You're ticklish," she chortled.

"This isn't very dignified," he muttered as she gave his bellybutton another slow lick.

"I'm not after your dignity." She closed her hand around his cock and gave him a long, lingering stroke. "I'm after something much bigger than that."

Her mouth came down over his cock and he stifled a yell. His hips pumped against his will and he knew he was just seconds from losing it.

Not yet...please not yet...

Rachel seemed to realize his predicament. She cupped his balls and gave them a lingering caress, just enough to bring him back from the edge.

"Christ, Rachel," he gasped, sagging against the bed. "You're killing me." There wasn't an inch of his body that wasn't completely aware of her every movement. If this wasn't being at her mercy, he didn't know what was.

She chuckled. "Not even close, Lover."

She opened her sweet mouth and took his cock deep into her throat. Luc's hips arched, his mouth opening on a silent moan of pleasure as she began suckling him. Slow and hot, her mouth and talented hands moved over him as she took him back toward the edge of release. She gave a soft hum of pleasure and he almost shot off the bed as the vibrations ran down his cock and shot straight up his spine.

Her eyes were closed and her expression was a symphony of erotic decadence as she worked her mouth over his flesh. Luc lost track of everything except for the woman bending over him. He felt the thick brass of the bed rails give under his grip but he didn't care. All he wanted was to savor the pleasure this woman was giving him. He'd wondered what her plump, scarlet lips would look like wrapped around his cock. Now he knew: even better than he'd imagined.

Orgasm beckoned and this time she didn't try to stop him from release. He came with a wild shout; his body tensed and the headboard finally gave way as the spindles broke in his grasp. Rachel kept him deep in her mouth, soothing him with her hands as she swallowed every last drop of fluid.

When the storm passed, Luc went limp on the bed. His breath raged in his lungs and his heart thudded so hard he thought it might explode from his chest. Rachel released him and moved up beside him. Curling onto his side, he draped an arm around her.

"How was that?" he panted.

She chuckled and slid her bare thigh along his. "It will do, for now."

* * * * *

Luc teased her with one, long, slow lick. Her soft curls tickled his nose and he inhaled the fragrant scent of her damp pussy. Her moan was long and ragged causing him to lift his head. Her slim wrists were bound to the damaged headboard with his red silk sash and the muscles in her arms strained as she fought both for and against his mouth.

He grinned and took full advantage of her captive situation to bathe her flesh with his tongue. He swirled along the soft damp folds letting her moans and cries guide him in his prolonged torment of her body.

"Luc, please," she moaned. Her hips thrust toward his mouth and still he refused to touch her clit. He wanted to make sure she lost her mind as he had his.

"I love to hear you beg, babe." He nipped one plump lip.

"Pppppplease…"

Her moan was music to his ears. He gave her the needed stroke with his tongue, eliciting a scream. Her back arched and he zeroed in on her clit and suckled it. She moaned again and her movements became more frantic as she strained against him, searching for release.

He slid one finger inside her tight pussy and she came with a wild scream, her vagina clenching his finger as her tight body came against his tongue. She was gasping for air when he moved from between her thighs. After releasing her from her bonds, he curled up next to her. Taking her by the waist, he rolled over until she covered him like a limp, human blanket.

Parting her thighs, the broad head of his cock broached her sweet cunt. Her head came up. He saw the satisfaction and renewed arousal lingered in her eyes. Bracing her hands against his chest, she sat up and guided her pussy over him, sliding down millimeter by millimeter until he was buried deep within her.

She was too sweet, too tight, for him to last long.

He thrust upward and she followed his movement with a gentle ripple of her inner muscles. Her breasts swayed and her rosy nipples thrust outward, begging for his touch. She surrounded him like a silken glove and he almost came at the second thrust. Her eyes slid closed and she moved over him, her expression a portrait of dreamy sensuality and her damp, fuck-me lips parted in a half-smile.

Her back arched, her breasts bobbed over him and he reached for them, trailing his fingertips over the lush globes and taut tips. Her lashes fluttered and she gave a loud moan. He thrust upward even harder and she fell forward against his chest as he began to ruthlessly push into her. She was too beautiful, too sexy for him to withstand more of her erotic magic.

She braced her body against his chest and his hands gripped her hips, holding her in place for his thrusts. Reality receded as their bodies strained for completion. Her head dipped toward his throat and he knew what she was asking. The most intimate act a vampire could do was to drink from their lover. It was an act that bordered on sacred among their kind and never before had it felt right to him to allow the act to occur.

Luc tilted his head to the side and Rachel's hot little mouth touched his flesh. He felt the slight sting of her fangs as she sank them into his flesh and he drove into her so hard he lifted both their bodies from the mattress. He'd never taken a woman who was this tight, this lush, and allowed her to drink from him.

The feel of her lips moving on his neck was so erotic that he lost himself in the sensuality of the moment. His grip tightened on her waist and Luc took her without mercy, his hips hammering into hers. Her climax was abrupt, her pussy gripping him so tight he thought he might have stopped breathing for a few seconds. The thrilling clasp of her flesh tossed him over the edge and he came deep inside her with an intensity he'd never felt before.

Rachel released his throat and together they sank into a morass of liquid heat. Their hearts beat in unison and, slowly, the storm passed. Luc wrapped his arms around her, never wanting to let go.

* * * * *

Dawn was fast approaching when Rachel slipped from Luc's bed. In the silence of early morning, she gathered her clothing, wanting to make her escape without him waking. Mentally chastising herself for staying this late, she located an errant shoe under a pile of bedclothes that had slid off the end of the bed.

Clutching her clothing to her chest, she rose. Golden candlelight from a single candle spilled across his fallen angel face and his sinner's mouth. Her heart clenched. Lucius deVille was more wonderful than she'd ever imagined a man could be. Before she'd set out on this quest, she'd known he was leaving New Orleans and had embraced that fact knowing they'd have their one night together and there was no danger they'd ever see each other again. This way no one would get hurt—least of all her.

Her fist clenched. If that was so, why did her heart ache so much?

* * * * *

The *Chat Noir* had changed little in the intervening weeks since last she'd been there. The Halloween costumes were long gone and the interior was decorated with tinsel and hundreds of white Christmas lights. The scent of fried food and beer hung in the air as Rachel wound her way though the crowd toward the bar.

Finding an empty seat near the server stand, she slid into it.

Around her people laughed and drank toasts to the coming holidays and she wasn't sure why she'd come here. She'd spent the past six weeks holed up in her house subsisting on her stockpile of frozen blood products and piles of romance novels. When she found herself rereading the same novel for the third time, she knew she needed to get out of the house for a few hours.

She looked around the bar and her stomach clenched. Though why she'd come here she didn't know.

Because you were here with him…

Her heart twisted. She'd done little more than think about Luc, wonder if he was doing okay wherever he was. Her original plan might've been for a one-night stand with a handsome stranger who didn't endanger her heart, but it sure as hell felt broken anyway.

There wasn't an hour gone by in the past six weeks that she hadn't thought about him. Even in her dark sleep, she'd dreamt of him, his laughter, and the feel of his hands on her body, his wicked mouth on her flesh —

"You look like hell, Rachel." Tom appeared behind the bar with a frown between his brows.

"Thanks." She gave him a wan smile. "Drink, please."

His brow arched. "Not the kitty again, I hope?"

She shook her head. "Just the straight stuff."

"Sure thing, darlin'." Tom turned away to get her drink, leaving her alone with her dark thoughts.

One of the things that bothered her the most was that she didn't dream of Wyatt, her human lover, any longer. A night or so after her evening with Luc, she'd dreamt of him one last time. Wyatt had been smiling and he'd given her a quick wave before he turned and walked away. It was as though he was letting her know that it was okay that she'd moved on. She was both oddly soothed and bothered by this dream. She'd met the man of her dreams, Luc, only to lose the man who'd inhabited her dreams and her life for forty-some years.

"Here you go, Rach." Tom set the mug on the bar before her and the scent of warm blood made her senses come alive. "Here's to your health," he hoisted a glass of mineral water in his direction.

She smiled and picked up her drink. "And to yours, my friend."

The first taste soothed her tangled nerves and she drained the mug. Human blood, unlike were-blood, did not have the tendency to knock a vampire on their behind if imbibed quickly.

Around her the party continued and Rachel wanted nothing more than to be curled up at home in her bed. Feeling unbearably lonely, she pulled out a few dollar bills and dropped them on the bar. Sliding off the stool she turned to leave, stopping dead when she realized a man stood in her way.

It was Luc.

A smile played at the edges of his mouth. "It's about time you showed up."

Rachel's heart stuttered and she stepped backward. "You're supposed to be gone…"

He shook his head. "I never intend to leave New Orleans. After many long years, I'm finally home. If you had stuck around, you'd have learned that for yourself."

She shook her head. "I don't understand…"

"The night we met, that bit of business upstairs, I'd finalized the deal to buy a house here in New Orleans."

A loud rushing noise filled Rachel's ears. Luc lived here now? He was staying in New Orleans? Her knees wobbled. How could she continue to live here knowing she'd run into him sooner or later? Sooner or later a man as handsome as Luc was sure to have girlfriends and she wasn't about to watch him parade around town with another women.

"Congratulations." Her lips felt curiously numb as she started to move past him.

"Where do you think you're going?" He moved to block her escape.

"Home. I have to go home." She refused to look at him.

"Why did you leave me that night, Rachel?"

Her heart breaking, she forced her gaze to his, letting him see the pain and the love she felt. "I was afraid," she whispered.

His gaze sharpened. "Of me?"

She nodded. "And of myself. I loved someone once before and I almost died when he passed away. I didn't think I could risk my heart ever again." Tears began streaming down her face. "You were supposed to leave," she whispered.

"And now that I'm not?" He pulled her into his arms.

"I'm so confused." She mumbled against his chest.

He chuckled. "Then let me make it easy on you." He caught her chin and forced her head back. "We don't know each other very well, but I think I love you. You've bewitched me with your smile, the way you bite your lip, and your sexy ass."

She blinked. "You think you love me?"

"Yes, does that clarify things for you?" He dropped his head and kissed her on the nose. "It would be a crime if you left now and we didn't explore what's going on between us." His grip tightened.

Her heart swelled and her jaw refused to work. Not trusting herself to speak, she just nodded.

"Good. So, um, so…you'll be going home with me, then?

She swallowed hard and nodded again.

"Good." He took her arm and walked her toward the door. "We need to talk about how you're going to make it up to me for that little abandonment stunt you pulled."

She stopped and gaped at him. "Make it up to you?" she spluttered.

"Yes, make it up to me." He pulled her toward the door again. "You left me all alone and I really needed to cuddle that morning but noooooo, you left without a word." He nuzzled her ear and whispered. "You know, a man really needs to cuddle for a while after mind-blowing sex."

Rachel wrapped her arms around his waist, hardly daring to believe it was Luc walking beside her. The night air was cool and damp and a light rain had begun to fall, but she didn't care if the heavens chose that moment to open up and dump torrents of rain on them. Nothing could spoil her happiness.

"Okay, Stud, how do I go about making things up to you?"

He pretended to consider that for a moment. "Well, letting me watch you go down on me would be good for a start…"

About the author:

J.C. welcomes mail from readers. You can write to her c/o Ellora's Cave Publishing at 1337 Commerce Drive, Suite 13, Stow OH 44224.

Also by J.C. Wilder writing as Dominique Adair:

Last Kiss
Tied With A Bow
Party Favors
Xanthra Chronicles: Blood Law

TAIL OF THE TIGER

R. Casteel

Chapter 1

Dearest Father had ruined enough people's lives.

Cedric Deverone Jr. sat at the large oak desk going through the hundreds of disks left to him by his father, Cedric Deverone Sr. His eyes felt like someone had poured sand in them. With his food cold, forgotten, and a bottle of his father's most expensive imported cognac in his hand, he read the information on the screen. It had taken him five hours to break the security code on the last disk.

Now, in all truth, he wished he hadn't been successful. He knew his father was a brilliant scientist and the founder of Ever-Alive, the leading institute for the cloning of humans. He hadn't known until now of his father's sickly perverted experiments — or that he was his father's bid for immortality.

He, Cedric Deverone Jr., was another of his father's misbegotten clones.

Cedric lifted the crystal bottle to his lips, took a long swallow, and felt the fire wash over him. In anger, he threw the bottle at the large portrait over the fireplace. The bottle broke, soaking the canvas and filling the room with the heady aroma. Glass fell to the floor and glistened in the reflected light of the fire.

Rage boiled up inside him, releasing the bloodlust he fought so hard to control. He wished now, more than ever, that Cedric Deverone Sr. had never been born.

* * * * *

Cedric watched the island take shape on the horizon and adjusted his course. He had sailed out of Brazil a week ago, one month to the day after having found the damning file. Stocks wavered and fell as the news spread of the redistribution and liquidation of the Deverone fortunes.

It had been assumed when his father died, that he would step in and fill his shoes. Board members from a dozen companies, firms, and charities were now scrambling to fill the vacant seat.

Some said he was abandoning his responsibilities, others that he owed his father to keep Ever-Alive going. Cedric saw it the other way around. He owed Cedric Deverone Sr., nothing.

On the sea charts, Deverone Island was only a dot in an endless ocean of blue. It was his island now, the only piece of real estate not for sale. As he watched the foliage take the shape of large trees, excitement began to rush through him.

The beauty of the island, the danger of the unknown, and dread of discovering that the story on the disk was true caused a varied mixture of emotions to swirl in his mind. According to the records, the half-ling woman wasn't the first. Were there more of his father's *mistakes* on the island?

There came to him another emotion, one he hadn't felt in years. A feeling that frightened him more than finding out the secrets of his father's work were not, after all, the fanatical ravings of a sick man. For the first time in more years than he could remember, Cedric Deverone felt he was coming home.

Circling the island, he anchored his sailboat in a small, protected cove and took the dingy to the narrow white beach. A swell from the tide pushed him onto the sand and he hopped out. His heart pounded painfully in his chest as he knelt to examine a single set of footprints leading to the dense cover of the tropical forest.

Ten feet away, he found a clean, distinct handprint and then another. It was true, every word of horror his father wrote. She walked upright like a human and ran on all fours like the beast. The prints bore clear proof that the half-ling clone still lived.

Cedric stood, wiped the sweat from his palms, and followed the trail into the underbrush.

* * * * *

Watching from the high branches of the canopy, she studied the man as he entered the forest. The simmering heat lifted his spoor and she tasted his fear. Yet he worked his way slowly and silently along the trail like a predator instead of the prey. Kat melted into the shadows as he lifted his head, his eyes searching among the treetops.

For a human, he wasn't bad looking. A thin white shirt clung to his body, revealing broad muscular shoulders and a narrow waist. His long, curly black hair stirred in the ocean breeze. Humans had visited her island before, but few ever ventured off the beach. Those who did — seldom returned. He stopped directly under her, studying the ground and listening.

"Kat, I know you are watching me." He kept his voice low like he knew she was close by. "I only hope you can understand what I'm saying."

Panic gripped her heart. The tip of her long tail twitched nervously. *How does he know my name?*

"I do not wish to harm you. Please, you have to believe me." He stood, leaned against her tree, and waited.

Her fingers brushed a pinecone and it fell, landing at his feet. She heard his soft chuckle as he reached down and picked it up.

"Sorry, Kat. I didn't bring anything for you from my boat. If you'll come down to the beach tonight, I'll have something for you there." He walked away, back down the path.

Leaping surefooted from limb to limb, Kat descended to the ground. His scent filled her senses, excited her. For some reason, this human had come seeking her out. Sinking to all fours, she crept through the underbrush.

She watched him start a small pile of sticks on fire and as the flames grew, he added more wood. Humans were strange creatures, always wanting fire. She knew how to harness the power but had no real need of it.

Her guardian, the only human she had ever trusted, had taught her about it and their language. It had been so long now since his passing, she missed the long nights under the stars, listening to him tell about a mysterious world that she would never know.

This was her home, her sanctuary. From her earliest memories, she had run through the trees, caught fish in the small stream, and lived off the land. She felt safe here, unless humans came.

* * * * *

Cedric spent the remainder of the day gathering wood for his fire and exploring along the beach. Through the shadows and dense foliage, he caught fleeting glimpses of her as she watched him from a distance. He had taken a risk going into the thick tropical canopy and invading her territory. Was she stalking his every movement out of curiosity, or was she waiting for him to venture back into the tree line where she could spring from hiding and kill him?

Along a small fresh-water inlet, he found more of her footprints and knelt to examine them more closely. Kat was so close that he could feel her presence and hear her shallow breathing. Cedric slowly turned his head and stared into the dense cover. Brilliant amber eyes glared back at him.

Cupping his hand, he dipped it into the water and lifted it to his mouth never taking his eyes off of hers. They held him spellbound. If she attacked now, he would be powerless to protect himself.

"You have beautiful eyes, Kat." He decided to trust his feelings instead of centuries-old inbred instincts. Cedric turned his back to her, stood, and walked away.

His eyes were black as night, and seemed as fathomless. Their compelling depths had nearly drawn her out of hiding. She crept back into the darkening forest and followed his movements down the beach. Upon reaching his small campsite, he stretched and began removing his clothes.

Laughter filled her chest at the sight. Men were so helpless without clothes. *They can't even run through the forest for fear of hurting their little...*she searched for the words she had heard from other humans...*cocks, pricks, dicks, so many names for something so small.*

Kat crept forward in the encroaching darkness. Curious about him, she lay on the beach and watched him in the water. He moved closer, and she bunched her muscles, ready to flee at the slightest danger.

He couldn't believe his eyes. She had actually come out of the forest. "Please, don't go."

"Who are you and how did you know I was here?" Her tail swept across the sand.

"Oh! Wow! You do talk." Although her English was good, with just a hint of New England accent, her words were slow as if she seldom used speech to communicate.

He started to move closer and she lifted her hips in the air.

"I don't blame you for being afraid." Holding his hands up, he stopped and backed away. "My name is Cedric. I found out about you from going through my father's files."

"I was told a man would come one day and that I should kill him to make the world a safer place."

"Regrettably, the person you speak of was my father and he is already dead."

"Come out of the water, Cedric, before you fall prey to the large creatures of the sea. I believe you call them...sharks."

She backed up as he drew near.

Picking up a piece of wood, he added it to the fire and sat down. Kat came out of the darkness into the flickering light of the fire.

Cedric stared open mouthed at the beauty of the half-ling. Amber eyes caught the fire and flashed in the night. Her dark rose-colored hair flowed around her face in a wavy halo before falling to just below her shoulders. Except for orange and black-striped skin on her forehead, it could have been her image cast on movie theaters, television screens, and magazines around the world.

Human skin covered most of her chest. Her large breasts sagged slightly from years without wearing support. The rest of her, covered with the short orange and black-striped fur of a tiger, intrigued him.

"You find me repulsive?" Kat crossed her arms over her breasts.

"Different, but never repulsive." Cedric lay back on the sand, turned on his side, and propped his head on his arm. "I see your mother in you."

"My mother?" Quicker than his eye could follow, she sprang across the fire and crouched within reach. "You knew my mother?"

"Not personally." He watched the corded muscles in her legs and arms quiver. "Since discovering my father's files, I've watched every movie of her I could get my hands on."

"Movie, what is a…movie?"

"I can show you on my boat." He lifted his arm and pointed out towards the cove. "I thought you might want to see her."

She sniffed the air and whipped her head back to glare into his eyes. " There is no one on your boat."

"No, I have a picture of her." Cedric watched the indecision play across her face. Her long sleek tail swished in the sand.

"I will see this picture, and if it is not as you say…" she trailed off and smiled.

Kat didn't need to say any more. Two large canine teeth glistened in the light of the fire. "Come with me, and I will show you." Cedric stood and held out his hand.

Slowly, she raised her hand to take his. He felt her tension pulsating through her fingers. Even this small measure of trust elated him and he smiled.

Surprisingly, she smiled back.

Chapter 2

On the short ride in the dinghy, Kat rode crouched down in the bow, her tail brushing his legs and knees as she scanned the waters ahead. Upon reaching his sailboat, she sprang to the deck and sniffed along its length from stern to bow.

Cedric climbed aboard, went below, and started the generator. Kat hissed and drew back. "Sorry, I should have warned you. It's a little noisy but necessary for the lights."

Crossing the small cabin, he loaded a DVD into the player and turned it on. "It's a little cramped in here." Picking up the remote, he stretched out on the bed, and turned the television on. You might be more comfortable sitting over here." He pointed to the bed.

Fascinated by the images coming over the screen, Kat eased onto the foot of the bed and curled up to watch. "There is so much about your world that I do not understand."

Cedric exhaled a breath in a long sigh. "I lived in it every day, and I feel the same way."

"Look!" she sprang to all fours. "Is she my mother?"

His eyes darted to the screen. "Yes, Kat. Cynthia Marcella is your mother."

"She is so beautiful." She stretched out on the bed like the half-cat she was with her legs tucked up underneath her.

"So are you." The words slipped out of his mouth before he realized it.

"I do not look like her," she hissed. "I am ugly."

He felt sorry for her. "No, Kat. You are different from your mother...*Hell*, you are different from anyone else in the world, but you are *not* ugly." He fought an overpowering urge to touch her. "You have your mother's face, her body, and even her smile — minus the couple differences in your teeth."

Turning her head, she gazed at him for several long seconds. "You are a strange human, Cedric." She turned back to watch the screen.

"Tell me more about my mother."

"Well, as you can see, she was a beautiful woman. Cynthia was a talented movie star, but it became an obsession with her. She couldn't accept the fact of growing old and when my father informed her of his own dreams and research, she insisted on being included."

"Did she...know about me?"

"No. Your mother never knew about you, or the other creatures created from his sick, twisted mind."

"I wish I could have known her," she sighed wistfully as she watched the screen.

Kat's tail never stayed still for long. He soon realized it was a good indicator of her emotions as it swayed back and forth across the bed. When Cynthia's face appeared it lifted with the tip twitching like the tail of a snake.

Several times, it brushed across his lap. The soft fur against his skin felt strangely erotic. The way she was lying on the bed, gave him a close-up and interesting view of her female genitals.

Kat, in that area, was totally woman.

Come on Cedric, she is a half-ling. Okay, a beautiful half-ling, but you're not going to get a stiff dick over her. Despite his self-admonishment, his cock began to stir from its bed of hair.

Raising her head off the bed, Kat sniffed the air. Her body shifted, her hips lifted and wiggled as she arched her tail.

Moving her head to the side, her eyes traveled from his toes, up along her legs, and zeroed in on his erection. Sniffing the air again, she turned on the bed to face him.

Her intense gaze at his cock only intensified his emotions and made him uncomfortable.

Confusion spread across her face. "You…wish to mate with me?"

"No!" He looked down at his betraying cock and a little voice from somewhere whispered in his ear. *Liar.*

"I have seen your kind mating on the beach. It was always from a distance though, never up close." She lowered her head to within a couple inches of his cock. "I smell the same strong scent from you, as I did from them."

Cedric gripped the sheets to keep from running his fingers through her hair and forcing her to take him. He had never forced a woman and just because she was a half-ling, he wasn't about to start with her.

"Does it hurt, when you are like this?"

"No, not so much in physical pain." He relaxed his hold on the sheets but didn't let go.

Her head moved from side to side. "Then why do you grab the sheets as though you are in great pain?"

"I was afraid if I touched you, you would run away and I would never see you again." He released the sheets and folded his arms across his chest.

Kat curled up and watched the television for a few minutes. "I won't run away."

Come on, Cedric get a grip! His hands shook as he reached out and his fingers touched the long thick strands of her hair. It was coarse and tangled from neglect. Reaching over to the small shelf beside the bed, he picked up his hairbrush.

"Sit up and I'll brush your hair."

"What is that?" She reached out to touch it.

He noticed for the first time the difference in her hands. Short cat-like claws protruded from the tips her fingers. Their pale, needle-sharp points glistened in the dim cabin light.

"It's called a hairbrush, used for taking the tangles out of your hair." He ran his fingers through her thick tresses. "If you don't like it, I will stop."

She sat up with her back to him and he began working his way through the wavy mass of dark-rose strands. A low rumble became noticeable in the cabin. Kat was purring.

He tried to keep his mind off of her by counting the brush strokes but he soon gave up. The more he brushed, the softer it was to touch, and he wanted that much more to caress her whole body. Her damn purring didn't help matters one bit.

"I'm finished." He laid the brush down. "Run your fingers through your hair and feel the difference."

"Oh!" she lifted the long strands and let them slide through her fingers. "Its so soft, it doesn't even feel like my hair.

"What are they doing?" She pointed to her mother on the screen.

"They are kissing."

"Why do people kiss?" Kat lay back on the other pillow and watched her mother and the man engage in an open mouthed, tongue-probing kiss.

He chuckled. "There are several reasons really — when greeting a close friend, affection between family members, a way of saying thank you, or showing passion and desire between two lovers."

"Then how do you tell them apart?" She rolled onto her side facing him. Her breasts touched his arm and he felt her heat roll across him like a warm tropical breeze.

"It's difficult to describe, but I'll…"

"Show me the difference."

Her words knocked him off balance. "Are you sure?" Playing with fire around gasoline would be safer.

Kat briefly hesitated. "Yes."

Leaning over, he brushed the hair from her face. "A friendship kiss is light, and normally on the cheek." Cedric gave her a soft kiss. His lips left a warm feeling that spread across her face.

"Then we have the family embrace." His mouth puckered and gently touched her lips. The heat began to spread and her heart skipped a beat.

"I wasn't ready for that one. Can we do it again?" She followed his example and puckered her lips.

Cedric gave her a second kiss on the lips and watched her smile. "That was more enjoyable."

Kat lifted her hand and touched his face. His eyes flashed with an emotion she didn't understand. She brushed his cheek again and he captured her fingers with his hand.

"Next..." His voice grew husky and vibrated with nervousness. He kissed her fingers and then, turning her hand over, he placed a longer kiss in her palm. "Is between lovers." He kissed her arm where her skin began to change, "and is usually longer, more intimate, and placed — anywhere on the body."

"Anywhere?" She licked her suddenly dry lips and turned away from the intensity of Cedric's eyes.

Visions of women on the beach with their mates licking them and kissing their breasts swam before her eyes. His touch brought her back to the present. Light as his fingers were on her breasts, they sent out tiny shock waves.

"Everywhere." His head drew closer, lowered, and his lips lingered on her skin.

"Oh!" Lifting her hand, her fingers glided along his side and back. It grew warm within the cabin. The heat seemed to center between her legs and tail, and spread outward.

Cedric lifted her breast and kissed her nipple, drawing it into his mouth. Her fingers dug into his skin and her breath came in rapid shallow pants. Rolling onto her back, she brought her other hand up to curl her fingers through his hair.

He lifted his head. "Last of the kisses," he whispered, "is the most sensuous and shared between lovers.

His mouth covered hers. His tongue traced her lips, delved between them, and coaxed her to do the same. Cedric captured her tongue and sucked on it.

Driven by the wild new sensations, her fingers raked along his back. Her tail cracked like a whip against the bed and she hung onto Cedric for fear of falling into the unknown world before her.

His hand caressed her fur, sliding lower along her side and over her leg. A finger traced wet, swollen, female flesh between her legs. Her tail lifted and curled into a protective barrier shielding herself from him.

Cedric broke the kiss. "I lied earlier."

His rough hurried breathing caressed her cheek. Her sensitive ears picked up his increased heartbeat.

"I do want to mate with you. I want you more than any woman I have ever known."

The heavy, musky scent of his need and hers swirled together in the air. Looking into the black depths of his storm-tossed eyes, she could see the truth of his words. Slowly, she lowered her tail, reached up, and pulled his lips back to hers.

His finger dipped inside her and she stiffened.

"Relax," he whispered in her ear.

Her body reacted to the rhythm of his finger sliding across her inner flesh. She could no more stop the purring than she wanted Cedric to stop what he was doing. A feeling of loss swept over as he removed his finger from inside her.

As he moved between her legs, she looked down at his hard, swollen, and dripping cock. She experienced a moment of doubt as he placed it at her opening and slid inside her.

The surprise rushed from her throat in a long gasp as she stretched to accommodate his length. She marveled at the warmth radiating into her from his cock. She looked into his eyes and surrendered to their compelling depth.

Lifting her tail, she brought its thick base into contact with the sack hanging below his cock. With the tip of her curled tail, she caressed the length of his back. She flicked it, and it snapped against his flesh. A startled look flashed momentarily across his face. Cedric smiled, lifted an eyebrow, and rammed his hard length into her.

It became a teasing game. Every time he stopped, she smacked him with her tail. Each time she did, he took her to a higher level of sensation until her body began to demand more than he was giving. Kat felt an intense pressure building up inside her. His face blurred before her eyes. He shoved into her over and over again, every swing of her tail landing somewhere on his flesh.

His low grunts filled her ears.

She dug her fingers into his back and the mouth-watering odor of fresh blood filled the cabin. At his startled gasp, Kate tried to focus on his face. There was something different about...his eyes. They were bright red.

As she rode the crest of the next sensuous wave, Cedric's body stiffened. She felt the intense heat flow into her and her body responded with its own blinding release. Her legs locked around his waist, holding him in place as she soared through the dizzying sensations. The air in her lungs rushed out in a strangled cry and she buried her face in the hollow of his neck.

Kat whimpered as he pulled out of her flesh and lay beside her. She opened her eyes and saw a look of contentment in his tender smile. "That wasn't what I expected," she whispered.

He started to speak and she placed a finger over his lips. "It was better."

"We may have to tie up your tail and clip your claws." He laughed and lifted a strand of hair from her face, "before you remove my skin."

She lifted her tail in the air and brushed the tip gently across his cock. "I thought you liked it."

Leaning over, he kissed her. "I did."

"My claws?" She knew the damage she could create with just one swipe of their deadly tips. Kate noticed the sheet was splattered with blood and she checked his back.

"Where did all this blood come from?" she looked at the faint red scratches on his skin.

"It could be yours," he smiled. "Most women bleed the first time."

She sniffed the bed sheet. "Its not mine."

"Then there is nothing to worry about," he patted the bed beside him. "As you can see for yourself, I'm not bleeding." *At least not anymore, thanks to Father.*

Kat lay beside him and curled up in a little ball. She began to purr loudly and fell asleep.

As the warmth of the morning sun inched across her body, she woke and leapt quietly from the bed. Going on deck, Kat stretched and rubbed her fur against the railing. She watched the shoreline, wishing she had the chance for her morning meal, but the presence of dark fins kept her from swimming to shore.

"Morning, Kat," Cedric called from the cabin door. "I trust you slept well."

"Yes, I did." Walking over to him, she gave him a kiss on the cheek.

"That's all I get after last night?" He placed his hand on her arm.

"Last night we were lovers. Today...we are friends." Turning, she hid her face from him. She couldn't allow herself to become attached to him. Her loneliness would only worsen if she did. Better to have things remain the way they were.

"Why?" Reaching up, he placed a finger beside her face, gently turned her around, and wiped the moisture from her cheek. "What caused this sudden change?"

"How can we be lovers when you will be leaving?" her lips quivered.

"Leaving? I never said anything about going." His fingers brushed through her hair.

"They all do. None of those who come here ever stay."

"My lovely Kat." Cedric pulled her into his arms and kissed her hair. "I intend to make this island my home as I have no desire to be anywhere else."

His lips met hers in a long kiss. At last she had a mate, hope for the future, and someone who desired her as a woman. The tip of her tail twitched as she curled it around his legs.

"Show me around your island, Kat." Cedric led her over to the boarding ladder. "I need to decide where to build my new home."

"I must warn you. My half-sister may not receive you as openly as I did." Kat smiled as she remembered last night's mating.

"So, there *is* another like you here?" She heard the keen interest in his voice.

"Yes, but she stays near the mountain," Kat sighed. "The man who raised me said she was born without a human heart and was evil as the night in which she hides."

"Where is this man you speak of?" Cedric asked.

"He died...somewhere on the mountain." Sorrow crept into her heart. "I believe she killed him."

Chapter 3

They rode to the shore in silence. Kat leapt from the small raft and ran off into the woods. A short time later she returned to the beach where he waited.

"It should be safe during the day as long as you don't wander off. The night is when danger walks through the forest and it is not safe to be out."

"I thought you said your half-sister stayed near the mountain." He followed her across the sand and into the tree line.

"There are other evils lurking about besides her."

Kat stopped on the trail and froze. The tip of her tail shook like a rattler. A noise up ahead in the bush drew his attention. A wild pig burst from the foliage, turned to face them, and pawed the ground. Its long sharp tusks gleamed a deadly white.

Cedric felt the bloodlust well up inside him. This time he welcomed it, freely embracing the part of his life that he had kept hidden. He hurdled Kat's crouching body and charged the beast.

"Cedric! No!"

He ignored her scream and met the charging animal in a flurry of dust and crashing brush. The wild pig lifted its head and the razor sharp tusks grazed his arm. Cedric wrestled the squealing, twisting flesh to the ground and sank his teeth into its neck. The rich metallic taste of hot blood filled his mouth and he drank greedily as the animal grew still and died.

Looking up, he observed the confusion written across her face. He smiled, trying to reassure her. No one else had ever seen this side of him...and lived.

"Humans don't drink blood." His eyes had again changed from black to red, just like when they had mated. *Had he been so close to taking my life?* The thought gave her pause as she considered it.

"I never said I was all human." He tossed the bloodless carcass over to Kat. "Most of the time, I've been able to hide the dark side of who I am."

"What of those times when you could not hide this…dark side? She ripped open the animal and began eating the still warm meat.

"Then someone died." Cedric wasn't happy with the knowledge that he had taken the lives of others. Their faces swam before him in the damning hours of darkness and they would plague his conscious for eternity.

"Being more human than I am, I can see it troubles you." She tore off more meat and continued eating. "Humans visit the island and those who venture far inland seldom return."

"You have taken human life as well?" He was seeing a new side to Kat, a part of her that he could identify with and understand.

"Yes. Although I take no pleasure in their deaths, they do not trouble me in the way they do you."

She finished eating, took the rest of the wild pig between her jaws, and raced up a nearby tree where she placed the animal in the fork of a large branch. Leaping from the limb, she landed with a soft thud beside him.

"It will be safe up there." Kat turned and started off down the narrow trail. "I will get it later for you to cook over the fire."

With Kat walking ahead of him, bent over sniffing the ground, he had a difficult time keeping his eyes on the trail and his surroundings. Ever time she lifted her tail or swished it back and forth, he had an erotic view of her soft pink womanly flesh.

His erection throbbed with longing and his breathing became labored. In college, women had thrown themselves at him and into his bed in an effort to latch onto the Deverone fortunes. Perhaps because of this, he had become jaded to the point sex no longer held a fascination for him.

Kat was different. She wasn't after his money, or to be in the social spotlight with the most eligible bachelor on the marriage market.

He wanted her again. It wasn't about sex, or the novelty of fucking a woman who was also half-tiger. Something deep inside wanted to reach out and hold her forever. Unless he broke his own self-imposed rule, the most he could hope for would be a few short years.

They broke through the thick ground cover into a small clearing at the base of a steep cliff. A large pool of water glistened in the sunlight. From the movement of the water, Cedric realized it was fed from a source deep underground.

Kat went to the edge of the pool, lowered her face to the water, and began to drink. A groan of raw desire rumbled in his chest at the sight of her fur-covered ass raised in the air and the gaping flesh of her pussy.

She sniffed the air and turned her head to look at his crotch. Before he could blink, Kat spun around and rubbed her face against the material of his shorts. With deft fingers, she unfastened them and pulled them down around his ankles.

Her coarse tongue caressed his balls and slowly traveled up the length of his swollen cock.

Cedric's legs shook and knees threatened to buckle. "Ahh!" The air rushed from his lungs in a ragged sigh.

Kat smiled, turned, and once again lifted her hips. Cedric dropped to his knees in the soft, damp dirt and in one quick thrust, buried his hard cock inside her. She lifted her head and her low cat-like growl filled the clearing, causing the birds to scatter from the nearby trees.

She began to purr, softly at first, but with each thrust into her wet flesh it grew louder. Her whole body began to vibrate. He felt it surround his cock and invade his body, driving him to heights he had never before imagined possible.

Everything around him—the trees, the clouds in the sky, even Kat with her shoulders on the ground and her ass rubbing against him—became a blur. He felt like he was on a sensual merry-go-round that just kept going faster and faster.

No longer able to hold on, Cedric's body let go in a sudden rush of hot release. He found himself floating with Kat as the loud, wild roar of the tiger filled his ears. Collapsing forward on her back, his body shook as he gasped for air.

Kat turned her head and licked his face.

A loud scream filled the air and sent a chill down his back.

Cedric and Kat lifted their heads. At the apex of the cliff, a black shadow slithered in and out of the rocks. As it came closer he saw it was a giant black panther.

"Run, Cedric!" Kat cried. "Go back to you boat. I'll try and hold her off."

"Who," Cedric asked, "are you going to hold off?"

"Zalorna, my half-sister!"

At that moment, a sleek, black body launched itself from about fifty feet up the cliff and landed on the other side of the pool.

Cedric stared in amazement at the similarities and distinct differences between the two. They both had the same facial features, but Zalorna's body was sleeker, more streamlined, with small breasts, and she was covered with a black, shiny coat of fur.

Zalorna snarled, bared her teeth, and crouched. "How dare you lift your tail to a human? If you won't kill him then move out of the way and I will."

Cedric pulled up his shorts and allowed the threat to summon his dark side.

"I won't let you." Kat growled. "I've taken him to mate and if you want him, you will have to go through me. Besides, he is only part human, like we are."

"You lie!" Zalorna hissed. "My eyes do not deceive me. I have killed enough of them to know he is human."

"Do humans have these?" Cedric flashed his own fangs at the bitch and was rewarded with the startled look on her face.

"Sis, this is one fight you do not want," Kat argued. "I have seem him attack and kill a tusker."

"You dare to compare me to a *tusker*?"

Zalorna spit out the word like it was pig shit and Cedric laughed. "Kat did not mean to insult your ability, but to warn you that I'm not going to cower and run from you."

Her lips parted into a sinister smile. "A human who is not afraid of me. How interesting."

"Go on back to your mountain cave, sister, and leave us alone. Cedric means you no harm."

The black beast paced on the other side of the pool. Cedric kept his own fangs visible and never took his eyes off of her.

"I will go. Be warned, sister, if he comes near..."

Zalorna flashed her razor-sharp fangs one last time as a reminder and disappeared into the dense underbrush surrounding the pool.

Cedric willed his dark side back and felt his fangs recede.

"I fear she will not be content to stay near her mountain and leave us in peace." Kat stood erect, staring in the direction Zalorna had gone. "The island is too small to avoid all contact. Promise me you will not go into the jungle alone."

"I promise." Cedric trailed his fingers along her cheek. "But do not fear so for my life. I will not die easily. See," he raised his arm, "the injury from the tusker is healed."

Kat gave him a kiss. "It is not only your life I am worried about, but my half-sister as well." She turned and waded into the pool. "Come on in, Cedric, the cool water feels good on a hot day."

He peeled off his clothes and waded out to her. The water reached his balls and he gasped. She was mistaken about the water being cool. It was downright cold. Cedric shivered as he lowered himself deeper into the pool.

She reached between his legs and laughed. "If it gets any shorter, I may have to go looking for it."

"Hey, give me a break, at least you're wearing fur." A strong sensation of being watched crept over him. Cedric glanced to the cliff. "She's up there...watching us."

"I know...let her watch." Kat drew closer, placed her arms around him, and gave him a long, seductive kiss. "She could have joined us if she had not been such a..."

"Bitch," he finished for her.

"I am not familiar with that word, but it sounds right." Kat snuggled him and playfully nipped at his ear."

"You wish to share what we have with Zalorna?" He wasn't sure he wanted to be that close to the half-sister. Yet once Kat placed the idea in his head, he didn't find the idea revolting. Stupid maybe, but definitely something he could at least fantasize over.

"Why not?" Kat purred. "After all, she is my half-sister."

"Humans don't normally want to share what we have."

"Ahh, but then we are not humans in the true sense, are we?" She let go and started for the edge of the pool. "The cold is finding its way through me as well."

Cedric followed her and received a shower as she shook the water from her orange and black-stripped fur.

Kat sat on a large flat rock at the pool's edge and began grooming her fur like any ordinary cat. As he watched her tongue glide over her body, he became aroused.

"Does your cock grow from wanting me again so soon, or are you thinking about Zalorna?" She gave him a sly glance, lifted her breasts, and began to lick them dry.

"Do you want me to think about your sister?" Cedric sat beside her, stretched out on the rock, and ran his fingers through her coarse fur.

"Not while you are with me." Kat lay back, scooted next to him, and turned onto her side facing him.

"It would be impossible to think about anyone else when making love to you." He knew that in all sincerity, he wanted the words to be true but even now, he knew the question would always be in the back of his mind. Cedric closed his eyes. *What would it be like if...?*

He was brought back to reality as Kat's tongue took a detour and licked the tip of his now throbbing cock.

"Still thinking about that black sister of mine?"

"No."

"Liar," she laughed and sat up. "I want you to think about mating with her."

"Why?

"Then you will not be so quick to kill her when you meet." Her fingers fluttered over his chest and caressed his cheek. "I would like for the three of us to live in peace on this island."

"I want that too," Cedric pulled her head down to his and kissed her, "more than you know."

Chapter 4

Cedric sat on the edge of the bluff overlooking the small, protected cove. Kat lay curled up beside him contentedly purring while he stroked her soft fur. The site was perfect for their home.

With all his vast wealth, he could've had a mansion built, but there was something invigorating about working with his hands and building it himself. Besides, what did he need of luxury, when he had Kat?

She leapt to her feet and snarled. Every hair on her back stood, her tail lowered, and she crouched as if ready to attack anything that moved.

"What is it, love?" His body began to respond as her nervous awareness surrounded him.

"I...I do not know," she growled. "Danger is coming. I can feel it. Run for the cave." She spun and charged across the partially cleared plateau.

Her sense of impending danger brought his dark side to the surface as he followed her. His heart kicked into overdrive and sent blood surging through his veins. With the force of a jackhammer, it pounded behind his eyes, and filled his ears with a roar. His fangs slammed into place with enough force to bring pain to his face.

A bright, blinding light exploded around him. A blast of intense heat swept over him like a steamroller, knocking him to the ground.

Oh, my God! A nuclear bomb!

Dazed and in shock, his perception and reasoning slowly returned. Kat crawled over to him and licked his face.

"What happened, Cedric? It is so hot I can barely breath."

What the hell did happen? The grass seemed to wither before his eyes.

"I don't know, but we need to reach the cave." He staggered to his feet. "We have to get out of the sun."

"Cedric," panic filled her voice, "look at the sky. It is on fire."

Lifting his eyes, he stared in wonder and fear. What appeared to be tongues of flame rolled overhead like angry storm clouds. For as far as he could see, the heavens were burning.

"We must seek shelter at once." Cedric forced his legs to carry him forward.

Further up the slope from the plateau, a dead tree burst into flames. *Is this the end?* his mind questioned.

They reached the relative safety of the cool cave. Dropping to the floor, Cedric forced his breathing to deepen and calm. If he stayed the way he was, if the blood-lust continued for much longer, he would need to feed the craving. Right now, he couldn't allow that to happen. Kat was the only source of fresh blood and he would rather die first.

"I'm frightened," Kat confessed.

Cedric looked out at the orange-red sky and watched as first one pine tree and then another, ignited and burned like a torch. He wasn't frightened, he was scared to death, but he couldn't let it show.

"Come here." He lifted his arms to her.

Kat crawled into his lap and wrapped her arms around his neck. Cedric rocked her as they observed their world going up in flames.

It felt like his skin was being removed, one layer at a time. He had been burned in the few minutes it had taken them to reach shelter. Blisters on his arms and chest gave testimony to just how lucky they had been to reach shelter.

Finally, after burning far into the next morning, the fire in the sky flickered out. Tired, hungry, and parched with thirst, Cedric emerged from the cave with Kat walking beside him. The heat surrounded them, sucking the air from their lungs.

The trees that hadn't burned had their leaves curled and shriveled. Overnight, the grass had turned brown. In scattered areas of the island many fires still raged. Walking to the edge of the cliff, he scanned the devastation below. Miraculously, his boat still floated in the cove.

Not knowing of Zalorna's fate, Kat stood up, looking toward the tall mountain peak in the center of the island. His heart went out to her half-sister, but their own survival came first.

"Cedric, I don't hear any birds."

Suddenly, he heard it too…the sound of silence. It sent a foreboding chill up his spine, and he strained to hear even the slightest sound of life.

"I know." Lifting his eyes to the sky, he looked for the ever-present sea gulls and found none.

Out on the horizon where the blue sky merged with the ocean, a line began to form. He stood rooted in fear as it grew larger, stretching from the east to the west as far as he could see.

Cedric swallowed the panic lodged in his throat. "Kat, you have to find Zalorna just as fast as you can and bring her to the boat." He started running toward the path leading down cliff.

"Why?" she asked as she fell in beside him.

"Trust me, Kat." His lungs burned as the hot dry air filled his lungs. "There isn't time to explain."

She bounded ahead of him and was gone.

There may not be any time left for us if I don't save the boat.

Reaching the cove, he dove into the water and started swimming. There wasn't time to haul the dingy to the water. Cedric reached the boat, scrambled up the ladder, and hauled in the anchor. Forcing himself to remain calm, he started lashing down and stowing away everything he could.

Finished with the topside, he glanced towards the beach for any sign of the females. Seeing no movement on land, he went below and prepared the cabin for getting underway. He had to be ready, but if they didn't make it back it wouldn't matter what he did.

Back on deck, he saw Kat and Zalorna looking around as if wondering what to do. Thankfully, the boat had drifted closer to the beach.

"Swim for it!" he yelled. "Hurry!"

They didn't question but hit the water at a run. Time seemed to drag by while he waited. "Come on, girls," he muttered. "Swim faster."

Kat was the first to reach the boat and climb aboard. She collapsed on deck as Zalorna lifted her black head above the gunnels.

Loose portions of skin hung from broken blisters. He couldn't imagine the pain she must be going through. There would be time to tend to both of them later...if they survived.

"Get below," he pointed to the hatch leading to the cabin, "and brace yourselves. It's going to get rough."

Cedric started the engine, thankful that he had a full tank of fuel. He gave the wheel a spin and opened the throttle. If he made it to the far side of the island, they might stand a chance, but even then, he questioned their odds.

He cleared the mouth of the cove and looked to the north and his heart sank. A wall of water bore down on them. With no time left, he spun the wheel, locked it in place, and dove for the hatch.

Kat was waiting. Her blanched face registered her fear as she slammed the door behind him. The stern began to rise and the small sailing yacht shuddered.

With the quickness of her cat instincts, Kat threw herself at him and locked her arms around his chest. They crashed into the bulkhead, bounced off the small kitchen counter, and then hit the overhead as the boat rolled over beneath the onslaught of the wave.

Time seemed to stand still. Everything moved in slow motion. Zalorna flew past them to crash into the forward bulkhead. Somehow, she managed to land on all fours, only to be lifted and slammed into the overhead.

It seemed like forever, but the boat slowly righted and popped to the surface like a cork. "Kat, Zalorna—are you okay?"

"Yes." They answered with shaky voices. "What happened?"

"A giant tidal wave hit us."

Shaken and bruised, they had come through it alive. The engine had stalled. At least, he hoped that was all and nothing more serious had happened.

He opened the hatch and went on deck. The top half of the mast was gone. If he couldn't repair it, they would be forced to rely on the engine for as long as the fuel lasted. After that, they would be adrift.

"The island!" Zalorna's startled cry turned him around.

Water lapped along the edge of the cliff where only a few short hours before he had been building his home. The island had been reduced to a small ridge of land that even as he watched, grew smaller in size.

A chunk of ice, bigger than his boat, bobbed in the water nearby. He shuddered at the thought of what would've happened had they been hit by it while riding out the wave.

"What happened, Cedric?" Kat watched the ice floating past the boat.

"Only one thing could've caused this. The polar ice caps have melted."

"Oh…what are ice caps?"

He suddenly realized the world that they were heading to would be so drastically changed that trying to describe the old world would be nearly impossible. "They were large areas of that stuff," he pointed to the berg, "for as far as the eye could see."

"And whatever happened yesterday...melted them?" Zalorna frowned.

"It's the only answer I have for...this." Cedric spread his hand out toward the island. Even as he spoke, he could see the land slowly disappear beneath the waves.

Starting the motor, he pulled back to the island. "Kat, see if there are tools stowed away for cutting wood."

"Zalorna, can you jump into that tree?"

"Well, yes." She had a funny, disgusted look on her face.

"Sorry, I didn't mean to imply you couldn't...when I get close enough. I need you to tie a rope off higher in the tree."

He broke out the anchor rope, removed the anchor, and handed her the end of the rope. Drawing closer to a tall pine that had miraculously not burned, he stopped the engine.

Zalorna jumped for the branches of the tree, clawed her way towards the solid trunk, and climbed towards the top.

"Okay," he yelled. "Tie it off."

Kat came back on deck with a small handsaw and campfire hatchet. Cedric reached for them but she backed away.

"I'm a better climber than you are." She looked up the tree to where Zalorna sat clinging to the branches. "Tell me what you want done."

How the hell do you argue with a woman when you know she's right?

"Clean all the branches from as far up as you can safely reach and work down. I'll try to pull some of the branches aboard to use as shade. When I think you have trimmed enough of the main trunk, I'll let you know."

He brought out a small line and tied it to the tools. "When you reach the tree, pull the tools to you and whatever you do, don't lose them. Without them, we don't stand a chance."

She got ready to jump into the water and he grabbed her arm. "Kat, be careful." He pulled her into his arms and gave her a kiss. "I love you."

"You are just now realizing that?" Kat gave him a big smile and jumped.

She reached the tree, retrieved the tools, and worked her way towards the top. When she could go no further, she started back down, cutting branches as she went. When she reached Zalorna, the two of them worked side-by-side sending wood chips flying and branches crashing into the rising water below.

"Okay!" he yelled. "That should be enough. Cut the main trunk off below the rope."

Time seemed to drag by as the sun beat down upon them. The small saw handled the branches just fine, but on the bigger section of the trunk it was slow going.

He heard the wood crack and the top begin to sway. Zalorna gave a push and the top broke fee. She lost her balance and fell.

Cedric watched in horror as she clawed the branches fighting for a hold. She hit with a splash and resurfaced spitting water. With a triumphant smile on her face she lifted her hand in the air. To his amazement, she was still holding the hatchet.

With both females back aboard, wet but thankfully no worse off, Cedric gave each a big hug and kiss. Much to his surprise and Kat's, Zalorna returned the kiss. Grabbing the rope, he began hauling in the section of tree. *If this doesn't work in splicing the mast...I have to think positive, this will work.*

With their prize on board and secured, both cat-women collapsed under a makeshift canopy of pine branches. Cedric turned his eyes back to the island in time to see the top of the tree they had cut disappear beneath the waves.

Going below, he checked out the radio and GPS locator. Both were dead. Taking note of the direction they were drifting and their speed, he went back on deck, crawled in between Kat and Zalorna, and fell asleep.

Chapter 5

"I'm scared Kat. I am really frightened."

"Me too. After all we have been through, I do not think we will survive. If it were not for Cedric and his boat..."

"I know, and I take back everything I said about him. Cedric is not like other humans."

Cedric lay listening to the females as they sat nearby. They thought that he was still asleep. Their soft voices echoed his thoughts. He knew how much water and food remained on board. Even if by chance he managed to catch any fish, they needed fresh water.

There was one answer, but it saddened him to even have to contemplate it.

"Zalorna, I want you to mate with Cedric."

Kat's words startled him. He had dismissed their earlier conversation as idle ramblings. Was she testing her half-sister, or...was she serious?

"Why?"

Yeah, I'd like to know the reason too.

"Because," Kat whispered, "you are my sister and I don't want you to feel lonely anymore, or feeling like you don't belong here."

She's serious. I damn well don't believe it.

"Besides, it is time you mated. Why do you think we were kept separated from humans? You have seen the fear in their eyes. We may never find another mate willing to accept us."

"I will think about it," Zalorna promised.

"Aahhmmm," he feigned a yawn. "What are you two doing?"

"Talking," Kat answered, "watching the stars..."

"And wondering if there is anything out there that survived." Zalorna voiced the thoughts he had been purposefully shutting out.

Climbing out from under the branches, he stood and stretched. "It's cooler now. Let's get this mast fixed and find out."

The sun was up and blaring down on them by the time he finished tying the last line holding the splice in place. With fingers crossed, Cedric hoisted the main sail and watched with trepidation as the canvas caught the wind and billowed out. Wood creaked, moaned, and bent under the strain.

"Whoow!" Cedric breathed a loud sigh of relief. "I thought for a minute it wasn't going to hold." Changing course, he locked the rudder and turned to hug the females.

Kat gave him a passionate, open-mouthed, tongue-probing kiss, which left him wanting more. She broke the embrace, stepped back, and gave her sister a nod of encouragement.

Zalorna touched her lips to his. "I am not very good at this," she whispered. "Will you teach me?"

Stepping away from her, he took Kat's hand and half–dragged her to the bow. "I overheard you two talking. Is that the only reason you are pushing this?"

"I think you know the other reason," she snapped. "It is the three of us out here on this little boat and if we don't have fresh food and water real soon, we will not survive." Kat placed her hands on her hips. "If we are to die, I want her to know the pleasure of your love the way I do."

Running his fingers through his windblown hair, he turned to stare out at the empty ocean.

Kat grabbed his arm. Her sharp talon-like nails dug into his skin. "Well?"

His shoulders sank and his heart broke. "Neither of you shall die." *You swore you would never create another like yourself. How can you even contemplate such a thing?*

"Please, Cedric," Kat begged.

No!

Strangely enough, he could see the logic in what she was asking. Living like they had, growing up on an island where the beast ruled every aspect of their lives, sharing a mate would only be natural.

"Very well." Turning away, he walked to the stern where Zalorna waited. *Fuck her if you want to, but don't turn her into what you are!*

Lifting a hand to her face, Cedric brushed a tendril of hair behind her ear, lowered his lips to hers, and set out on a course of seduction to change her life forever. Leaving the soft contour of her lips, he places light tender kisses along her jaw. "Don't be nervous," he whispered.

"I'm not."

Cedric chuckled. "Your tail is twitching."

"It is not."

He gently blew in her long, black, furry cat's ear.

"Okay, maybe it is…a little."

"Zalorna, I won't hurt you." *Liar!* His conscious screamed at him even as his left hand worked up her side and his fingers caressed her breast.

She started purring. "I have watched you mate with Kat."

"Did you think that I was going to hurt her?" Lowering his head, he hovered over the other nipple, licked it with his tongue, and blew his heated breath across her breast.

"At first." A shudder coursed through her body, and he smiled against her flesh. "Then I became curious."

"I can stop, if you want me to." Cedric playfully bit at her nipple and heard her gasp.

"What will happen if we find land?" Her voice shook and her fingers dug into his shoulders.

Cedric lifted his head.

"Will you leave us?"

Her question caught him off guard. "No, I will not leave the two of you alone."

A tentative smile lifted the corners of her mouth. "Then I will mate with you." Zalorna led him to the shelter of the branches and ducked underneath.

Cedric dropped his shorts and crawled in beside her.

"Let us be honest with each other." She lay back on the soft bed of needles. "I do not expect you to have the same feelings toward me as you do for Kat. She has always been more human. For me, this is a natural, physical act, and nothing more. Maybe that *something* I see in her eyes when she looks at you...will come later. If it does, fine."

His fingers played in the short, black fur covering her legs. "I think there is more woman inside you than you realize. It's a matter of which one you allow to be dominant."

A steady low rumbling vibrated through her body. Her eyes closed as his hands traveled further up her body. Cedric's palm brushed the distended flesh of her nipple. With the sudden flaring of her nose, her breast lifted, seeking more contact.

Leaning closer, he used the tip of his tongue to touch the passion-inflamed flesh.

Kat paced back and forth on the deck, in and out of what little shade the sail provided. Her two instincts clashed, as they had on several occasions since Cedric came to the island, but nothing compared to what she was now going through. No matter how much she wanted this bonding between Zalorna and Cedric, a part of her hated them, and herself.

Both halves of her inner self tried not to watch or listen to the contented purring and shallow moans of her sister. *So what, big deal, they are mating… I wish she was not so vocal about it or that Cedric did not appear to enjoy it so much… With what we have gone through, this makes sense… It had to happen sooner or later… If they do not mate, they may kill each other for food…*

Zalorna fought against the growing passion within her. She wanted this over with, without any emotional ties between them. Her human half grew stronger, and began to assert itself.

His mouth came back to hers. Zalorna parted her lips, and his tongue touched hers, darting in and out of her mouth. The sensation overpowered her and she grabbed his hair with both hands, holding him in place as she ravaged his mouth.

Strange new emotions sent the blood racing through her as Cedric nestled between her legs and his hard shaft touched her wet flesh. Instincts long embedded in her genes took over and she rubbed herself against him. With one quick thrust, he entered her.

Shock, surprise, and wanton desire clashed. Desire won out, and she wrapped her legs around his hips. With each plunge of his shaft inside her, she met him with one of her own. The intensity grew, blocking out everything around. Her sharp claw-like nails dug into his flesh.

Zalorna relished the feeling of being a woman for the first time in her life. Standing on the edge of a sensuous cliff, she felt liberated, free, and alive. A soft cry burst from her chest as her body seemed about ready to explode.

She snarled as Cedric pulled out of her.

"Turn over." His hands gave a gentle tug on her hips and she rolled onto her stomach.

Cedric lifted her tail and sensing what he wanted, she lifted her hips in the air.

His fingers curled into her short black hair covering her body. This new position was more exciting, more natural, and sent her newfound passions soaring even higher.

Zalorna clawed at the blanket beneath her as she ground her hips and womanly flesh against Cedric. Cat-like growls and snarls poured from her throat. Harder and faster he drove deep into her wet flesh.

She was flung off the edge and fell into the blissful void of passion's release.

Even as her body strained and shook beneath his, Cedric felt his dark side emerging, taking control. With one final thrust into her quivering flesh, he lifted his head, and bared his fangs. As he felt the heated rush of release being pumped into Zalorna, he fell across her quivering back and sank his fangs deep into her neck.

"No!" Kat's strangled cry reached his ears moments before her body crashed into his. They rolled across the deck, locked in each other's arms.

Filled with the taste of Zalorna's blood, Cedric wrestled with Kat. Empowered by his dark-side craving, he turned his bared fangs on Kat.

Kill her, kill them both, and spare them your torment and guilt. He took enough of her blood to mix with his own, and in a moment of self-loathing, injected it back into his beloved Kat.

She stopped her struggles and as her eyes drifted shut, her lips formed a silent question. "Why?"

"Because, I love you," he whispered. "Please, don't hate me for what I have done."

Cedric picked up her limp body, carried it back under the shade of the tree branches, and gently laid her beside her sister. Beads of sweat already formed on Zalorna's brow. Filling a bucket with sea water, he bathed her face, neck, and chest. Within moments, he noticed Kat's body drenched with sweat too.

Their temperatures soared for the next several hours. In his desire to save their lives, had he instead hastened their deaths? As he kept their flesh cool, a difficult task in itself with the extreme heat, Cedric noticed a gradual healing of their sun-scorched skin.

Their fevers broke.

The setting sun did little to relieve the heat. The whole world it seemed had been turned into a giant greenhouse. A thick haze hung suspended in the sky blotting out all but the brightest of the stars.

Cedric checked on their location using what stars he could recognize and adjusted their direction. They were headed home, back to America. Hopefully, there would be something left to come home to.

The trade winds were holding true. Their mast held against the billowing canvas. He checked the rigging, went to the bow, and sat with his feet hanging over the edge. Sometime later, Kat and Zalorna sat one on either side of him and wrapped their arms around him.

He gave Kat a kiss, turned his head, and kissed Zalorna.

The sound of waves breaking on the bow breached the stillness of the night as the wind carried them toward an unknown and uncertain future.

Cedric had always hated what he was—a *daywalker*. But were it not for the altered DNA of a slain vampire fused with his father's when he was cloned, he and the half-ling creatures beside him wouldn't stand a chance in this new world.

"Whatever happens, whatever we find out there, we'll be together and," Cedric gave them a reassuring hug, "we will survive."

About the author:

Romance author R Casteel retired from the US Navy in 1990. He enjoys the outdoors, loves to Scuba Dive, and is a Search and Rescue Diver. With twenty years of military service, which included experience as flight crewman, search and rescue, and four years as a Military Police Officer, it is of little wonder that his books are filled with suspense and intrigue. As to his ability to write romance, Gloria for Best Reviews writes "I had thought Leigh Greenwood was the only man who wrote wonderful romance...I was wrong...Rod Casteel is right there too!"

Mr. Casteel lives in his hometown of Lancaster, Missouri and would love to hear from you.

R. Casteel welcomes mail from readers. You can write to him c/o Ellora's Cave Publishing at 1337 Commerce Drive, Suite 13, Stow OH 44224.

Also by R. Casteel:

The Crimson Rose
Taneika: Daughter of the Wolf
Texas Thunder
Mistress of Table Rock
The Toymaker

DRAGON'S LAW: MACE

Alicia Sparks

Chapter One

Near Waydon, a small village near Tyr on the planet Tyr-LaRoche. Modern Day.

The wind howled, forcing the tiny hairs on Eleanora's neck to stand at attention. She swallowed the lump that had formed in her throat and waited. The night birds that had been singing their welcome to the moon only seconds before were quiet now, as if they anticipated the arrival of some menacing force that would rip them from the sky. The clearing was illuminated by the light moon as the dark one hung, a black circle in the night's sky, signaling what would soon be coming.

The thunderous footsteps seemed to echo as they approached. Eleanora listened as tree branches snapped and leaves crunched beneath the power of the beast that made its way to the sacrificial site. Perspiration formed on her hands as they remained tethered in place. She was prepared for whatever the fates had deemed would be her destiny. As the dragon approached, she raised her chin, willing herself to face her death as her sisters had faced theirs. If only she could be the last sacrifice, a guarantee that the villagers would no longer strive to sate the dragon's blood lust.

The dragon crouched before her and let out a piercing growl, forcing her to flinch, her bravery fleeing. A slow chill crept up her back as her eyes ran over the dragon's frame. He was no bigger than a man, but his domineering presence in the clearing was enough to make that chill break into a full-blown shudder. She had never seen a dragon at such close range and had no idea what to expect of him. This was certainly not it. Still, he was commanding enough to make her rethink her plan of attack, which was to use magick to free herself and render him helpless. She cringed when she caught sight of his tail, which swished like a cat's and was double the length of his body. The tail looked harmless at first glance, but the spines there were known for the poison they injected into his victims. Her hands clutched into fists as she contemplated her best plan of attack. A wave of nausea threatened to overtake her. In spite of her trepidation, she was held spellbound by the strength of his frame.

She raked her eyes over his scaly body and bit her lip as she raised her head, daring to look at his face. The profile was almost human, but there was nothing human about the way he lingered over her body, prepared to make her his latest meal as his hot breath swept across her face.

The howl echoed once more, conjuring tremors throughout her body, but his approach ceased when he lifted his head to sniff the air as if he sensed someone else here. Her hands froze, and her entire body stood stock-still. The dragon caught her eyes only for a second, but she felt the image of raw pain that reflected in those gray pools.

He turned and flicked his tail back and forth before he pounced.

The dragon covered her body as he let out a howl that sounded like pain. Eleanora tried to steady her breathing, tried to recover from her moment in the dragon's eyes, but her body refused to cooperate. She should act now and save herself, but her arms wouldn't move. The piercing sound of the dragon's roar forced her into action. The jolt of electricity that shot through her body at the sound of his cry was enough to move her once-frozen limbs.

The words were said in an instant, almost before she could think her way through the spell. As soon as they fled her lips, the shackles fell to the ground, releasing her from her temporary prison. Only now, two dragons hindered her move toward safety.

Her passage was blocked as the black one, the one whose eyes she had seen so clearly. Then the red one advanced, charging forward, challenging the black one for dominance.

Eleanora was trapped, unable to move between or around the dragons, unable to save herself. Cowering to the ground, Eleanora lay spellbound as the black dragon covered her body, protecting her from the fury of the red.

In the next seconds, the black let out a howl and blood flowed from the long razor cuts along its back. It circled around the red, the two looking like wild animals challenging one another for a meal. She swallowed hard. If they sensed she was still here in the darkness, neither gave notice.

She drew in her breath, once more determined to end the wreckage brought upon her village by the dragons. Every ounce of courage she may have had hours ago died inside her as she contemplated her approach. Two ferocious beasts fought just a few yards away from her. And never before had she felt as inconsequential as she did at this moment.

Then, at the last moment, the red dragon misjudged. He caught sight of her, distracting him enough to give the black an advantage. Bleeding, howling in pain, the black leapt, sinking his teeth into the jugular.

The red didn't fall as she expected. She knew dragons must lose much more blood than a shallow cut could render. And they healed more quickly than humans. But the black hadn't given up his quest. Eleanora's eyes widened as he leapt once more, this time practically ripping the vein from his opponent's neck.

The black turned now, having worn the red to weakness. The red lay in a heap under the moonlight, his blood already ceasing to flow. Before she had time to react, everything went black.

* * * * *

Eleanora trembled, thinking that she must be dead. The last thing she remembered before the blackness engulfed her was the flash of red hair and the sting of the dragon's tail as it pierced her skin, biting into her shoulder. The red hair hadn't belonged to the dragon, whose flesh was as black as the night. And it wasn't her own — unless…

She lifted a weakened hand to her hair, wondering if it had been covered with blood. Her eyes slowly opened, peering at the night sky between the veil of consciousness and unconsciousness. How long had she been out? The dragon that threatened to suck her blood from her body would return to finish the deed.

She tried to sit up, only to be assaulted by a weak dizziness. She reminded herself to move slowly, take shallow breaths, gain control of her body before she attempted to escape the clearing and hide in the woods. She began by flexing her toes and then her feet, satisfied that her body was still intact. The sensation moved up her legs until, finally, she lifted her neck without waves of nausea consuming her.

Bracing herself, raising up to a sitting position, she waited for the ground to stop spinning. What in the name of the gods had happened here tonight? It took a second for her heart to stop its hammering in her chest and slow to a steady rhythm as she remembered. The two dragons had fought for dominance, and she had, apparently, been spared.

She stretched her arms over her head. The movement wasn't the graceful cat-like movement it would have been if she were waking from a nice, long slumber. Her thin arms seemed to glow beneath the moonlight as the eclipse ended and the light moon once more peeked its head out. Eleanora brushed her long dark hair off her shoulders, wishing she had something to tie it out of the way. Her body refused to move, her motions pained, contrived, and her shoulder ached as her blood pounded in her skull. Why hadn't she died?

Her first attempt to stand made a wave of nausea hit her once more. She rolled onto her stomach in hopes of coming up onto her knees first and then moving from there. It was then that she saw the possessor of the red hair from her earlier memory.

The man was maybe a foot from where she lay. His head almost touched hers, and his masses of blood-red hair resembled a pool of the precious liquid on the ground. Had Eleanora not been close enough to touch the silky strands, she would have assumed it was his life's essence poured out onto the dirt. As it was, the sight was frightening enough. He didn't move as she reached for him.

She adjusted her body, crawling the two paces to his side. Her breath caught in her throat and her hand went to her chest, covering her heart. She hadn't prepared herself for the sight.

An audible gasp caught in her throat as he groaned. Thank the gods, he lived! His badly scarred body was covered with dried blood, none of which was hers. A gash at his neck proved his battle, which must have taken place in order to save her from the dragons that threatened certain death between their teeth. He must be the reason the dragons had given up their quest. The thought alone made her heart swell, but it also caused other sensations she couldn't define yet, sensations that were heightened by his nakedness.

He was beautifully, gloriously naked. Her eyes roamed across his bare torso—taut, tanned, firm. They went to his perfectly formed pectorals as her fingers ached to run along his flesh. They strayed next to his member, his, his...*manhood*. She tore her eyes from that part of his body before she could define the sensations it stirred, before she licked her lips and wondered...

No one had ever fought for her before.

Before tonight, there had been no need to protect her life save for the fact that she was destined to be a dragon's sacrifice, just like her sisters before her. The village men knew this and therefore had never lifted a hand to aid her in any of her misadventures. Only this man, this stranger, had come to her aid. Surely he was knight, though she had never seen him before. He certainly could not be from Waydon.

The wound on her shoulder pulsed as she feared the dragon's poison had made its way into her system. Rather than weakening her as she thought it should, it somehow caused her heart to quicken, her senses to awaken. Desires she had never before known surfaced all at once. Her fingers itched to reach out and touch the man's flesh. She wanted to run her hands all over him. Instead, she placed a hand on his hard chest, feeling for a heartbeat. Her hand instantly jerked away, seared by the heat from his body. The fever had entered and would kill him if she didn't do something to lower it.

Eleanora knew she wasn't much use to the villagers. She was a half-wit when it came to herbal remedies. Even though she was being trained as a healer, it wasn't her gift. Her older sister held the gift, but her life was taken from her too soon by a dragon. Still, to honor her memory and take her place in her community, she forced herself to attempt the arts. Even if she did nothing but annoy Liesel, the high priestess and healer.

She wrung her hands, frantically searching for an answer to her dilemma. The man was so large, she doubted she could move him alone. And she had nowhere to take him. If she returned to the village, she would surely be exiled for not fulfilling her destiny at the ends of the dragon's talons. If they stayed here, in the clearing, he would likely die.

She had no choice but to take him to Liesel's empty cottage, which was far enough from the rest of the village to serve as a means of protection from both the villagers and future dragons. She hoped.

Pulling herself up to standing position and contemplating the man on the ground, she knew he couldn't possibly walk. He was feverish and mumbling in a language she couldn't understand. She bent over to lift him, pulling at his injured shoulders. When he let out a howl in his sleep, she knew she couldn't move him. Not like this, anyway.

She wiped her sweaty palms onto the skirt of her dress. Minutes ago, she'd survived a dragon attack. Surely, she could save a man.

He was heavier than she'd imagined. Still, he was somewhat responsive as she hauled him, using her upper body to brace him while she moved him forward. He groaned low and long as they proceeded through the dense woods to the cabin. When she dumped him onto the low mattress, curses spilled from his lips and his skin flamed. She knew she must bring his fever down or he would suffer the brain disease. And then he would die.

Something in her gut protested this notion. She would not allow him to die. It didn't matter what she must do to keep him alive, she vowed to do it.

She gathered her long, messy hair into a mass on top of her head and stuck a few of Liesel's pins into it to hold it in place. Then she began her labors on the patient. First she cleaned his wounds, starting with the most severe one on his neck.

As she worked, she tried not to think about running her hands along his flesh or the heat that was now radiating down from her shoulder and into her chest. She had heard tales of the poison dragons injected into their victims and had no idea what to expect from the small gash on her shoulder.

She dipped the sponge into the herbal diffusion she'd put together. The sweet smell from the herbs hit her nostrils at once. When it mixed with his manly scent, it was enough to make her hand shake. She squeezed out the excess solution and then ran the sponge slowly along his face.

His nose was pointed, aristocratic. It gave way to a perfectly sculpted square jaw. His eyes were wide-set. She wondered what color they were as she ran the sponge along his commanding forehead. She tried not to look at his lips when she traced the sponge along his jaw line. Beautiful, full, perfect lips. They tormented her, making her wonder for the first time ever how it would feel to kiss a man.

She shook the thought from her head and let the sponge trail down his neck. He had a long, thick neck that melted into the broadest shoulders she'd ever seen. His battle-scarred chest was smooth, hairless. Waiting to be explored. She sucked in her breath, letting her gaze and hands stray further down to his belly.

It lay right there, solid as a stone, pressing against his belly. She tried not to look at it, but her eyes couldn't stay away. She had never seen a naked man before, but her instincts told her this one was not like the rest. His member was large, demanding her attention. The hood that normally lay over it was stretched, thanks to his state of...*arousal*?

She brought the sponge down to his legs, first one then the other, her eyes never leaving his *thing*. Her fingers brushed against the light covering of hair on his massive thighs. She closed her eyes to the sensation, embarrassed when a tiny moan escaped her lips. She imagined those powerful thighs lying on top of her while the other...

Eleanora stopped. He was wounded. Her patient. She must remember that.

Still, as she washed his feet, her eyes continued to stray to the mass of blood-red curls beckoning her. Making her wonder how *it* would feel.

She knew about mating. Knew that it was necessary to maintain the race. But ever since she and her sisters were chosen for the dragons, she knew mating would never be hers. She would never know the touch of a man's skin against her own, the feel of a kiss. The heat of...oh, gods! The heat.

She pressed her thighs tightly together, hoping to rid herself of the need that grew in her belly. And lower, as if the heat from her wound had moved into her innermost core, making her fully aware of the man who lay before her and the needs that seemed to grow by the second. Quivering at the thought of having him on top of her, inside her, she bit her bottom lip until the salty taste of blood brought her back to the task at hand.

Her hands worked to cover him with Liesel's sheet as she carefully avoided contact with his skin. Then she began mixing the herbal tea for him to help lower his fever. As she worked, she thought about the wound at his neck, which was not as bad as it had appeared at first. In fact, it looked much better here in the candlelight than it had under the moonlight, making her wonder if it had been life threatening at all. Maybe it was her panic making her think the wound was severe.

She glanced back at her patient, who still had not moved though he continued to mumble incoherently. Leaving the tea to steep for a few minutes, she made her way to the adjoining wash room and began peeling her clothes off her sweat-soaked body while she tried to keep her mind off the man in the next room.

He's unconscious, she said to herself, ashamed. *What if he has a wife? Children?* She had never seen him before tonight, but that did not mean that he was alone. Somebody probably loved him, was looking for him. It was her duty to heal him and return him to those who needed him.

And then she would leave the village. She was as good as dead if she stayed. Liesel spoke wonders about the land that lay beyond the mountains. Children's tales, she knew. But it was a land of riches beyond her wildest imaginings. Filled with princes and finery. Artificial lights graced large dining halls. Food that was not just a necessity but was a delight for the senses.

Yes, there she would have a future. She had skills as a seamstress, a wonderful cook, and, if she saved this man, maybe even a decent healer.

She decided a quick bath would help ease her nerves. Besides, her clothing had been ruined and her body soiled by the night's events. Turning on the water, she tried to quell her daydreams about the man in the next room, the man who had so selflessly saved her. The water ran warm beneath her hand, bringing her back to reality. Liesel enchanted the hot spring and forced it to flow into her well. Eleanora had only bathed here once before and the sensation had been too much for her then. Combined with the man in the next room, she was sure to give in to the excesses completely. No, she mustn't. She had to save the man. It was the only way for her to repay his kindness, leave her village, and have a life.

She cringed at the tears in the seams and the gash in the shoulder as she tossed her gown to the side. It would still be useful, but she planned to replace it with one of Liesel's gray gowns as soon as she was clean. Taking the sponge into her hand, she dabbed the blood from her shoulder, noting that her wound, which on second glance was little more than a scratch, was already beginning to heal. The throbbing in her shoulder had not ceased though, and had truly awakened every nerve in her body, making her fear the results of being poisoned by a dragon. If she died tonight, no one would save the man who so desperately needed her attentions.

Eleanora reached for her undergarment and began sliding it down her thighs. Only then was she aware of the dampness. *There*. The scent wafted up to her, a combination of sweat and something else. She remembered being told how women became ready to mate with their men. They open for them, cover them with a liquid that invites the men inside. She never imagined she would experience such a sensation.

Fever burned through her in a way she had never known before. It was as if she couldn't control her hand as it roamed down her body and she dared to touch herself. No one ever need know. The mass of curls was damp as her finger slid deeper down, seeking something. Trying to find the place that ached the most. When her fingers made contact with her tiny bud, she inhaled sharply. This was the place. This hardened *thing*. This was where the heat radiated from. But not the liquid.

She wanted to explore. Her instincts told her there was unimaginable pleasure waiting inside her own body. Slipping a finger down lower, she uncovered the source of the wetness. There. Oh, yes, there. Her lips parted and the juices coated her fingers. The opening. She knew about this place that Liesel called the sheath for the love sword. She'd giggled like a girl when she first heard talk of mating, but now her womanly curiosity got the better of her. This was where her lover would be. He would take her, lowering himself on top of her, sliding himself into her.

Shaking herself, trying to remove the fever from her head from her body, she forced her thoughts back to the sleeping man, the only man she wished to have touching her. The one she knew would be so unlike anyone she'd ever met.

"What are you doing?" Eleanora chastised herself. She moved her hand quickly. He was ill, likely dying, and she was in here doing something she shouldn't.

Plunging herself into the water, her nerve endings awoke when the warmth hit her woman-head, visions of a lover flooding her mind. Suddenly things she had never experienced before poured into her brain, almost as if they had come from an outside source. Almost as if the dragon's poison had created the thoughts, the sensations. Her breathing quickened, and her body began to quake wondering how a lover's tongue would feel running along her body.

You know nothing of lovers. Now bathe and get to the task at hand.

She ran the cloth over her body as quickly as possible. There was no need to dally, especially since the tea would be ready now. She dunked her head into the water, quickly lathered her tangled hair and then dunked it once more to rinse. The tangles she would work out later.

She quickly sprang from the tub and roughly dried her body, ignoring the throbbing between her thighs. She pressed them together. Later. She promised herself later she would explore her own depths. She didn't need a man for that, did she?

Liesel's dress clung to her body, Liesel being much smaller than Eleanora. Her ample hips threatened to burst from the seams and her breasts almost spilled from the bodice. Still, it fit. She bit her lip again, realizing she had no clean undergarments. The wicked thought occurred to her to go without them and allow the night air to caress her the way the water had earlier. Pulling her damp curls from the back of the dress, she allowed her hair to hang loose around her waist.

The man still hadn't stirred, which was ironic considering all the new things stirring inside her. She whispered one of Liesel's chants as she poured the tea into a cup. "Give him strength," she demanded.

The bed creaked and groaned when she sat next to him, proof of both its age and the heavy burden it already bore. She lifted his head into her lap, allowing his red mane to spill out over the gray dress making it look drab and ordinary. She raised the cup to his lips, coaxing him by running her fingers along his cheek.

Please, drink.

The first few drops of liquid spilled out the side of his mouth and trickled onto her dress. The second attempt was successful, his sensual lips opening enough to allow the liquid to move inside. She watched it go down his throat as he swallowed. It would heal him, she was certain.

She moved, placing his head back onto the pillow, her lap feeling emptier than before. She ran a hand along his forehead. Her fingers stayed in place even though the skin there seared them. The tea would break the fever, but how long would it take? She nervously bit her lip and tried to look somewhere other than at his beautiful face.

She examined the wound, which was all but healed. The cut must not have been as deep as she'd imagined. But there was still a chance of the dragon's poison, a chemical she knew nothing about. Would it render him blind? Deaf? Her heart raced at the prospect. The woman who loved him would mourn for him.

She leaned over him, her hair accidentally brushing his face. Her voice caught in her throat, her heart ceased beating, and her breath stopped completely as his eyes opened and his hand encircled her wrist.

The last thing she saw before he pulled her down into him was the golden glow of his eyes. Then his lips were on hers, his body rigid against her, his hand a vise around her wrist, bruising it. His lips fiercely moved against hers, rendering them swollen, hot. He was delusional. He must think she was his wife.

She pushed her hand onto his chest to no avail. Her lips parted in a gasp at her exertion. It was then that he probed his tongue into her mouth, causing the heat she'd held at bay to come pouring out of her opening. His teeth grazed her lips. His free hand sought her beneath the folds of her dress.

When it made contact with her wet, throbbing flesh, she closed her eyes. His rough fingers forced the fabric away from her body. The fur separating them had already tangled and fallen to the side. His rod was now stone still and pressing against her.

It only took one motion for him to enter her body. She couldn't control her own actions. He impaled her and she allowed it, ruining herself for another man as her juices combined with blood to allow him entrance. Her scream pierced her ears while the shivers that overtook her body rendered her helpless.

She looked down at the man who had savagely entered her body. His eyes were closed. He was asleep.

Chapter Two

Eleanora sat as still as she could manage with the fire raging inside her. She wanted to move off him. With all her strength and will, she wanted it. Terrified, she held tight to his chest. She watched his breathing, the beautiful muscles rise and fall with his slumber. The low, guttural sound of his snore. This was a change from earlier. He hadn't made a sound then. He would live. But right now, her most desperate concern was how to move off of him. And the fact that it was the last thing in the world she wanted.

She lifted herself, feeling his powerful body slide almost all the way out. The juices shot from her, oozing out around him. Every instinct she had told her to remove herself from him now. Every instinct except the one forcing her to remain mounted and allow him access to her inner core.

He gave no indication of feeling her. She lifted herself once more only to slide back down until his belly and her belly met, his red curls mixing with her black ones. She quivered around him as a sob escaped her throat.

No one would ever know she had mounted him, had mated with him, had given him her maidenhead. No one would need to know. She could tell her husband about being savagely raped while crossing the mountains. Or she could refuse to take a husband, living on her own means.

She looked down at his beautiful face. She would not wish for a husband after this night. He may not touch her, may not even be aware of her, but she was aware of him.

She shook again, tightening around him. Ten thousand sensations assaulted her at once. The most important was the need to move now. Quickly.

She rose above him once more then counted to three as he slid back into her. Again. Again. Again. This time, she increased the intensity. She rocked her hips back and forth, taking all of him into her body. She quivered, she pressed against him, she stroked his chest.

Tension built inside her and threatened to drive her mad. She continued to spill juices out onto his body. She wanted to stop now. Needed to stop. She knew what she was doing was wrong. He was not hers. He belonged to another. A man as beautiful as this one must have a wife. Children.

She bent over to kiss his lips one last time, the thought of children more than she could bear. It was then that the sensation took over, threatening to destroy her.

It started somewhere deep inside, the place where he rested against her. And it worked its way up to her chest and down to her toes. She was inches away from his face when it hit. She let out a long, low moan as the spasms wrecked her body.

His eyes opened again. This time, there was no golden glimmer. This time, they were green. And angry.

He captured her wrist roughly and hauled her against his chest. The words he muttered through his roughened throat were in another language but held the acid o f a curse. Her breath hung in her throat, afraid to escape. Afraid of her sin. Would he kill her now for using him so?

The dragon frightened her, but this man looked fiercer than a dragon ever had. What made her think he was beautiful? His face twisted into a sneer, his lips snarled, revealing perfectly whiteteeth. The growl erupting from his belly made her shiver, forgetting the fact that she was still quite literally impaled onto him.

His breath ran across her face, heating it while the fever inside him seared her skin. And his eyes. He could slay dragons with those eyes. They were soulless, empty, dangerous.

Her ragged breathing and pounding heart kept her tears at bay while she waited for him to kill her. One flick of his wrist could snap her arm as if it were a twig. If his hands moved to her throat, he could either suffocate her or break her neck. Either option seemed extremely painful. She didn't dare move when his lips parted again. What once would have seemed sensual had her on the verge of tears. This man couldn't be the one who saved her last night. If he were, why did he look at her as if she were the enemy?

"What are you doing?" Anger colored the growl erupting from his chest.

"I, I—" She shifted, trying to break free of his hold on her wrist, struggling against his shaft.

"You, what? You wished to tame me?"

"No, I..." Her voice trailed off, tears threatened to spill out.

"You wished to mate with me, then?"

She whimpered, hating herself for her obvious weakness. She stood down a dragon, took it upon herself to mate with a stranger. Her strength would see her through whatever he intended to do to her.

"Speak, whore!" he commanded, his voice forcing her to face him.

Still embedded deep inside her, Mace flipped her over so that her back was flat against her bed. She wanted to fuck a dragon? Mating with a dragon served no purpose for mortal women. None save the obvious pleasures of the experience. It was not with them as it was with dragons—dragons were forced to mate with humans in order to maintain control over their transformations.

Last night, he had been weakened after his battle with Damon and then forced into a human state after only striking the female once with his poisoned tail. Weakness did not sit well with him, even if he had managed to rip the amulet from Damon's neck and toss it into the abyss created by the eclipse. Weakness was a human quality, not a dragon one. Now that his strength was back, he could transform, frighten her, rip her body in half with his massive cock.

He smelled her sex as it wafted up to him. She had come, obviously under the influence of the powerful aphrodisiac in the poison. The woman had pleasured herself on his dragon dick, having poisoned him with the vile liquid she fed him. He had only loosely been aware of it. Now, as the scents of the room assaulted him, causing his nostrils to flare, he understood her game. She wished to drug him, control him. For what purpose he did not understand, but he would have answers. First, he would have her flesh.

"I want you to look at me," he demanded when she squeezed her eyes shut. Her body was rigid, her pussy gripping his dick like a tight fist.

"I can't," she whimpered.

"Yes, you can." He took her face into his hands, roughly holding her head level, keeping her from burying it in the furs. He would pound into her flesh so hard, so brutally, she would never seek to control him again. "Look at me."

Her eyes fluttered open. When they did, tears spilled out. The dragon inside him cried out for justice, hating the deception. It wanted to hold her down, tie her to her own bed and render her defenseless just as she had rendered him. Hold her prisoner.

His dick stiffened at the thought. He liked his sex rough and dirty. Yes, the dragon would love nothing more than to pound away, ravage her body, cover it with bruises. Mace's breathing quickened and he fought for control, fought to beat down the beast that loomed inside him. Just as he was beginning to gain control, the scent attacked him. There was something else mixed with her come. Blood.

His hand moved against her woman's lips, which quivered when his fingers moved them aside and ran along the base of his cock. His suspicions were confirmed when he brought the fingers to his lips. This woman, whoever she was, had spilled her virgin blood on his cock, rendering him completely defenseless against her. And the dragon deep inside, the one who had raged filled with the desire to hurt her, now subdued itself as Mace considered this knowledge.

A virgin? What would a virgin want with a dragon? More importantly, who was responsible for this deception? If he knew anything, he knew this plan sounded suspiciously like the doings of his brother, Damon. He even smelled his scent on the woman's cunt, as if Damon had chained her to the rock, leaving her there for Mace to find and battle over. The real battle had not been for the woman but had been for control over Tyr, something Mace would not give up easily.

"I should kill you." He held her face still, holding her eyes with his. "But I think I shall use you first. By the end of this moon time, you will come to crave my touch. And you shall tell me why you brought me here, why you sought to control me with your body. And who is responsible for spilling your blood on my dick." He meant the words to be harsh, though the emotion behind them was not genuine. Swallowing hard, he removed the last of the dragon's rage from his head and concentrated on the woman before him.

She visibly shook at his words. "I spilled the blood." He sensed her fear. But there was something else in there, too.

"Yes, you did." He pushed further into her, against her womb.

"I wanted you…I wanted to thank you for…" Her voice trailed off.

"For?" He slid out of her and then slid back in, slowly. He hid his smile when she closed her eyes and sank her teeth into her bottom lip.

"For saving me from the dragon last night."

"Saving you?" He held the laughter in his voice at bay. Saving her? From a dragon? Holy fuck. Did the woman not know whose dick was buried inside of her?

"Yes, but please, you can't tell anyone."

He moved again, out then back in, watching her eyes smolder with each movement. He pulled out one more time, waiting, his dick barely inside her tight, wet hole. When she arched her back lightly, he drove into her fully, impaling her on his shaft. The moan that escaped her lips was exactly what he expected. A virgin who liked to fuck. A virgin who could be controlled by his cock.

Damon had mistakenly chosen this one. Maybe he had teased her pussy himself. Licking it. Holding her hostage as he played with her lips, ran his tongue along the edges of her folds. Maybe he even dipped his tongue inside to taste her cream. Either way, he created a woman who loved sex. And that was his first mistake. Mace could easily control her. He would fuck her every day and at length, teaching her what pleased him, erasing Damon's tongue from her mind. And when the moon ended, he would send her back to his brother, ruined. She would be *his* whore, not Damon's. And she would bring him his brother's secrets.

A smile crossed his lips. "Thank me, little one," he coaxed.

Eleanora's body reacted to his the only way it knew how. It opened for him, pressing against him, begging for release. He was wild and untamed. Dangerous. Everything about him told her she was in trouble. In over her uneducated, never-had-sex-before-tonight head.

His body pressed hers into the mattress as he rocked into her slowly, holding her on the verge of something. But his eyes told her she wasn't telling him what he wanted to hear. He didn't believe her or trust her even as he tortured her with longing for sweet release.

"You're thinking of a way out now, aren't you?" He smiled down at her.

"No, I…" What? She had no answer for him.

"Hush now," he demanded, a finger covering her lips. "Let me give you what you want."

Her body opened for him, expanding to fit his ever growing size. Right now, she couldn't think. Not with it sliding in and out of her, stretching her, filling her, driving her to the edge and back again.

She clung to him, her ragged nails biting into the taut skin on his shoulders. She squeezed her eyes shut only to open then when his hand lightly slapped against her cheek. His hand was large and rough, but it didn't aim to hurt her, which confused her more than if he'd pounded her face with his fist. It was a gentle touch on her cheek, reminding her to look at him.

Each time she opened, he gave her a half-smile, which resembled an animal's snarl more than a man's smile. So much about him was animal-like. The way he held his head, the way he growled low and long as he moved.

"You like my cock?" he cooed, sending another thrill through her at the seductive tone of his voice.

"Please, I…"

"Oh, now you wish to beg. Beg me. Beg me," he grunted.

"Please, don't…I need…" Pressure built somewhere deep inside her, and she felt that she couldn't control the thousands of thoughts that raced through her head. The man's eyes burned through her, his distaste obvious, yet he continued to take her body, to speak softly then harshly, to make her feel things she couldn't explain.

"I know what you need." Her legs had been trapped inside his as he moved slowly. She gasped when he raised himself above her and took her ankles in his hands, spreading her wide open. When he pushed back into her, she let out a yell. She could almost feel him in her throat he filled her so completely.

"Like that, huh?" His voice was rough now as he looked down at her, but his eyes were alive with desire, belying his insults.

She knew she pleased him, even if she couldn't answer his question. She clung to the edge of some black nothingness that threatened to control her, consume her. It was like liquid fire building and building. His slow movements increased. Her legs ached from being held outstretched. Everything else ached from his size.

"Are you ready to come for me?"

She had no idea what he meant. She knew she was ready for something. She nodded, her movements frenzied.

With each thrust, she held her breath. Was this how it felt to die? Had her sisters ever felt such a sensation before meeting their ends? She reached up for his arms, needing something to hold her steady, to keep her from falling over into the nothingness.

His face twisted into a fierce grimace when she touched him. His hair flew wildly about his frame as he moved, still stretching her open. He must be feeling the same thing she felt, out of control, filled with need, with longing. When he stiffened and let out a growl, she shivered as he shot liquid fire deep into her. The scream that came from her throat didn't sound human, but the release that came with it made her feel as if the whole world melted away and nothing was left except the two of them. She trembled and shook. And looked up into his eyes which once again glowed golden.

Too soon, he moved away from her, pulling himself from her body. She felt bruised but gloriously alive. The warmth he shot inside her still filled her, making her want to pull him back into her. As soon as the thought crossed her mind, he turned back to snarl at her, his eyes once again the malicious green.

"Clean yourself," he demanded. She looked down at the wet spot on the bed. It was streaked with blood, proof that he had been her first. Her only.

She would marry one day. This man tonight may have said horrible things to her, may have even hated her, but he started something inside her that she would never forget. But no man, not even her future husband, would be able to make her feel the myriad of feelings the stranger forced on her.

"I can't move." Eleanora tried to move her stiff legs, but found them weakened.

"Then I shall carry you. If you are to be mine for the next moon period, you will be clean when I take you. There will be no other scent on you save for mine."

To be mine. What did he mean? "I should explain," she began. Explain what? Explain that he slipped himself into her while he was unconscious, and she did nothing to protest. She welcomed the invasion?

"Yes, you should. And you shall. But first, you shall bathe. Then you shall change the bedding. And I want you to take off that dress. It doesn't suit you. It barely fits. You shall wear no clothing while you are in my care."

She watched as he strolled across the room, unaware or unconcerned with his nakedness. He was still fascinating. She watched his muscles tense and flex as he moved to the hearth to stoke a fire.

His back was covered with scars, some long, some mere scratches. All of them only adding to his beauty.

She watched as he crouched in front of the hearth, poking at the wood before standing and taking a few more pieces from the pile, added and then arranged them. He looked back at her once more and winked before turning back to the fire. Her heart leapt into her throat and she gasped, horrified when he leaned forward, took a deep breath, and blew fire from his mouth. The man and the dragon were the same. He had not saved her from the dragon's talons. Instead, he had injected her with poison, preying upon her sympathy for the man she thought was a knight, here to rescue her.

A moment of betrayal flew through her, but it was quickly replaced with fascination. Two dragons had fought for her, and this one had won. And now she felt as if her place in the world, her destiny, had changed.

Chapter Three

Guilt washed over him. Mace knew that she had been at the mercy of his poison, yet he had continued to take her body, to treat her with such disregard, attempting to conjure the dragon after he had taken so much time to subdue it. He was not angry with the woman. It was his brother who should pay for the deception.

Yet he could not appear weak in the eyes of an enemy no matter how innocent she was in the ways of men and women. Even if she had been taught desire, her body had never been entered, her defenses never broken. Mace had seen the dragon's poison at work so many times in the past, yet never had he seen one so innocent come to life so instantly. Every impulse inside him told him that she was indeed his brother's spy.

Still, as he watched her sleep, her tiny body wrapped in the thin bed covering, a fierce desire to protect her swept over him. He let out a low growl, knowing what was happening to him. It was the dragon's curse, set in place so many years ago by a woman scorned. When a dragon spills virgin blood, he is in danger of losing his heart.

Inwardly, he cringed as her leg shifted, allowing him to see the pain he had inflicted, the bruises on her thighs. The dark hair that curled between her legs was still wet from her bath, just as the long hair that covered the pillow still dripped. The woman had been too exhausted to do more than collapse on the bed. Again, guilt and regret swept through him, two emotions he was not accustomed to feeling.

Against his better judgement, Mace crawled into bed next to her, wrapping his arms around her sleeping frame, taking in her creamy white skin, which felt like the finest of fabrics against his rough body. Her eyes had been the color of the sky close to midnight. Closing his eyes, he tried to relax against her, tried to slow his breathing to match hers. It had been an eternity since he had slept in the same bed with a woman.

* * * * *

Her body never seemed to tire of him, which was frustrating beyond belief. Worse even, she awakened to his touch, arching her back, craving his fingers on her soft skin. Mace watched her eyes glaze over with desire every time he took her, waiting, hoping to see fear in there somewhere. Instead, he saw something else he couldn't quite define, something that shook him to the core. The poison had worn off, leaving her desire for him to be just that—desire, plain and simple. Whoever she was, wherever she had come from, she craved his touch in a way few had before her.

She had been his prisoner for three days now, and her body was covered with bruises from their fierce lovemaking that first night. They had begun to turn yellow, discoloring her skin, reminding him of his brutality. He had been determined to break her in those first few hours. Now, he feared his resolve was weakening rather than hers.

He turned onto his side and grumbled at the sight of her body lying next to him, stark naked. She was a beautiful woman. Her long, dark hair reminded him of the night sky, and her skin was as soft and fine as the whitest sands of his home. She knew no fear as she clung to him last night in wild abandon while he drove himself into her dark, wet warmth. Mace almost wished he knew how to love, wished he had experience in seduction without force. There was something about Eleanora that made him wish for things he had never wished before. Every impulse inside him told him that what he was feeling for her was nothing more than a result of having spilled her virgin blood. The curse was powerful, and he was at its mercy now more than ever before.

She mumbled in her sleep and snuggled against him, placing her head on his shoulder. Sleeping as soundly as a child, she scared the hell out of him. What was he supposed to do with her? He'd never known a woman who didn't cower from his size and strength. His brother, damn him, had trained her well, if she were his spy. The dragon inside him insisted that the woman was not to be trusted, but the man looked down at her sleeping frame and could not help but wonder where she came from and why she looked up at him with such trust when he had done nothing to warrant it.

His hand went to her breasts before he could stop it. She had amazing breasts, small but firm with rosy tips that begged for his touch. He caressed the nipple until it stood hard, waiting for his mouth. She moaned but didn't stir as he touched her. He shifted and placed her head onto the pillow. Her dark hair spilled out against the white sheets. She would look amazing against the red satin sheets in his bed at home.

He slid his hand down her thigh, parting her legs, searching her wetness. She was always wet! The thick patch of dark curls called to his mouth, beckoning him to touch her there, kiss her there, bring her to release with his tongue, his teeth, his hands. Her clit was already hard, awaiting his touch.

She moaned again and stirred enough to part her thighs completely, making room for him. It was all the encouragement he needed. She had taken him while he slept, now he would return the favor by taking her in her sleep.

His cock throbbed as he positioned it at her opening. The tip was instantly coated with her honey. In one swift motion, he filled her to the hilt, stopping only when his balls lay flush against her ass. He listened as she sucked in her breath. Her eyes shot open as he began to move in and out of her hole.

She raised her hands to caress his chest, but he refused to allow her touch. Capturing both tiny hands into one of his, he held her arms over her head, pressing her into the bed as he drove into her over and over. He refused to touch her clit even as she ground it into him. He refused to touch her nipples even as they begged for his mouth.

For three days, she had come for him, coating his cock with her juice. Squeezing him until he thought she would tear his cock from his body. No more. He wouldn't allow her to come, to find her release. From now on, there would be no pleasure in their mating. None for her anyway. He would come in her mouth, on her flat stomach, but would not give her the satisfaction of enjoying her own release. It would be a test. If she still desired him, it would be proof that something more was at work, something stronger than the bonds a spy had to her employer. No woman would stand for it unless she truly craved his touch.

He didn't speak, didn't look at her as he continued to move inside her. She bucked against him, meeting his every stroke with her raised ass. An ass that he vowed to fill as soon as he tired of her pussy. Another test of loyalty. Would she allow him to take her? His heart pounded in his ears and his thinking became unclear. Sensations to which he was not accustomed continued to pulse through his body, making him aware of the weakness he had been reduced to by this woman.

"Roll over," he demanded, freeing her hands. She obliged.

Her waist may be tiny, but her ass was fleshy and full. She raised it in the air, giving him a full view of her cream as it coated her outer lips.

"Have you ever been taken in the ass?" The thought made his dick throb. Her pussy was tight enough, he wondered how her ass would feel.

"No." She arched her back as he moved toward her, positioning his dick at her opening.

"You mean my brother didn't fuck your pretty little hole?" A test. The words pounded in his head even as he said the words, unsure of how else to treat the woman who had seemingly taken control of his body in a way so that he could no longer act save for taking her.

"I don't know your brother."

She had told him this several times, but the dragon inside didn't believe her. He knew she had Damon's scent on her while she rode his cock that first night. Mace bit his tongue, hoping again to subdue the dragon whose growl lay just on the edge of his consciousness.

"You don't know my brother," he mocked. "Yet he sent you here to be my slave, my whore." He slapped her ass and watched as the flesh jiggled under his touch.

"Perhaps I should beat you until you tell me all I wish to know." He slapped her again, this time with more intensity. Her pussy spilled out more of her sweet cream and her back arched to meet the contact of his hand against her flesh.

"Mmmm. You like that?" he cooed against her ear before gently grazing his hand against her again. Once more, she moaned and arched into him.

"You wish to break me," her voice was a low purr, humming all the way into him. "You will never control me."

He would control her. All of her. Mace wanted to drive himself into her and not think about how amazing she would feel squeezing around him, tight as a fist, but he resisted. There had to be a way to control the desire he felt for her, desire that seemed to be both blessing and curse. If he could allow the dragon inside to take her, he would frighten her, he was sure. But something about her steady eyes told him this one did not cower from dragons, and she contained enough magick to free herself from the bonds that had held her to the rock.

It was nothing more than the joining of two bodies when he took her, sliding into her wet warmth, resisting the urge to ride her ass as he had threatened. The sounds of her pleasure were enough to drive him mad, especially since her soft body was casting a spell on him he neither liked nor understood. He growled his release much sooner than he'd wanted, yet he was satisfied by the small fact that she hadn't come. That was part of his newly formed plan. He would keep her on the edge until she told him her secrets.

Gave him the key to defeating his brother.

Or told him the secret to how she had managed to get under his skin in such a short time, forcing him to question everything he'd ever known before.

Eleanora had learned several things in the past three days. The most important was her strength. She didn't fear Mace even though he wanted her to. She could tell by the fierce look in his eyes every time they met hers, but there was something soft and gentle in his touch, even when he sought to control her. He could have hurt her, killed her if he wanted. Instead, he loved her with wild abandon, using his strength to bring her to the edges of ecstasy.

She watched him sleep. Something inside her quivered and ached just looking at the square-set jaw. She feared what she knew to be true. The dragon didn't frighten her, but the man and the feelings growing deep inside her did. Mace did not know what a light sleeper she was. He was unaware that she had felt his hand on her face, filled with gentleness, night after night, whispering words into her ear, which made no sense. He pulled her into his embrace, resting her head on his chest, vowing to protect her from some force he thought wanted nothing more than her destruction.

She snuggled into his embrace and sought sleep. The answers would come in the morning.

"Wake up." Fingers grazed across her cheek, tickling her. She opened her eyes to see Mace standing over her, wearing clothing she had never seen.

"I'm awake," she smiled, wondering why his tone was so soft this morning.

"We must return to my home. My father will wonder about me. And I'm sure you're more than ready to see my brother."

"I told you I don't know your brother," she reminded him. "Where did you find those clothes?"

"They are mine. A dragon must always be prepared. I have a lair in the mountains."

Was that a slight smile at the corners of his lips as he spoke? When had Mace smiled? She had seen him do it once, when he thought she was asleep. He had been staring into oblivion, his hand stroking her hair, and then he had looked down at her and graced her supposed sleeping face with a smile unlike any she had ever seen before. It was then that she knew he was a man filled with conflict, filled with things she couldn't begin to understand. And now, he had shared a tiny secret with her about his lair. Perhaps the man was winning his battle with the dragon after all, but maybe not. There was still the question of what would take place when they returned to his father's house.

"What will you do with me?" Her heart raced as she asked, not out of concern for her safety, but out of concern for her sanity. Would he have her killed? Would she be able to watch as he returned to his wife, abandoning her? The aching in her chest grew as she wondered how she would return to normalcy now that she was just beginning to uncover the mystery to the man.

"What dragons always do with humans," he grumbled.

"And what would that be?"

He stood and ran his hands through his hair, a sign she knew to show his frustration. "You know I cannot leave you until the next dark moon. You know that I am your prisoner." The tone of his voice indicated defeat, though he did not seem to be a man who knew such an emotion.

"My prisoner?" Since when? Ever since her first night with him, she felt he held her in chains.

"Yes." He fell to his knees in front of the bed, startling her with the motion. "You know the code. You know that when a dragon and human mate it is for one moon period. Why do you deny this? Why do you insist that you do not know my brother?"

His fingers dug into her knees. She looked down at the pale flesh there. If she had learned nothing else about him, she knew Mace hated losing control. Apparently more than he hated his brother. If he really believed she were his brother's spy, he wouldn't adhere to any code. Then she realized if he were her prisoner for one moon period, when they parted ways, he may harm her.

"Will you kill me at the end of the moon time?"

"No. We do not kill humans. You know this already."

"Then you...?"

"You will be free to live as you please. As long as you never return to your village." He stood and turned his back on her, another sign of his frustration.

"My sisters!" She flew to her feet, hands on her hips. "My sisters are still alive?"

"I know not."

"My sisters, Isadore and Lucina. Surely you know them." Her heart pounded at the thought.

He nodded slowly. "I know them."

"Did you...?"

"No. They were not mine. They live in the palace now with two of my father's men. They are well cared for. Better than they would have been had they stayed in your village to starve."

"They're alive," she said to no one in particular, her heart soaring with the knowledge. Alive. She would go to them, ask them for help.

"You act as if you do not know this." When Mace turned to look at her this time, she saw something in his face akin to belief. Maybe she was finally getting through to him.

"Where is this land of yours?" she asked after they had eaten and prepared for their journey.

"Not far."

"And how will we get there?"

"You really don't wish to know."

"Yes, I do."

Mace eyed his mate. The dragon inside him raged, wanting to scream at her, frighten her to no end for the deception that had gotten him this far. Yet every time he tried, she faced him down as if she were the bravest of warriors instead of a wisp of a woman. She claimed no knowledge of his people and appeared truly fascinated by every new piece of information he provided. And Mace was quickly losing sight of the tests he had vowed to use in order to keep her under his control.

The change would be the evidence. He would change before her eyes and see if she feared him or not. He hoped to the gods she did for if she didn't, he would not be able to continue his façade. Something was happening deep inside him that he couldn't yet define. Didn't wish to define. All he knew was that he craved her soft skin, her gentle kisses, her passionate displays, almost as much as he craved breathing.

"I should leave Liesel a message, telling her we used her cabin," she said from somewhere behind him. He stopped in his tracks and turned.

"Liesel?"

"Yes, she is my mentor. She's away gathering herbs for the moon time. When she returns, I don't want her to think someone had broken in."

"The healer?" *Please let it not be the one.* He steadied his breathing, awaiting her reply.

"Yes, the healer. I am her charge."

The entire world came crashing around him, Eleanora's words echoing in his head. Then Liesel's words came back to him. *You shall meet her when you least expect, dear Mace. She will be the one to change your destiny.* "You are Liesel's charge?"

"Yes."

Mace, child, you are not so bad as you would like everyone to think. There is a woman who shall tame you, slay the dragon, eh? I am training her for you now. She will be of great service to you even though she has a ways to go in the arts.

He had demanded to know her name, threatened to seek her out. Liesel warned against it.

If you find her before the moon deems it to be, you shall destroy everything. You are meant to rule Tyr. You shall need her by your side.

"Mace?"

"Yes. We would not want her to worry." His voice didn't sound like his own and caused her to send him a wary look. He wondered if Liesel shared with her the secrets of their destiny. And wondered why it had taken him so long to piece the events together.

Chapter Four

Eleanora hadn't backed down from him when he transformed into the fierce dragon and crouched down for her to mount his back. She clung to his back during the journey over the mountains, all the while her breath warm on his neck. Something inside him was changing, had been changing ever since he met her. And now that he knew she was the one Liesel foresaw, all he could think of was learning the remainder of the prophecy, the part Liesel conveniently overlooked.

This woman was not a princess from a foreign land as Liesel had assured him his soul mate would be. She seemed nothing more than a sacrificial virgin, one who had come to crave his touch as much as he had come to crave hers. One who had gotten under his skin in the worst manner to leave him defenseless against her. One who would destroy him if given the chance.

What he thought had been love or emotion in her eyes was nothing more than cool dignity. She would not bow down to him, but this didn't mean she cared for him. The aching in his chest told him he cared much more than he desired. Feeling emotions was forbidden to him, had been taught out of him as a child. But something about her when she wrapped her strong legs around him made him want to feel for the first time in a long time. His mother would be disappointed. He would almost be willing to give up the throne to his brother if it meant becoming capable of feeling something for someone. No, not someone. For her.

He watched the reunion between his lovely captor and her sisters, determined not to be shaken by the love between them. And wondering why his own family never shared such an experience. His and Damon's mothers had fought ever since the brothers were born weeks apart so many years ago. Their father lived in a constant power struggle between the two women until his mother's death three years ago.

"You found her." The familiar voice caused him to turn and face the wise old crone.

"Aye, that I did." He kept his face set, not allowing Liesel to see into his mind.

"It won't work, child. I've known you since your birth. I was there the night you were destined to be king. And I know your heart. You love this girl."

Hearing the words out loud was more than he had prepared for. Love. Yes, he supposed he did. If love meant feeling an ache inside so strong it threatened to destroy your sanity. Feeling an insatiable passion that threatened to overrun common sense.

"Don't deny it. A new time is coming. One of peace. Your brother has found something special as well. A woman fit for a princess."

"I am to be king," he growled.

"And you shall. You shall both rule in peace. Two is better than one, eh?"

"I shall never rule with my brother!"

"Yes, you shall. At the end of the moon time, you shall see the truth in my words. Damon is a changed man. The change is under his skin as it is yours. Neither of you can deny it."

He didn't want to believe it. The feud between brothers had lasted his entire life. It drove him in his every action. There had never been a circumstance without the hatred. Until now. "Damon has returned, then?"

"Returned with several surprises." Liesel nodded toward Eleanora. "Go to her," she encouraged. "Take her into your world. Your real world. Into your heart. She is yours just as you are her prisoner."

As if on cue, Eleanora turned to smile at him. The smile slipped inside him, going into his darkest core and changing him, melting all the doubt and hatred. He returned the smile. Suddenly all he could think of was having her hair spread out on his red sheets. And loving her.

"Your dragon is handsome," Isadore commented.

"Yes, he is. But he doesn't trust me. He thinks I'm his brother's spy."

"Ah, yes. Damon. Another handsome one. Then again, I've not seen an unattractive dragon. Their feud is as old as they are, it seems. But I've been here for three years and I've never seen Mace smile as he does now." Lucina nodded toward the dragon.

"I should go." Eleanora tore her eyes from Mace's handsome face and hugged her sisters one more time. There were so many questions to ask. But now that she was here, she had been assured she would never return to her village. She held her breath as he approached and warily took his hand when he offered it.

"Do you like your new dress?"

"What do you care of my dress? You prefer me naked." She laced the words with as much bitterness as she could manage. The truth was, she preferred to be naked with him. And she was terrified he would give her up.

"That I do, little one, but if you are to be a member of my community now, you shall only be naked in the privacy of our chamber."

She flushed when he gave her hand a squeeze. "Our chamber?"

"Unless you prefer to do it in the open?" He laughed, showing her his perfect white teeth. "I see your blush. All the way to here." His fingers grazed along the top edge of her bodice. "I wonder if it trails down. To here." He brushed a hand across her nipple, which hardened instantly. "You are on fire for my touch."

Her eyes met his and held them. There was no way she could deny her desire for him. "I should like to see this chamber," she smiled, her boldness coming back.

"And you shall."

"Say my name." His voice was a growl. He bit into her shoulder as he drove himself into her tight hole over and over again. She bucked against him, meeting his every stroke. They barely made it to the chamber before her new dress lay in shreds at her feet.

"Mace." She panted his name, making his dick throb even more. To have a woman such as this panting and weakened at his touch, his loving empowered him.

"Yes, little one. Know that I am your master."

Her inner walls squeezed against him, fisting around him, reminding him that only days ago she had never known a man's touch. Now, she begged for his touch, his release. He grasped her hips, digging his fingers into her soft flesh while he rocked back and forth, slapping his balls against her hardened clit. He loved taking her from behind. Loved watching her ass move in time to the force of his thrusts. Mostly, he loved being inside her and planned to take her any and every way possible.

His balls spasmed and he knew his release was near. Pulling his throbbing cock from her pussy, he shot his white seed on her ass and ran his fingers through it, coating her tight rosette. He still hadn't taken her this way, but tonight he planned to. He rubbed his liquid into her hole, into her cunt, reveling in the way the orgasm shook her.

"Are you ready for me?"

"Yes."

He positioned himself at her opening and slid the head of his cock in enough to open her slightly. "Be still and I won't hurt you." His voice was meant to soothe her, but still she shook against him. Not out of fear. She wanted this as much as he did.

He could tell by the way she arched her back against him, begging him to fill her.

Slowly, slowly, he moved into her, feeling a tightness like he'd never known before. When his cock finally filled her completely, he slipped his fingers into her pussy and began stroking her to orgasm while his dick remained buried in her tight ass.

He let her set the rhythm. She moved her ass back and forth, taking him in and out. At first, she moved slowly and carefully. As the tension built inside her cunt, she stroked harder, faster, causing his hands to increase their intensity as well.

He felt her hand reach around to stroke her clit, a movement he'd taught her when he forced her to pleasure herself while he watched. She moaned, screamed, echoing his name throughout the chamber. He took his hand from her cunt and grabbed her hips, once again pounding toward his release. She reached behind her and grabbed his balls, sending him over the edge. The hot liquid shot against her inner walls and seeped out around his shaft.

He pulled her into his arms as he slipped his cock from her body. They lay there, panting, breathless, each spent. One hand cradled around her waist while the other stroked her breast.

"You have made me your prisoner," he whispered against her bruised shoulder. The teeth marks were already apparent and turning her skin purple.

"And I am your slave."

The word sank into his head. *Slave.* He had done this to her. Again, guilt took over, causing his heart to twist at the thought. Staring up at the ceiling, he counted his breaths, hoping to calm his hammering heart.

"I do not deserve you. You should not be here with a man like me." Pulling away from her, he sat on the edge of the bed. His shoulders sank away from her when she wrapped her arms around him and rested her head against his back.

"What is wrong with a man like you?"

"I have not done you justice. I have taken from you more than I have given you. And I swear to you I shall make it up to you. Starting now."

"Mace, I…"

"No. I do not need your words. I do not need your kindness or your soft kisses. What I need from you is your acceptance of me. Can you love a man who can hardly control his demon? A man whose dragon is a vicious, violent creature who is not easily subdued?" His breathing stopped completely as he waited for her answer.

"I need you. I have needed you ever since that first night. I can't explain what you do to my body."

He turned in her arms and pulled her into his lap. "I have a confession for you, one that you may not wish to hear."

"Yes?"

"That first night, you did not join with me of your own free will. You had been infected with my poison. It is a powerful aphrodisiac. It was responsible for our mating." And saying the words now, after so much time had passed, made their first night together feel like a betrayal. "I shall make this right for you."

"I do not care how the first time took place. All that matters now is that you and I have an understanding. I have seen your world. I understand your curse."

"How do you understand the curse?" He had not explained it to her.

"I sleep lightly. I have heard much of your nighttime musings. So you and I are even in our deception."

He took her face into his hands. "I want you to stay with me."

"I can't return to my home."

"I know. But I want you to stay with me. For all time. Be mine."

"You mean continue to be your slave, to make love to you?" There was a slight hint of laughter in her voice.

"Yes. But not as a slave. As..." he stopped as the words hung in his throat.

"As?" When she brushed her fingers over his lips, his cock sprang to attention again, remembering the feel of them against it earlier.

"As my wife." The words came out more as a grumble than he had hoped. He looked into her eyes, hoping for an answer there. They glistened with unshed tears. "Eleanora?"

"Yes," she nodded wildly, the tears now spilling out onto her cheeks and onto the sheets.

"Yes?"

"Yes, I will stay with you. I love you."

"And I love you. You and I will bring peace to this place." She pulled his head down to hers and brushed her lips against his.

"If you do that again, I shall take you once more." Her eyes gleamed with the fearlessness only his little one knew, and she pulled him to her again.

This time, he took her slowly, barely moving as she clung to him. He faced her, placing kisses on her eyes, her lips, her breasts. Then he raised above her, slowly driving himself into her, making her come over and over before he took his own release.

He looked down at her swollen lips, her swollen clit. He had been so rough with her, but she had reveled in their mating. Just as he had. He spread her lips open with his hand and watched as his cock moved in and out of her hole, spreading her cream onto the sheets, onto her lips, his balls, tangling in his hair and hers.

Finally, her pussy began to quiver, milking his life's blood from him. Soon, the sheets were coated with proof of their love. He collapsed on top of her and held her while they slept, knowing this was exactly where he was meant to be.

* * * * *

"Wake up, love."

Eleanora wasn't really asleep, but every morning she reveled in the different ways Mace found to wake her, reminding her of their first time together. This morning was no different. His breath brushed across her mound, which he had shaved bare last night and then pounded into until she thought she couldn't take anymore. A smile crossed her lips just thinking about the new sensations.

"I have something for you." His voice was gently coaxing, but she decided to wait just a little longer to see what he had in store.

She started when the cold object came into contact with her bare skin. What was that? He rubbed it around her outer lips, teasing her clit with it before slipping it inside her. Her opening widened instantly, stretching to hold the object. Whatever it was, it was not as large as his cock. She squeezed against its hardened surface.

"What is that?"

"A present for you."

She opened her eyes only to see him smiling at her. "What kind of present?"

"The kind that will remain inside you all day."

She sat up, feeling the slight pressure of the object against her insides. It wasn't uncomfortable, but it felt strange, as if it would fall out if she moved. "All day?"

"Yes. I have a meeting with my brother today. One which you will attend. And while you sit next to me, you will squeeze your muscles here," he ran his finger along her pussy lips, "and think of me."

"I always think of you."

"Ah, but today you will be filled. And while Damon and I discuss our plans, I shall remind you to squeeze and concentrate. You will sit next to me and I will rub your clit through your gown. You shall come over and over quietly while we meet. And tonight, when we return, I will remove it and slide myself easily into your tight hole."

"I can't keep this inside all day."

"Yes you can. And you will. If you do not, you will be very lonely tonight."

His warning was meant to be serious, but Eleanora knew he couldn't keep his hands off her. In the month they had known each other, they had made love every day, most of the time several times a day.

"Perhaps it is you who shall be lonely," she teased.

He pressed his hand against her pussy, pushing the item in further, making her quiver with delight. "All day."

"Yes, master," she smiled before pulling him into her for a kiss.

Mace thought he'd die if the meeting didn't end soon. Eleanora sat next to him, her pussy filled with his love toy, her juices spilling out around it every time she came. And she came so many times. Every time, she squeezed his knee with her hands, pressing her nails into his flesh beneath the cloth. Still, he kept a straight face while he continued to massage her clit and push the toy back into place beneath the folds of her gown.

Apparently, Damon had found a woman himself. For the first time, Mace realized he and his brother could work out a peace agreement. When the meeting ended and Mace and Eleanora were alone in the conference room, he turned to her.

"Lift your dress," he commanded. Her eyes were already glazed over with desire and he could see her tight nipples puckering beneath the fabric.

"But, my king, you said I should not remove this…whatever this is." Her protest was weak and topped off with a wicked smile.

"You shall not remove it. Perhaps I shall take you while it is still imbedded in your tight hole." Her eyes widened at the threat. "You can take two, can't you, love?"

"Surely you're joking." She bit her lip as he pulled her into his lap.

"Does this feel like a joke? You're primed and ready, love. You ever wonder how it would feel to fuck two men at the same time?"

"I can't."

"You can. And you will." He raised her up onto the table and pushed his chair back, raising her skirt to reveal her clean-shaven mound. "Your lips are quivering for me, trying to hold on to it."

"Mace," she moaned as he dipped his head down to take her clit between his teeth.

"Tell me what you desire, then. Would you like for me to love you gently?"

She was dripping. Her juices coated her ass, her clit, shining like sacred cream in the light. He ran his tongue up and down from her ass to her hard clit, biting along the way. "I don't think you have it in you."

"Is that a challenge?" a smile lit up his face. "Lay back." He pushed her gently all the way back so that her legs were spread wide open for him. Using his tongue and teeth, he forced her to the edge of orgasm again and then let up before she came. He knew her body so well, could play it like a fine instrument. He could make her come at will and stop her from coming as well. Three more times, he brought her to the edge, but refused to push her over.

"Please," she begged.

"Please what?" he teased against her lips.

"Please take me."

"Ah, but you said you wanted gentle."

"Anything. Just let me come."

He inhaled her scent and licked her one last time before pulling the toy out of her swollen lips. "It would be a tight fit if I tried this," he warned. "Perhaps we should retire to our room. There, I can show you just how gentle I can be."

"I don't care. Please."

He knew this kind of wanting. It was what he felt every time he looked at her. He stood and placed his cock at her opening, his attempts at moving slowly feeling unnatural. Calming his breathing, trying to steady his beating heart, Mace slowly slid his swollen head in, parting her lips, stretching them even further, opening her so wide that her clit turned down to brush against the hilt of his cock as it slipped into her.

He filled her to the hilt, his balls resting against her ass. He smiled when she gasped and clung to him, her nails digging in to his forearms, her head thrown back in ecstasy, her hardened nipples puckering beneath the gauze of her dress.

When he began stroking, he set the rhythm, trying to move slowly, trying to focus on the sensations that swept through his body as he felt every slight spasm of her pussy as it wrapped around him. He had not been one to concentrate before, having spent most of his years only taking. Eleanora had changed him, had made him want to be different, want to be something more.

The slow strokes were maddening, driving him to the edge of somewhere he had never been before. Then, the edge was there and he threatened to slide over as her clit rubbed itself on his cock and his strokes increased, bringing her the release she sought as her nails dug into his shoulders. When her pussy fisted around him, coaxing his cum to pour out, she screamed loudly enough to alert all the guards. No one opened the door, as they all were accustomed to Mace's love play.

"That's it, love. Come for me. Scream for me. Let everyone know you are mine."

Her cries echoed in the room, blending in with the sound of his cock rubbing into her juices, slapping against her inner walls.

She shook against him, her own orgasm so intense she threatened to bruise him.

He pulled himself from her body and looked down at the woman who had changed him. Mace wanted to bury himself in her again, to make up to her the abuse he had caused, the betrayal and mistrust of their meeting. His cock sprang to life and easily slipped inside her. She lay back, her arms thrown over her head, her body open for him. Only when he came did she cling once more to him and whimper against his shoulder.

"I love you," he managed while gasping to catch his breath.

"I love you, dragon."

She reached up to stroke his chin, sending another shiver through his body. "Let's get you back to bed."

"Whatever you wish."

She clung to him as he carried her up the back stairwell to his—their—chamber. They only stopped once to ride each other against the wall. He threatened to impale her on his cock and carry her up the stairs the remainder of the way to their room. She only smiled and ground herself into him further. When Mace finally placed her on the bed, he knew she held his heart. He looked down into her face, her eyes wild from their lovemaking and from anticipation.

A new peace was coming. If he could find love, anything was possible. He watched the candlelight flicker, softening her face, and knew his world would never be the same.

About the author:

Alicia's interest in romance began as a child when she used to hide out reading her mom's forbidden romance novels. She remembers very distinctly the first time she ever read Gone with the Wind and was instantly hooked on the concept of the Southern gentlemanly rake. She likes to think that there's a little bit of Rhett in all of her heroes, whether they be sexy cowboys or dark and brooding rock stars.

Always writing against a soundtrack, Alicia finds inspiration for her cowboys and contemporary heroes from country musicians such as Kenny Chesney. Her love for the gothadelic sounds of Type O Negative has inspired several vampire stories and stories about tragically beautiful musicians. Other inspirations include the music of Saliva, Van Halen, Santana, Blake Shelton, and Prince. (She's a Gemini. That explains the wide variety of influences!)

Alicia has completed several manuscripts ranging from comedic contemporaries to dark, sexy paranormals and fantastical futuristics.

Her favorite ice cream is Godiva's dark chocolate truffle. Eaten straight from the container, it is almost—almost—as good as reading erotica!

Alicia welcomes mail from readers. You can write to her c/o Ellora's Cave Publishing at 1337 Commerce Drive, Suite 13, Stow OH 44224.

Also by Alicia Sparks:

Better Than Ice Cream

TAMING JACK

Angela Knight

Prologue

He'd known the call to report to the Sheriff's office couldn't be good, and he was right.

"Jack, this isn't easy for me to say, but I don't have a choice," Sheriff Steve Jones said after Ramsey had settled into the lone chair in front of the big man's desk. "You're endangering the case. You're going to have to back off."

"What case?" In his frustration, Ramsey forgot any pretense of diplomacy. "Dammit! It's been three weeks since Heather was murdered and we don't have shit. Not a suspect, not a clue. Nothing."

The sheriff's long, homely face hardened. "Watch your tone, Deputy. I've been willing to allow you a certain amount of slack under the circumstances, but you're pushing it. Hard."

"Sheriff, she was my baby sister." A barely controlled fury rumbled in his voice. Ramsey clenched his fists as his mind flashed back to that day three weeks ago when he'd found Heather lying on the floor of her apartment.

Naked, raped and strangled. All her wit and loving spirit gone, sacrificed to a psycho's sick lust.

She'd been just fifteen when their parents died in a car crash the year Jack was a college senior. He'd put aside his own law school dreams and became a cop so he could support her.

It had been worth it. Heather — bright, pretty Heather — had deserved the best he could give her.

And she'd given him her best right back.

Heather was determined to become a trauma surgeon so she could save people like their parents, and she'd devoted everything to that dream. In college, she worked so hard and so brilliantly, she'd won a medical scholarship to Duke University. Ramsey had been so damn proud of her, he'd cried without shame at her college graduation.

But the week before she was supposed to leave for med school, some sick fuck had extinguished all her bright promise and gutted Jack Ramsey's soul.

He had nothing left — not for himself, not even for Lark Anderson, the woman he loved and had once planned to marry. Like his dreams for his sister, that plan was ashes now. He knew Lark deserved more than the hollow man he'd become.

Now all that drove him was the search for Heather's killer. And he didn't much care what he had to do to find him.

He'd raged through town like an avenging angel, questioning anybody and everybody who might know anything about Heather's death. And sometimes he hadn't been particularly polite in his methods, particularly with certain lowlife thugs of his acquaintance.

Which might be why the Sheriff had finally drawn the line.

Now Jones sighed, rubbing his hands over his face. "Jack, for once think like a cop instead of the victim's big brother. Let's say all that cowboying around town you're doing does bear fruit, and you shake loose a lead — or even a confession. You know what the killer's lawyer will do with that?"

"At least we'd have an arrest," Ramsey growled.

"Which is no damn good without a conviction." The sheriff glared at Jack, frustration pouring off him in waves that were almost visible. "And we won't get one, because the defense will claim you were on a vendetta, that in your grief you arrested an innocent man because you were so hungry to see somebody — anybody — pay. And that argument's going to sound awfully convincing to a jury, considering you're not even a detective."

Jack stiffened. "That doesn't mean I don't know my job."

Jones threw up his big hands in a gesture of disgust. "Oh, for God's sake, you're a motorcycle cop, Jack! You're supposed to catch speeders and write traffic tickets, not solve murders."

"Sheriff…"

"Look, I know you're trying to get Heather justice, but this isn't the way to do it." Jones caught him in a hard, level stare. "I'm giving you a direct order, Deputy Ramsey. Back off. Take your bereavement leave and let us do our jobs. Spend some time with that girl of yours and get your head screwed on straight." The sheriff's mouth tightened. "Before you blow your career straight to hell."

Ramsey stalked outside toward his cycle, his boots ringing on the pavement, his strides long and angry. His sister's murder was turning into one of the whodunits cops hated, the kind that never got solved.

Now every day that passed put the department further from catching the killer. And Jones had just forbidden him to do anything to bring the bastard to justice.

He wanted to howl.

Ramsey's shoulders slumped. Maybe the sheriff was right and it was time to pay Lark a visit. He'd been avoiding her since Heather's funeral, unwilling to expose his psychic wounds to her pity. All he wanted now was to go to her, talk to her. Maybe…

"Jack Ramsey?"

Impatiently, Ramsey turned to see an elderly woman standing in the parking lot under the light of a street lamp. She was dressed entirely in pink, from the pillbox hat perched on her lavender curls to her neat pink dress, right on down to her pink flats. Over one arm, she carried a huge pink straw purse that seemed to be moving. Ramsey shot it a wary glance in time to see a little Yorkshire terrier thrust up its fuzzy black head from the purse's pink depths.

"You are Jack Ramsey, are you not?" the old woman asked in a reedy voice.

Great. She probably wanted to complain about some neighbor who liked to play his boom box too loud. Controlling his sigh, Ramsey walked over to find out what she wanted. "That's me. What can I do for you, ma'am?"

Blue eyes met his, astonishingly sharp in that wrinkled face. "It's what I can do for you, young man." She reached into the bag and pulled out the Yorkie. Holding the dog out to him, she said, "This is Gav."

Ramsey looked down at the little animal, which stared back at him with perked ears. "Cute dog. Look, ma'am, if you need help, the desk officer inside can…"

"Do you want to catch your sister's killer, or don't you?" the old woman demanded.

He stiffened, his gaze narrowing on hers. "What do you know about that?"

She thrust the Yorkie at him again. "Take Gav, and all your questions will be answered."

Impatiently, Ramsey reached for the dog. "Ma'am, what is it you have to…?"

The instant his hands closed around the animal's furry ribs, the Yorkie began to glow. Jack glanced down in surprise. He barely had time to yelp before a beam of raw force shot from the dog's eyes and into his.

As the energy blasted into him, his body jolted as if he'd seized a live electric line. Pain ripped through him. He couldn't even force a scream past his straining vocal cords.

When the beam finally cut off, Jack toppled backward like a felled tree to hit the sidewalk flat on his back.

The dog was gone.

The old woman looked down at him as he stared blindly at the stars, arms and legs still jerking. "Now, isn't that better?"

With a satisfied nod, she turned around and headed back toward her car. Distantly, Jack heard the purr of a big car's engine as she drove away.

Chapter One
Six Months Later

On some level, Lark Anderson knew she was dreaming again. Jack wasn't really with her. She was alone in the big bed she'd once shared with her lover, alone as she'd been for all the months since Jack had lost his sister.

But knowing better didn't stop the dream. It never did. And she didn't want it to.

Dreams were all she had of him now.

Jack looked up at her over the curve of her breast, his breath gusting warmly over one hard pink nipple. "God," he whispered, his voice silky and very male, "I just love your breasts." He gave the little peak a teasing lick, and Lark moaned.

He laughed at the helpless sound and traced his fingers over her sensitive ribs until she wiggled. "Like that?" His white teeth flashed. "I certainly do. You taste so sweet and hot."

Lark looked up at him, feeling a bubble of passionate love swelling within her until she thought she'd burst with it.

He lay on his side next to her, his chest forming a powerful curve, muscle shifting in his biceps as he teased her with those big hands. She loved looking at him, watching the subtle way muscle rippled in his pecs and abdomen when he moved. He was just so damn male, so damn arousing. So damn big. Six-foot-five, every inch of him built like a brick wall.

Yet despite the linebacker build, when he made love to her he was exquisitely gentle, as though she were precious and breakable. Every touch and stroke seemed to proclaim silently how much he loved her.

As Lark watched, breathless with hunger, Jack lowered his head and closed his hot mouth over her nipple. His tongue flicked and swirled around the sensitive flesh until she arched under him. Instinctively, she eased her legs apart. He took the gesture for the invitation it was and slipped one hand between her thighs. Long, strong fingers found her opening, eased inside through thick cream. He smiled into her eyes. "Oh, you are ready, aren't you?"

"You've...AH!...got a real gift for understatement, you know that?" She rolled her hips and closed her eyes, letting the pleasure spin through her in long, silken streamers.

He smiled lazily and rolled over on top of her. "Well, in that case..." She caught her breath as he settled that big body between her thighs, blanketing her in warmth and strength. He felt so good...

And even better when he slid his thick cock slowly into her creamy core. He groaned in pleasure. "God, Lark, you make me so hot!"

She grinned up at him. "Same – AH! – here..."

He'd begun thrusting, slow and gentle, the big shaft teasing its way in and out of her, stroking her pleasure rapidly toward a quivering peak. Panting, Lark watched him as he moved over her, riding her in that easy way he had. His handsome face was absorbed as he gazed down at her. "I love you, Lark," he whispered.

"I love you too, Jack."

The heat rolled up her spine, and she tossed back her head, coming, convulsing around him. "I love you!" She screamed it this time, the words borne on a wave of searing pleasure.

Her own cry jolted Lark awake. Instinctively, she looked around for Jack, missing the warm strength of his body.

The bed was cool and empty.

Then she remembered.

He wasn't there. He'd turned his back on her, cut off all communication months ago, a bare three weeks after Heather's murder.

Without explanation. Without a word.

Tears stung the back of Lark's lids. Biting her lip against her moan of grief, she curled on her side in her cold bed and wrapped her arms around herself.

Since Jack had left, they were the only ones that ever held her.

* * * * *

Lark looked up at the deli's neon sign. She hadn't had any real interest in food since Jack had dumped her. Today her appetite was even worse than usual, an effect of the depression that had nagged at her since last night's dream.

You're pitiful, Anderson, she told herself. *Pining away for that son of a bitch when he doesn't give a damn about you.*

She ought to make herself eat something. Maybe some soup. She'd worked all day at the bookstore; by rights, she should have worked up an appetite.

What the hell, Lark decided. Might as well give the deli a try. After all, she and Jack had never eaten there, so it should be mercifully free of painful memories—the way he threw back his head when he boomed out that rich male laugh, the little crinkle around his dark eyes when he was about to make some truly awful pun.

The way his impressive cock rose high and hard when she modeled her latest extravagance from Victoria's Secret...

Wimp, she thought at herself, disgusted, shoving the deli's door open and stalking to the counter. *It's been six months. It's time to cut him out of your heart the way he did you. Assuming he even had a heart to begin with, the big jerk.*

Then she sighed. Unfortunately, it was painfully obvious Jack did have a heart, or Heather's murder wouldn't have butchered it so thoroughly.

Dammit, the least he could have done is let her comfort him. That's what people in love did—turn to one another for solace in times of pain.

Which proves he never loved you to begin with, Lark told herself. Deal with it.

As she studied the menu written on the menu board behind the counter, she felt something furry brush against her ankles. Lark looked down to meet a pair of brilliant green eyes.

"*Meow?*"

"Hi, there, kitty." The cat looked like some kind of longhair mix with its pointed little face and abundance of silky black fur. It meowed up at her again and rose on its hind legs, stretching its soft paws up her thigh. "What're you doing in here, other than violating a slew of health codes?"

"Some things are more important than rules," a frail female voice said. "Like soothing people who are hurting. Cats are good at that."

Lark looked up to meet the gaze of the old woman who'd just stepped up behind the cash register. She was wearing a pink waitress uniform, an old-fashioned pink frilled cap resting on her lavender curls.

The cat chose that moment to extend its claws delicately, gently pricking Lark's leg as if to reclaim her attention. She smiled down at the animal and stooped to pick it up. "I've always liked cats," she said, as the little beast settled against her chest, purring and silken.

"And she seems to like you," the waitress said.

Lark thought of Jack. "Glad somebody does." Absently, she reached to scratch behind the cat's pointed ears.

Then it lifted its black head and met her gaze. An energy beam stabbed from its eyes, driving into her skull like a red-hot ice pick. She opened her mouth to scream, but her body wouldn't obey as pain ripped through her.

She didn't even feel herself hit the floor.

Distantly, Lark was aware of the elderly waitress moving past her to hang the "Closed" sign over the door. "There," she said. "We wouldn't want you and Xedda to be interrupted, would we?"

Lark didn't care.

Something alien was in her head.

At first that was all she knew, all she cared about — the alien thing that didn't belong, that filled her skull with its invasive presence. She began to fight, everything in her howling in frantic rebellion as she fought to force the invader away. *Get out!* her mind shrieked. *GET OUT! Getoutgetoutgetout!*

"*I won't hurt you,*" the voice said, soothing and female. "*I'm here to help. Help you and Jack Ramsey both.*"

I don't care! Get out!

"*He's in danger, Lark.*"

Suddenly an image flashed through her mind, like the flickering impression from a nightmare. Jack, battling savagely against twisted caricatures of men who pounded back at him with hammer blows. Men she somehow knew were raw evil in human form.

He grabbed one of them. Red light flared around the two men as they struggled, Jack's powerful arms bunched as he held on until the evil thing slumped in his arms.

But even as it died, Jack's handsome face twisted, his eyes burning with something wild, something tortured and mad.

"*He's killing them,*" the alien voice said, "*but they're destroying him. We have to save him before it's too late.*"

The bottom seemed to drop out of Lark's stomach. She knew this had to be some kind of trick, knew she shouldn't listen to this...whatever it was.

And yet...

What if Jack really did need her? Everything inside Lark rebelled at the idea of allowing this *thing* to stay another second. But remembering Jack's distorted face, the despair in his eyes, she knew she couldn't turn her back on him. No matter what it cost her.

Who — what — are you? And what were those things fighting him?

"*My name is Xedda, and I am a Spirit Rider. Those he battles are Dark Ones.*"

Are they . . .human? They looked like men. In a way. But there was a sense of evil there, as if they were something more. Something worse.

"*Only in part. Listen, child, and I'll tell you what they are. What we are. Where we come from. And I'll tell you how you can save him.*"

Feeling as if she'd been trapped in a dream, Lark listened as Xedda told her the incredible story of her kind, a race of immortal energy beings.

They'd evolved on a gas giant hundreds of light years away, eventually splitting into three separate races. Among them were those like Xedda, who could feed on the ambient energy of the planet around them. Another race, the Dark Ones, preyed on Xedda's kind, absorbing their life force to power their own.

A third species, now called Paladins, fed on the Dark Ones. They formed a kind of partnership with Xedda's people, both protecting them and using them as bait to attract the Dark Ones.

But then the sun their world orbited became a red giant as it aged, swelling and flaming across the sky, making their world uninhabitable. All three races were in danger of extinction when a group of alien methane breathers came to their planet to observe its death throes.

In desperation, Xedda and her sisters managed to enter the minds of the some of the aliens, possessing them. The Dark Ones and the Paladins had quickly followed suit.

Unfortunately, the hosts weren't really compatible. So once they were all on their way from their dying world, the energy creatures sought new species to possess. Physical bodies, after all, were able to use tools and equipment to protect themselves, skills the energy creatures now knew they badly needed.

Soon afterward — about two thousand years before the birth of Christ — the creatures and their hosts discovered Earth. The energy beings were delighted to find humans were more compatible than their current hosts, so they began possessing the new life forms at once.

The Dark Ones soon discovered they could prey on human life force just as they'd always preyed on Xedda's people. But because they were incorporeal, they needed human hosts to do their killing.

The Paladins, for their part, used their hosts to hunt Dark Ones, just as they always had.

Spirit Riders like Xedda still assisted the Paladins. Yet now they did so by keeping the Paladins' hosts sane and stable, since absorbing a Dark Rider's energies tended to have a negative effect on the human mind.

Despite the risk, the beings' hosts found there were advantages to harboring one of the spirit races. All the Riders formed symbiotic relationships with their hosts. imbuing their human vessels with fantastic abilities, such as super strength or the ability to heal.

Even so, finding those partners was no easy task.

Fortunately, the energy creatures learned to assume physical form for short periods—usually some small animal like a dog or a cat. Another Rider already in a human host would help them find someone suitable. In the case of Lark—and, according to Xedda, Jack—that had been the elderly lady in pink.

The question was, did Lark want to be one of those symbiotes?

"Now," Xedda asked, when she'd finished answering Lark's tumble of questions, *"will you help me?"*

And Lark, remembering the madness she's seen growing in Jack's eyes, knew there was only one possible answer. *Yes.*

Chapter Two
A week later

"*Pull over here,*" the spirit said.

Lark hit the brakes, peering out the Honda's windshield at the darkened street. "Are you sure, Xedda?" The sole surviving streetlight along the sidewalk revealed boarded windows, piles of garbage, and graffiti-splattered brick that did not fill her with confidence. "I don't like the looks of this."

Oh, hell, who was she trying to kid? It looked like just the kind of place Jack would head for in his holy mission to find his sister's killer.

As she glanced around, she spotted the flash of rotating blue lights coming from the entrance of a nearby ally. Her heart leapt into her throat.

"Oh, yeah, he's here all right," Lark muttered. "Figures."

Her gaze locked on that flashing light, she pulled the Honda into the nearest empty spot and turned off the engine. Thrusting the driver's door open with an impatient hand, she got out and promptly stepped in something that squished under her high-heeled foot. "Shit." Lark stepped out of the puddle of slime and slammed the car door closed, hitting the remote locks on her key fob. "I hope to hell you'll appreciate what I'm going through for you, Jack," she grumbled.

"We're gonna kill you, you fuckin' cop bastard!" The male bellow snapped her gaze toward the alley.

"Dream on, asshole," a male voice snarled back. Lark frowned. It sounded like Jack's, but with a deep, rumbling quality she'd never heard before. "I'm not one of those helpless women you like to prey on."

Glass shattered, mixing with male grunts of effort and the scrape of feet over pavement as Lark broke into a run. She had to dodge broken malt liquor bottles and twisted chunks of metal as she made for the alley. It figured she and Xedda would find Jack the day she'd decided to wear a short skirt and three-inch heels to work.

As she skidded between the two boarded-up buildings, the first thing Lark saw was a police motorcycle dumped on its side, its engine still rumbling. Two men fought in the illumination of its rotating bubble light, exchanging merciless blows.

Despite the circumstances, Lark's heart leapt. Finally, after more than a week of fruitless searching, she'd found Jack Ramsey.

Then she got a closer look at him. "God, Jack," she muttered, "what the hell have you done to yourself?"

At least the being that had possessed him hadn't changed that powerful body. He was still the biggest damn motorcycle cop Lark had ever seen, looking like one of her kinkier fantasies in those polished knee-high bike boots. Bunching biceps strained at the short sleeves of his uniform shirt as he pounded blow after blow into his opponent. Muscle worked up and down his broad back under the thin blue shirt, and his thighs bunched as he threw his weight into every punch.

The face under his helmet was thinner than it had been six months ago, and there were deep hollows beneath his high, chiseled cheekbones. Lines of bitterness and suffering bracketed the wide mouth under his thick sable mustache. His sister's murder had aged him. Lark could almost feel the pain that ate at his soul.

But it was the cold, feral determination burning in his deep-set black eyes that sent a chill through her. This wasn't the laughing lover she'd hoped to marry. This man was a driven avenger, as willing to destroy himself as those he hunted.

The current target of all that holy rage was just as big and brawny as Ramsey himself, despite the beer gut sagging over the man's huge silver belt buckle.

At first glance, he looked like every redneck thug Lark had ever seen. Tangled, greasy hair tumbled around his bull shoulders, and his snarl revealed missing teeth.

But when Lark met his gaze for an instant in the cycle's strobing light, she realized he was something much, much worse than the crude bruiser he appeared. There was more than malice and cruelty in those bloodshot eyes. There was evil, an evil so profound and alien that it was no longer quite human.

Like Lark and Ramsey himself, the thug had been possessed. But unlike them, there was nothing remotely good in whatever it was that had moved into his mind.

"We've got to help the girl," Xedda whispered.

"What girl?" Lark demanded, tearing her eyes away from the battle.

"There," the spirit said, directing her eyes toward a pitiful figure lying near the cycle.

It was no wonder Lark hadn't spotted her. She looked like nothing more than a pile of rags.

"What the hell did that thing do to her?" Lark hurried toward the girl, only to break step as she got close enough to see the victim clearly. The woman's blood-smeared T-shirt was up over her breasts, and her jeans jerked down to her shins. The halves of her bra flopped open across her chest, as though the thug had simply sliced it apart between her breasts. Something dark and wet gleamed on her bare thighs. Lark's stomach lurched as she realized it was blood.

Dropping to one knee beside the woman, she noticed an object on the ground beside the woman's head, shining in her pale tangled hair.

A knife.

"Jack stopped him before he could finish her," Xedda whispered. *"Yet still her life drains away."*

"What do I do?" Lark licked her dry lips, barely aware of the meaty thud of a body hitting a brick wall somewhere down the alley. "I don't even have a first aid kit!"

She could sense the spirit's amusement. *"You don't need one. Just touch her. I'll do the rest."*

Lark's heart gave another nervous thump. *Is this going to hurt?* she wondered, then, with a glance at all the blood, pushed that concern aside. Extending one shaking hand, she touched the victim's pale face.

Her skin felt cool under Lark's fingers, despite the warm summer night. She was in shock. They didn't have much time. *Okay, do it,* Lark thought to the spirit.

Something... opened inside her. Suddenly it seemed Lark was *in* the woman's mind as numbing cold stole up her arms and legs like frost, climbing for her heart. She fought her instinct to shrink away. "What...what's that?"

"Death," the spirit said. *"But it won't have her. We won't let it."*

Whoom!

Energy came roaring out of Lark's body in a burning flood. As one, she and the victim screamed, spines arching, arms flinging wide as Xedda poured magic into the girl's battered, torn body, forcing it to heal itself with mystical speed.

And bringing her back to life.

Then it was over, and Lark hit the ground beside the woman she'd saved, dazed, burning, and exhilarated. She'd never experienced anything like it. "Oooh," she muttered. "Now *that* was a rush!"

"What...?" the girl murmured. "What happened?" Her name, Lark suddenly knew, was Carolyn Jennings. She'd come into the neighborhood in search of a little weed for her boyfriend, and had ended up attacked by...something that looked like a man, but wasn't.

"Just be still," Lark managed. "Rest."

"They're fighting," Carolyn said, trying pitifully to rise. "The cop and... Oh, I've got to get out of here. They'll..."

Somehow sensing what to do, Lark extended a trembling hand and touched Carolyn's face. "Sleep now," she murmured. "We won't let anything hurt you."

This time the force that poured from her fingers was cool and soothing. The girl's eyes fluttered closed, and she slumped back.

"I can soften her memory of what happened," Xedda said. *"Make it less vivid, edit out the contact she had with Billy Simpson's Dark Rider. It would be best."*

Lark frowned. "Billy Simpson?"

"Simpson is the man Jack's fighting. A sadist and a killer even before he allowed himself to be possessed by one of the Dark Ones. Had Jack not stopped him, Billy would have killed the girl so his Rider could feed on her life force."

She grimaced. "Yeah, that sounds like the sort of thing a girl would be better off not remembering. Go for it."

Again, the spirit slid away into Carolyn's mind. As she worked, a thunderous bang brought Lark's head up. Her heart skipped a beat.

Simpson had slammed Jack into the side of a metal dumpster so hard the steel had dented around the officer's big body. Her lover hit the ground on all fours, dazed.

"Oh, you're dead now, fucker!" Simpson snarled, lifting both ham-like fists over the deputy's head, evidently meaning to smash them down on him.

One second, Jack was on his knees. The next, he'd flipped around and sent one booted foot scything across Simpson's calves, cutting his legs out from under him. Even as the big man went down with a startled bellow, the cop surged to his feet. Grabbing Simpson by his huge belt buckle, Jack snatched him right off the ground and heaved him into the brick wall.

Lark blinked. The spirit that had possessed Jack must have turned him into the next best thing to Superman; that bruiser easily weighed three hundred pounds.

Before Simpson could recover, her lover took a couple of running steps forward and slammed a fist into his beefy face. The impact rammed the bruiser's head into the wall behind him. Brick broke with a crunch. Jack followed the blow with two more to Simpson's beer gut, driving him halfway into the wall.

"Jesus," Lark breathed, "what the hell did Jack let move into his head?"

"*A Paladin – a guardian hunter spirit,*" Xedda said. "*It makes him far stronger than human, not to mention almost invulnerable.*"

With a roar, Simpson surged out of the wall, leaving a man-shaped indentation in the broken brick, and slammed his fist into Jack's face. The cop went flying to hit the ground on his back and skid ten feet down the alley.

"*Unfortunately, Simpson's equally powerful,*" Xedda said.

Fear clutched at Lark's heart. "I can't just stand here. What can we do to help?"

"*Nothing, at least right now. My powers are strictly mental – we don't have that kind of physical strength. Given the chance, Simpson's Dark Rider would feed on both of us. Then he'd use the power our lives would give him to kill Jack.*"

Lark bit her lip as every instinct rebelled at the thought of staying on the sidelines while the man she loved fought for his life. Unfortunately, it sounded as though getting involved would only hand his enemy another weapon. "Okay, so we sit this one out."

"Now," Simpson snarled. "I'm gonna feed!" He flung himself through the air to land directly on top of the cop.

"Jesus!" Lark said, surging to her feet and staring helplessly at the two men as they battered at one another on the ground.

There was a blur of motion. Suddenly Jack was on top of Simpson, driving his fist down into the man's face repeatedly, his muscled arm working like a piston. *"Suckered him in,"* Xedda said, sounding smug. *"He's got him."*

The cop rose to his feet and jerked Simpson upright, then spun him around. Before the big man could pull away, Jack wrapped both arms under his and around his head in a hammerlock. "Now," the cop growled. "We'll see who feeds!"

"Let go, you son of a bitch!" Simpson screamed and bucked in Jack's hold, but the cop held on despite his frantic writhing. "Get off!"

"Not a chance," Jack snarled. "You're going to pay for what you did to Heather!"

Lark stared. Oh, sweet God! *That* was the man who murdered Jack's sister?

"Noooo!" the killer screamed. Streamers of red, shimmering smoke began pouring from his eyes and mouth. Jack inhaled, drawing in the smoke, drinking it down. His own eyes flared bright crimson as his face twisted with an awful sort of triumph.

Lark caught her breath. *This was what I saw in my vision!*

As she stared, not even daring to breathe, Simpson seemed to shrink, as though transforming from a superhuman behemoth to nothing more than a somewhat tubby thug.

"That was just an appetizer," Jack growled in the killer's ear, his voice even deeper, rougher, and nastier, than it had been a minute ago. He barely sounded like himself at all. "Now this— *this* is for Heather." He tightened his grip on Simpson's head. "And all the other women you killed and raped, you sick fuck."

"He's lost control. He's going to kill Simpson," Xedda said urgently. *"Stop him!"*

Chapter Three

"Me?" Lark's heart began to pound. Dry-mouthed with fear, she stared at her lover as he prepared to snap Simpson's neck like a fistful of dry spaghetti. "How?"

"*Talk to him,*" the spirit said. "*Hurry!*"

Xedda was right. She couldn't just stand by and let Jack do this. It would destroy him in every sense of the word. "Stop!" Lark started across the alley as his biceps bunched, the cords working in those powerful arms as he tightened his grip on Simpson's head and prepared to jerk. "Jack, what the hell do you think you're doing?" she snapped with all the cold authority she could muster.

He looked up, startled by the sound of her voice. His eyes glowed with a red, demonic blaze that made her blood run cold.

"Lark? What the fuck are you doing here?" Getting a good look at her, he gaped, looking almost human again. "Jesus, you've got a Spirit Rider! Why in God's name did you let that thing move into your head?"

"To save you, Jack," Lark told him crisply. "And you need it. Let him go, dammit. You're a cop, not an executioner!"

"He killed Heather." Jack's grip tightened. "Not to mention four other women, plus the six he raped even before he let the Dark Rider possess him. If anybody deserves to die, it's him."

"Maybe, but how are you going to explain breaking his neck?" she demanded. "If you kill him, you're the one that'll end up charged with murder. Is that what Heather would want?"

He bared his teeth in a snarl as he looked down at the man he still held helplessly pinned. Simpson's head lolled. Either losing his Rider had knocked him cold, or the cop had somehow rendered him unconscious. Jack's face hardened as his grip suddenly tightened. "Maybe I'd be better off in jail."

"No!" She jumped forward and grabbed him by one thick shoulder. "Jack, don't you dare do this to me! I love you! I don't want to lose you."

He looked up at her. She almost stepped back from the molten shimmer in his eyes, but somehow caught herself in time. If she rejected him in any way now, he was lost. You don't even know me anymore. You have no idea what I've become or what I've done."

"I know all that matters. I know you're a decent man who loved his sister so much you were willing to embrace something alien to bring her killer to justice. I know you hunted him until you found him, and then you beat him and killed the thing inhabiting his body. That's enough, Jack. Let the system do its job."

"The system." He sneered the word. "All it takes is one crooked lawyer and one gullible juror, and he'll be out on the street killing again. The only way the rest of the world will ever be safe is if he's dead."

"I could see to it that he gives a complete confession, right down to the location of all the bodies," Xedda said. *"Johnny Cochran wouldn't be able to get him off."*

Quickly, Lark relayed what the spirit had said. "Jack, this would let all the families get closure. They'd all be able to confront him in court and see him get what he deserves. Don't they deserve that satisfaction after everything they've endured?"

Jack looked down at her. As she watched, tense with hope, his cold executioner's mask cracked. He opened his arms and let Simpson fall in a bloody heap to the pavement. "You're right," he said, his voice suddenly weary. "They have as much right to watch him get the death penalty as I do."

"Thank God!" Lark stepped around Simpson and flung her arms around Jack, hugging his hot, sweaty body with all her strength. Her eyes slipped closed in relief. "I don't know what I would have done if…"

For a moment, he went still. Then, with a low growl of hunger, his powerful hands closed over her waist and lifted her off her feet. Her eyes flew open as he dragged her tight against him.

Startled, Lark stared up into Jack's molten gaze. Damn, she'd forgotten how big he was—with biceps the size of her head and a broad, powerful chest that tapered to narrow hips. He felt like heated steel plastered against her this way.

Hungry heated steel.

For a long moment he stared into her face as though memorizing each and every feature. Then his lips curled into a wolfish smile, and he was kissing her, his mouth hot and open on hers, his tongue sweeping between her lips to tease and stroke.

With a muffled, famished groan, Lark lifted her arms and twined them around his neck again. The motorcycle helmet he wore felt cool and smooth under her fingers as she cupped the back of his head. God, it had been so long, and she'd missed him so badly.

She could feel her body awakening, cream flooding between her thighs. Judging from the hard ridge pressing against her belly, Jack was getting a hard-on to make a Clydesdale weep with envy.

Finally he drew back to stare down at her, his gaze feral with sensual demand. "The thing is, I've got all this energy I need to burn off. How'd you like to give me a hand with that?"

Lark felt her nipples harden, reacting to the demand in his gaze.

"What about it, Lark?" he purred. "Think you can tame me?"

She smiled dryly. "Not even with a whip and a chair."

Jack laughed a low, dark sound. "I like a woman who knows her limitations," he said, then lifted one bleeding hand to caress her cheek. "But think about it. Wouldn't it be fun to try?"

"You'd better do more than try, Lark," Xedda said suddenly. *"He needs us."*

Not as much as I need him.

His trailing finger slipped downward, brushed across the top of her breasts. Her eyes drifted closed.

"This is serious," Xedda insisted, even as Lark groaned while he thumbed one nipple. *"Simpson's Dark Rider isn't the first one Jack's taken over in the past six months. There've been at least three others — three too many, in fact. You saw how close he came to killing Simpson. Unless we can link with him psychically, anchor him, the next time he tries to absorb one of the Dark Riders, he could be lost. And then he'll become as big a danger as they are."*

Lark looked up at Ramsey, her brown eyes huge, her full lips parted. There was something catlike and delicate about her fine-boned face, enhanced by the cap of short, dark hair that left most of her long neck bare. In contrast, her body was lushly curved, with generous breasts, a narrow waist, and voluptuous hips. He knew she fretted constantly about the five pounds she thought she needed to lose, but to him she was perfect, a sensual meal he ached to sample.

God, suddenly he was starving. It had been too many months since he'd touched her, since he'd kissed the tiny mole over her right hip, since he'd licked the rich cream between her thighs. He wanted to back her up against the brick wall behind her, slide up that short little skirt, and drive hard into her.

Down boy, he told himself. Taking a Dark Rider always put a nasty edge on his appetite. Tonight it was even worse than usual.

Images spun through his mind: pinning Lark's lush body under his, raking her pink nipples erect with his teeth, licking and sucking until she begged him to take her in the long, ramming thrusts he craved. He growled in his throat, shifting on his booted feet as the hunger rolled in him.

Jack? Jack, you must listen! The familiar voice of his Paladin spoke in his mind, but he ignored it, unwilling to think about anything else but possessing Lark.

Then the urgency in Gav's voice penetrated the fog of need in his mind. *"We need to link with her and her Rider,"* the Paladin said. *"You're too strong for me, boy. I can't hold you alone."*

Hell, he knew that. He'd almost broken Simpson's fat neck when he'd seen the bastard's memory of murdering Heather. Not even Gav's desperate demands that he stop had been enough to drag him back from the edge. He doubted anyone but Lark could have reached him.

The Paladin was right, Jack realized. He needed Lark's help to maintain control.

But were she and her Rider strong enough to anchor him the next time he absorbed a Dark One? He'd met two other Spirit Women in the past six months, but both had retreated the minute they'd attempted a link, afraid he'd drag them into madness with him. They'd probably been right.

He'd hoped destroying his sister's murderer would sate the demons the Spirit Riders had sensed, but it hadn't. If anything, the hunger to kill the killers had grown worse.

He was becoming a monster. Now even Gav was afraid of him.

As he looked down into Lark's soft, dark eyes, he doubted she had the strength to drag him back from the edge. She was too…soft, too gentle for the darkness that fought to devour him.

Worse, what if she tried to help him, and he ended up destroying her?

She deserved better.

"So do you," Gav told him shortly. *"And since she's the only hope you've got, you'd better hope she can do the job. Because if she can't, I'll have to kill you myself in order to break the link that binds*

us. You're infecting me with the darkness, and I can't allow that. Or we'll become a monster as bad as anything we fight."

Lark watched as Jack summoned a patrol car to take Simpson to the county jail, along with an ambulance to treat the killer's victim. Xedda had healed the worst of Carolyn's injuries, but the spirit had deliberately left many of the surface bruises. Without their violent evidence, Simpson would have tried to argue that what he'd done to the girl had been consensual.

Then it was the killer's turn.

Following Xedda's instructions, Lark walked over to the thug's unconscious body and bent to place her fingers against his head. She felt the burning rush of energy as the spirit surged into his mind and went to work planting compulsions.

Why couldn't Jack do this? she wondered.

"The Paladin gives him great physical strength, but not psychic abilities," Xedda told her absently even as she fought to force her will on the killer.

As the spirit worked, Lark began to sense Simpson's mind through their connection. It was like being plunged into a nest of maggots. She shivered in revulsion. The viciousness of the man's thoughts, his perverted fantasies, his sheer sick evil shook her to the core.

The minute Xedda finished, Lark backed away, feeling as though she'd touched something vile. "Now I see why you wanted to kill the disgusting bastard," she said to Jack, who crouched by Carolyn's side, checking her pulse. The girl was still sleeping, deep in the grip of Xedda's spell.

"Yeah. With any luck, we may be able to get him the death penalty," Jack said, frowning over at the unconscious killer. "I don't want to risk him ever getting out of jail."

"Xedda made sure he'll take the detectives to the bodies he's dumped, so that should help," Lark told him.

"Good." He rose to his feet, reminding her again just how damn big he really was. "You do realize you're a witness?" he said. "You're going to have to testify about what you saw tonight."

She winced. "What do I say? I sure as hell can't tell them the truth."

Jack smiled slightly. "Sure you can, just not the whole truth. Describe the fight, but not the supernatural parts." He shrugged. "That's what I always do."

"But what about all this?" Lark gestured at the broken brick. "Two normal guys in a brawl wouldn't have done this much damage. And there's a lot more blood around Carolyn than you'd expect from her current injuries."

"*If we combine our powers,*" Xedda said, "*We might be able to clean up the scene just a bit.*"

Lark relayed the suggestion to Jack. "Yeah." He nodded thoughtfully, then shrugged. "It would give me something to do with all the energy I absorbed from Simpson's Rider. Gav and I can't do anything with it, but your Spirit Rider is another story."

He held out a big hand to her. She took it automatically. And gasped at the male hunger she sensed burning hot in his tight control. *Damn,* she thought nervously.

She could sense Xedda's dismay even as the spirit sent out a spell to clean away most of the blood and repair the damaged brick and dented steel. "*His mind — he's stronger than I expected,*" the spirit said.

Do you think we can do it — link with him and give him this anchor you mentioned?

"*I don't know. He may be too much for me.*"

Oh, hell, Lark thought as her heart sank. That was not what she wanted to hear.

Chapter Four

It was well past midnight by the time Lark started for home. She'd spent hours answering the questions of detectives and giving her statement; she should have been staggering with fatigue.

And she would have been, if not for the fact that Jack rode his big cycle right behind her. She knew when the two of them reached her bed, sleep would be nowhere on the agenda. At least, not judging by the looks he'd given her every time she'd been in sight.

Even as wet heat welled between Lark's thighs at the thought of being with him again, unease rode in her mind. This anchoring business had all the earmarks of being a bitch. Entirely too much rode on it, and she wasn't even sure she understood what she was supposed to do.

That was no surprise, since damn near everything else to do with the Riders was equally incomprehensible, illogical, or downright fantastic.

Blue lights flashed in her rearview mirror. Startled, she looked up to see Jack riding her bumper. He whipped the big cycle around her car and drew even with her.

As Lark looked over at him, he gestured to the side of the road ahead of them, then opened the throttle and roared out in front of her.

She blinked at his taillights. "He's pulling me over." A slow smile tugged at her lips. "Why, whatever does he have in mind?"

As Lark watched, the cycle's taillight veered off down a dirt road between a stand of trees. Smiling wickedly, she followed, lifting a brow at the Dead End sign she passed.

Evidently, Jack had this little stop all planned out.

They rounded a bend in the road. Lark grinned outright as she realized how completely hidden they were from any passing motorist. Ready for whatever naughty off-duty games Jack had in mind.

She already had a pretty good idea what those might be. She'd confessed a kinky fantasy along these lines months ago, one night when they'd killed a bottle of very nice red wine. Jack had been intrigued, but reluctantly told her the idea sounded like a great way for him to lose his job.

Lark could sense Xedda's amusement now. *Don't worry. I'll make sure nobody sees you.*

She laughed and flicked open the first button of her white silk blouse. "What a pal!" Glancing downward, she decided she needed more cleavage and unbuttoned two more.

Lark looked up in time to catch Jack's signal. She stopped and turned off the Honda's engine, watching with anticipation as he killed his blue lights, lowered the kickstand and swung off his bike. Her headlights illuminated his big, muscular body as he sauntered back toward her, moving in a long-legged swagger, a flashlight propped on his shoulder.

Before they'd headed for home, he'd showered in the Sheriff's Office locker room and changed into a fresh uniform. Now he looked like the embodiment of spit-and-polish authority as she rolled down the window and gave him her best innocent look. "What seems to be the problem, officer?"

Jack directed the flash into her face, then down at the cleavage she'd artistically revealed with those open buttons. "Step out of the car, Ma'am," he growled.

"But deputy, what did I do?" Lark purred, obediently opening the door as he stepped back. She got out, knowing perfectly well that her short skirt had ridden up, flashing leg all the way up to her crotch. At fact that wasn't lost on Jack, judging by his hooded gaze.

She stole a glance at his crotch. Yeah, he was already harder than his nine-millimeter—and looked damn near twice as long. Lark licked her lips.

"Assume the position," he growled.

She managed a startled blink. "But I haven't done anything!"

"You know exactly what you've done," Jack said in a heated rasp. "Now turn around, spread those feet apart, and brace your hands on the hood of the car."

Lark swallowed and obeyed, leaning down to brace her hands on the warm steel.

He stepped up behind her and lean down to rumble in her ear, "I said spread those legs." Her nipples hardened, rasping against the lace of her bra as she widened her stance. "Morrre," he purred. "I want you nice and open for me."

She did as he ordered, bracing her legs wide. She could feel cream trickling deep between her thighs.

"Very good. Now, let's see what you've got." Big, broad hands smoothed down the length of her arms, rubbing the silk of her sleeves against her skin. He took a step closer and leaned over her so that his hips snuggled against her butt. The hard ridge of his erection pressed between her bottom cheeks as he circled her waist with his warm, rough hands. As he slid them upward along her sensitive ribs, Lark let her eyes slip closed.

Without skipping a beat, he reached around and cupped her breasts. Her eyes flew wide as he boldly squeezed, rasping his thumbs over her hard nipples. Licking her lips, she remembered her role. "What...what do you think you're doing?"

Jack laughed, the sound dark and male. "Hey, you're the one who unbuttoned your shirt halfway to your navel. Guess you thought you could get out of a ticket by flashing a little cleavage." He lowered his head until he could breathe into her ear, "But I'm afraid it's gonna take a lot more than that."

Skillfully, he hooked his thumbs in the cups of her bra and pulled downward. Her nipples popped free into the warm summer air.

"Nice," he rumbled, pulling the bra down even further until it caught under her breasts, pushing them up and together. "I just love a speeder with luscious tits." He caught either side of her blouse and pulled. Buttons went flying.

"Deputy!" she gasped, feeling the hot burn of his eyes as he studied her bared flesh. Long fingers stroked over her jutting nipples, sending sweet jolts of pleasure along her nerves. Delicately, he caught the hard tips between the thumb and forefinger of each hand, squeezing, twisting, tugging, milking waves of delight from her breasts. She twisted in the cage of his arms.

"Sensitive," he mused. "Good. Let's see what else we've got."

Lark moaned in protest as he released her aching breasts and knelt behind her. His big hands circled her delicate ankles, then began to sweep up the length of her legs.

"You…shouldn't be doing this," she managed.

"Probably not, but there's something about a skirt this short. It just makes me want to…" Reaching her ass, he paused to squeeze. "…find out what's under it. Mmmm. Thigh-high stockings. You *are* a bad girl."

He leaned forward. She felt the cool brush of his helmet's visor, and then his tongue running tauntingly up her thigh, before he caught the underside of one butt cheek in a gentle bite.

Lark squirmed.

A big, warm hand touched the inside of her thigh as he drew his thumb across the crotch of her panties. "Why, Ms. Anderson. Your panties are wet. If I didn't know better, I'd think getting pulled over turned you on."

"Nooo." Yes. God, yes. She closed her eyes and moaned.

"I think this warrants further investigation." Before she could move, he caught the fragile silk in both fists and jerked.

Lark jolted in surprise as her panties ripped away from her body.

"What do you think you're doing?" she gasped, looking around to see him holding the shredded fabric up to his nose.

He inhaled deeply, breathing in the scent of her passion, before stuffing the handful of lace in a pocket. "Just seizing the evidence. And now..." He took her ass in both big hands and pried her slim cheeks apart. "Let's see what else we can find."

Lark caught her breath as he leaned forward and gave the seam of her pussy a long lick. "Just as I thought," he rumbled. "Creamy, and hot." A long, thick finger slid between her lips to find the tender opening. She drew in a breath as he began to enter. "And tiiight." He slid in all the way to the knuckle, gliding in the thick juice that filled her. Withdrawing, he thrust deep again, adding a second finger this time. Scissoring the two apart, he twisted his wrist and thumbed the taut bead of her clit.

"God, Jack!" Lark moaned, panting. "That feels so good."

"Yeaaahh." He pumped deep again. "Oh, baby, you're going to be doing some hard time." Then he took his hand away. "But not quite yet."

He stood. Instinctively, Lark arched her back, grinding her butt against him, feeling the long, thick length of his cock bulging against his zipper. "Jack, please," she gasped.

"I said, not yet." He grabbed one of her braced arms and pulled it behind her. She felt something cool close around her wrist with a click. As he grabbed her other wrist, she realized belatedly he was handcuffing her.

"Jack..." she whimpered, wildly excited.

"That's 'Deputy Ramsey' to you," he growled back. "And no, I'm not going to fuck you right now. It's been six months since I've had any, and I need to take the edge off." He pulled her around by one shoulder. One corner of his handsome mouth lifted in a dark grin that held more than a little sneer. "'Cause otherwise, I won't be able to give you the long, grinding fuck you deserve." Jack's glittering black eyes narrowed. "Get down on your knees." He reached for his fly.

Dazed, shivering, Lark dropped to her knees on the hard-packed dirt road. She didn't even spare a thought to her expensive stockings. All she cared about was watching those big hands unzip his pants.

Leaving his gun belt on, Jack reached inside to liberate his massive cock from the placket of his jockies. As it jutted out at her, almost as thick as her wrist, she swallowed.

He stepped up to her, planting his booted feet on either side of her thighs. Threading one hand through her hair, he caught the base of his cock with the other and aimed it for her lips. "Open your mouth," Jack growled. "I'm going to blow my first load down your throat."

With a whimper of need, she leaned forward and took him deep.

As Lark's soft, wet mouth closed over his cock, it was all Jack could do not to climax on the spot. It had been so damn long since he'd touched her.

All he'd known for months was the driving compulsion to bring Heather's killer to justice. Well, he'd done that. The D.A. had told him tonight that the confession Simpson had given them would guarantee a death sentence. Jack was finally free.

Free to touch Lark again.

And he had no intention of thinking about the darkness that shadowed him, or even Gav's threat to kill him if he couldn't regain control. If this was all the time he'd ever have with her, he'd make the best of it. He'd protect her when the time came, but right now, he needed this. He'd earned it.

God, it felt so damn good, the way she sucked the head of his cock in long, eager pulls that made his balls draw tight. She gave him her mouth as she never had before. Each lick and nibble and suck felt so hot and demanding, it filled him with a burning pleasure. Maddened, he found himself thrusting, fucking Lark's face in short, delicious digs.

Jack shuddered, hunger clawing at his mind as he looked down at her, kneeling in the dirt working him with such single-minded hunger.

He'd never dominated her like this, never wanted to. But now, the darkness that had been growing in him demanded it— demanded he fuck and claim her, mark her as his own.

What astonished him was the way she responded, submitting eagerly, as if the act answered some hidden need of hers as well.

Gasping, he tightened his grip on her hair and dragged her close, feeling his full length sliding into her mouth as, impossibly, she swallowed him down. Savage pleasure spun the length of his aching cock, and his balls tightened.

Then, with a last, drawing suck, she catapulted him right over the edge. Jack bellowed out his pleasure as he stiffened, shooting his cum down her eager throat.

Normally, an orgasm of such mind-blowing intensity would have finished him for the night. But that was the old, merely human Jack. This Jack, the Paladin Jack, still seethed with dark energies.

And he hadn't had nearly enough Lark.

She had swallowed the last of his seed and was still gently suckling his softening shaft when he reached down, caught her under her arms, and jerked her off the ground. Lark yelped in surprise as he waltzed her backward, lifted her, and bent her back over the hood of the car so he could reach those rosy little nipples. Ravenous for her, he immediately began to suckle each tight peak in turn as he squeezed and stroked her soft breasts.

"Jack!" she gasped, instinctively lifting both long legs to wrap them around his waist. With her wrists still handcuffed behind her, it was the only way she could hold onto him.

"You taste so damn good," he growled. Closing his lips over the nearest nipple, he sucked and tongued the sweet, erect flesh. "And I've missed you so damn bad."

And now, at last, he had her.

Chapter Five

Lark tightened her legs around Jack's waist and moaned as each fierce pull of his lips wrung another delicious jolt of pleasure from her nipple.

She couldn't remember the last time she'd been this hot. Kneeling at Jack's feet sucking him off had been one of the kinkiest things she'd ever done in her life. Not so much the act itself, but the way he'd demanded it of her, the way he'd fucked her throat like a conqueror.

Before, he'd always been a careful, gentle lover who treated her like spun glass. Now he was wild, fierce, and hot, and she loved it.

Reaching between her legs with one big hand, Jack sought the tight opening of her pussy. Lark caught her breath as he found it and slid inside. "You're wet," he growled, lifting his head to fix her in his glittering black gaze. "That's good. You need to be, because I'm about to fuck you." His mouth curled up in a tight grin. "Hard." The finger slid out, then slicked back inside. "Do you want it?"

Lark caught her breath as erotic delight coiled a tight knot in her sex. "Oh, *yesssss*! Please, Jack!"

He circled her clit with his thumb and added another finger. It stretched her lusciously until she writhed in pleasure. "Begging. I like that. How do you want it?"

"Deep." She groaned and arched her back, lifting her weight off her bound arms and thrusting her breasts upward. "Don't hold back. You've got such a …AH!…big cock, Jack…"

"And you're so tiny. I always wanted to pound into you, but I was afraid I'd hurt your delicate little pussy." He added a third finger to the ones stretching her snug core. "Now you're so slick and tight, I don't think I can resist. I've just got to spread you wide open and cram every single inch of my dick all the way inside. And then…then I'm going to ride you *hard*."

Lark moaned as she lifted her high-heeled feet to brace them on the hood, spreading herself in voluptuous invitation. "Yeah," she moaned. "Now—God, please, Jack, fuck me now!"

He looked down at her wet flesh as he stroked his fingers deep. "I don't know, babe. I'm not sure you're ready for what I'm going to do to you. I think I'd better get you a little hotter first."

Catching her ass in both big hands, he bent his head and fastened his mouth over her pussy. Lark gasped, arching her body in ecstasy as he thrust his tongue right up her tight core.

As he lapped between her lips and around her hard clit, he reached up her body for her bare, aching breasts. Strong fingers pinched and rolled her nipples while his long, clever tongue danced over sensitive flesh.

The orgasm took her by surprise, rolling out of nowhere to trip-hammer through her cunt and up her spine. Lark convulsed, screaming. "Jaaaaack!"

And still he suckled and stroked and flicked, dragging pulse after hot, orgasmic pulse from her sex. Until at last she collapsed on the car's cooling hood, limp, boneless, and dazed.

Jack straightened to look down at her, his eyes dark with possessive satisfaction. Then he stepped back, grabbed her by one hip, and flipped her onto her belly. She blinked and lifted her head to look around at him. "Jack?"

"Here it comes, baby." His eyes glittered with lust as he put the smooth head of his cock against her cream-slicked opening. His grin was a savage slash of white under his mustache. "Oh, yeah, here it comes."

"Jack!" Lark whimpered the instant before he rammed the entire thing inside in one shattering stroke.

As he stuffed her with that long, relentless thrust, she threw back her head in shock. She felt his massive cock raking through wet, sensitized tissues as he drove himself in all the way to the balls. Until, completely impaled, she could only squirm on the hood of the car. "Oohhhhhhh!"

For a moment he didn't move, as though savoring the tight grip of her wet cunt. At last he lowered his head and said into her ear, "Now *this* is where I've wanted to be for the past six months."

"I hope," she wheezed, "it lives up to your expectations!"

He laughed and slowly began pulling out. "Oh, yeah. You are anything but a disappointment."

Eyes lit in dark joy, he started fucking her, just as mercilessly as he'd threatened.

As many times as they'd made love, he'd never taken her like this—in long, almost brutal thrusts that jarred her ass every time he pounded home. It was almost too much, even as aroused as she was. Bound, stretched across the cool metal of the car hood as he covered her with his powerful body, all she could do was writhe as his cock tunneled in and out. She'd never felt as helpless in her life...or as turned on.

Reaching under her body with both hands, he caught her breasts and began tugging and twisting her nipples. The sweet pleasure enhanced the torturous delight of his thickness stroking her core. "Jack!" she panted, as the first hot pulse of her climax squeezed around his cock. "I love you!"

"I...love...you!" he groaned, his sweat-slick body grinding against hers as he cradled her, jamming as deep as he could reach.

She felt so impossibly slick and tight around his cock, so soft and fragile in his arms. For months, he'd dreamed of this in his cold bed—not just taking her, but being with her. Then he felt her tiny muscles clamping hard around his cock.

"*Jaaaaaaaaaaaaaaaack!*" She threw up her head, writhing in his arms, coming.

The naked pleasure of it tightened around his balls like a fist. With a shout of raw pleasure, he shoved to his full length as the climax hit, hammering through him. Hot pulses of cum shot deep inside her velvet grip. "Lark! God, Lark!"

Still the orgasm went on, lashing along his nervous system like a velvet whip. Hot, burning strokes that made him writhe in a pleasure so glorious it was almost pain.

Until, at last, it was over.

Panting, he sagged against the car, feeling boneless, with Lark still wrapped in his arms like the erotic treasure she was.

But even as he thought about collapsing with her into the grass, Gav's voice rang in his mind.

"Don't go to sleep, lad," the Paladin said. *"We've still got work to do. And, unfortunately, this is the perfect time to do it."*

Jack stirred, drawing Lark protectively close. "What? What are you…?"

"Brace yourselves, children," whispered an unfamiliar female presence. *"Here it comes."*

A hammer blow slammed into his mind. He felt something crack.

Pressure. Light. Voices babbling at once.

Jack reeled as minds that didn't belong to him stuffed their way into his skull—not just Gav's, but others. He could feel them pressing in on him, crowding him. Panicked fury rose, and he gathered himself to force them out. Gav was more than enough. He was damned if he'd allow…

"Jack?" Warmth. Love. A sweet, glowing presence he knew so well.

"Lark?" He stopped dead, arresting the wave of mental force he'd started to fling against the invaders.

Yes. Lark.

Something deep and primal in him recognized the essence of his woman. His hostile fury drained away.

"You're...in my head?" she asked. He could sense her confusion, a perfect mirror for his own.

"I think you're in mine."

"Actually, you're both just where you've always been," the female voice said. He realized suddenly it was Lark's Spirit Rider, Xedda. *"We've just opened a link between you."*

The last of Jack's panic disappeared, replaced by startled joy. Lark was with him. They'd done it—forged the link he'd never been able to form with any of the others. The link he needed to save him from becoming one of the monsters he fought.

"Are you going to resist us any longer?" Xedda asked, sounding cautious. He saw in her thoughts that he was much stronger than she'd expected.

"Resist this?" Jack stroked Lark's nipple as he cradled her in his arms. He could feel how each caress felt to her, and he groaned in pleasure. Withdrawing his softened cock from her wet depths, he turned her in his arms. She smiled up at him, and he felt the love in her like warm sunshine spilling through the cold darkness that had filled him for so long. He sent his own love back in all its sweet intensity.

"God, what sane man would resist this?" Jack asked aloud. "We're both exactly where we belong."

As he lowered his head to kiss her, he knew there'd be other Dark Riders to pursue, other killers to capture, but his soul was no longer in danger.

He had Lark. And nothing, no matter how evil, could ever touch the hot, sweet love between them.

The End

About the author:

Angela welcomes mail from readers. You can write to her c/o Ellora's Cave Publishing at 1337 Commerce Drive, Suite 13, Stow OH 44224.

Also by Angela Knight:

Captive Dreams
Mercenaries
Mercenaries: The Thrall

Why an electronic book?

We live in the Information Age — an exciting time in the history of human civilization in which technology rules supreme and continues to progress in leaps and bounds every minute of every hour of every day. For a multitude of reasons, more and more avid literary fans are opting to purchase e-books instead of paperbacks. The question to those not yet initiated to the world of electronic reading is simply: *why?*

1. *Price.* An electronic title at Ellora's Cave Publishing runs anywhere from 40-75% less than the cover price of the <u>exact same title</u> in paperback format. Why? Cold mathematics. It is less expensive to publish an e-book than it is to publish a paperback, so the savings are passed along to the consumer.

2. *Space.* Running out of room to house your paperback books? That is one worry you will never have with electronic novels. For a low one-time cost, you can purchase a handheld computer designed specifically for e-reading purposes. Many e-readers are larger than the average handheld, giving you plenty of screen room. Better yet, hundreds of titles can be stored within your new library — a single microchip. (Please note that Ellora's Cave does not endorse any specific brands. You can check our website at www.ellorascave.com for

customer recommendations we make available to new consumers.)

3. *Mobility.* Because your new library now consists of only a microchip, your entire cache of books can be taken with you wherever you go.

4. *Personal preferences are accounted for.* Are the words you are currently reading too small? Too large? Too...**ANNOYING**? Paperback books cannot be modified according to personal preferences, but e-books can.

5. *Innovation.* The way you read a book is not the only advancement the Information Age has gifted the literary community with. There is also the factor of what you can read. Ellora's Cave Publishing will be introducing a new line of interactive titles that are available in e-book format only.

6. *Instant gratification.* Is it the middle of the night and all the bookstores are closed? Are you tired of waiting days—sometimes weeks—for online and offline bookstores to ship the novels you bought? Ellora's Cave Publishing sells instantaneous downloads 24 hours a day, 7 days a week, 365 days a year. Our e-book delivery system is 100% automated, meaning your order is filled as soon as you pay for it.

Those are a few of the top reasons why electronic novels are displacing paperbacks for many an avid reader. As always, Ellora's Cave Publishing welcomes your questions and comments. We invite you to email us at service@ellorascave.com or write to us directly at: 1337 Commerce Drive, Suite 13, Stow OH 44224.